Cover Design and Interior Format

THE SCOT'S BETRAYAL

HIGHLAND SWORDS

KEIRA MONTCLAIR

A NOTE FROM KEIRA

Many times I have asked you to suspend your beliefs of the real world when you join me on a journey. Whether it's a magical pony, an owl protector, a lass capable of seeing the future, or an odd storm, my books are filled with the kind of remarkable happenings many people in the Celtic world whole-heartedly believed in.

This one is no exception.

Those of you who have read my previous books may recognize the four characters at the center of this series—the three Grant lads born on the same night at the same time and their indomitable female cousin—but this is a standalone series that can be followed by anyone. In it, we will embark on a journey into the magical underworld of the Grants. I'm not sure where this journey will take us, but I am excited about it!

You will see a few true historical facts interwoven with my fictional world, but this novel and its companions are primarily the workings of my own creative mind.

Welcome to my world! I hope you choose to stay for a while.

Keira Montclair

PROLOGUE

And so the story was told for generation after generation.

Alasdair, dark-haired son of Jake (John) Grant and Aline Carron.

Elshander, fair-haired son of Jamie (James) Grant and Gracie Grant, and

Alick, fire-haired son of Kyla Grant and Finlay MacNicol.

All three were born on the same day, at the same exact time, all descendants of the renowned Alexander Grant, the finest swordsman in all the land.

When their time comes, the three shall lead Clan Grant together to be one of the strongest clans in Scottish history.

Their time has come.

CHAPTER ONE

Scotland
Late summer, 1304

A HIGH-PITCHED SCREAM OF TERROR RIPPED through the air as Alasdair Grant and his cousins emerged from a ravine in the middle of the Lowlands.

It was a sound he never wished to hear again.

Just ahead of them, a group of travelers on horseback was being attacked by reivers. One of the bastards had plucked a raven-haired woman off her horse and ridden away from the clash, leaving most of his fellow thieves behind. Two men rode with him, one on either side, to serve as protection.

Alasdair waved his hand to his two cousins, Alick and Elshander, indicating they were to go to battle while he went after the kidnapped woman.

Arrows began to fly, taking the villains out one by one, and he smirked, knowing exactly who was firing those arrows.

The reivers didn't stand a chance. His cousin was the best archer in all of Scotland. Dyna had signaled them a few moments ago, before they'd heard any sounds of a skirmish, and then peeled off to tie up her horse and position herself in the trees. The lass had an uncanny way of knowing things she should not know, sensing danger before it happened.

The fact that she was correct so many times unsettled him, but he was grateful for her insights. And for her arrows.

He urged his horse into a fast gallop after the villain mishandling the dark-haired woman. The man had made a mistake, thankfully—he'd chosen to ride off into a meadow rather than into the ravine from which Alasdair and his cousins had emerged. An arrow sluiced through the sky, taking out the reiver riding to the kidnapper's right. Alasdair brought his black steed up to the other guard.

They were probably English—no identifiable plaid, no fighting skills, no horseback riding expertise. The bastards had probably thought there'd be no repercussions to attacking a group of Scots. Their present monarch, King Edward, known also as Longshanks because he was so tall, certainly would not care. Relations between the two nations were more sour than a jug of two-week-old goat's milk. Longshanks hated the Scots, had even massacred most of Berwick before taking it in England's name, and didn't hesitate to let everyone know his true feelings. Even so, he fancied himself their rightful ruler, daring to overtake much of the Lowlands from the Scots, and giving land that had been in Scots' families for centuries over to English noblemen.

Alasdair spit off to the side of his horse at the thought of all that had transpired in his beloved

Scotland.

King Alexander III's death had thrown Scotland into turmoil, and after his daughter Margaret passed on several years later, there were fourteen rivals who had vied for the illustrious title of king of the Scots. King Edward had chosen John Balliol to be king, but the man had been little better than a puppet and had been removed.

Truth be told, Edward considered himself the king of both England and Scotland, and after asserting his dominance over the past several years, was attempting to ease into a peaceful agreement with Scotland. He'd returned some land, appointed many Scottish sheriffs, but much of the north still didn't trust him. Some had sworn fealty while others held out. Now it was a waiting game.

The Scots wished for their own king. William Wallace had fought hard for that role, his courage lighting a fire of fury in the heart of every Scotsman and Scotswoman, and Robert the Bruce and John Comyn had also made cases for themselves. But Edward had no intention of relinquishing control. His reprisals were brutal and he constantly sent his men into Scotland, giving them free license to take over any Scots' property and do what they wanted with the occupants, including the women.

The past few years had brought many new battles with the English, whether a literal skirmish or a less direct push for land, power, and dominance.

The English had done enough to wound his people. Alasdair would not let these English bastards hurt a Scots woman.

Shouting the Grant battle cry, he swung his sword the way he'd practiced over a thousand times in the lists and in battle, slicing the fool across his side, eliminating the second guard. Blood blossomed from the cut as he fell to the ground, his horse struggling to stay up. Two down, only one left. The kidnapper's horse had been driven wild by the sounds of fighting and the sluice of arrows, and the bastard atop the stallion struggled to stay mounted. Alasdair had to fall back to keep the panicked horse from taking him out.

The fool struggled to keep his saddle, partly because he didn't have any discernable riding skills and partly because his captive was fighting him with all her might.

"Don't give up," he yelled to her. Then he urged his animal on. "Come on, Midnight, just a wee bit closer. I've got two apples left." His horse was a powerful animal, named after the famous war horse that had carried his grandsire, the famous warrior Alexander Grant, through the Battle of Largs. The stallion's bloodline had given him the right to the name.

The graceful beast slipped him close enough for Alasdair to reach out and grab the man's tunic, yanking him off his horse and tossing him to the ground. A shout ripped through the air, and he didn't need to look back to know an arrow had struck the kidnapper on his way down.

That left the woman. She fought to stay on the spooked horse, grabbing its mane to right herself.

The animal looked liable to buck her off, however,

and Alasdair decided there was an easier way. He reached over, his long legs and arms assisting him in his endeavor, snaked an arm around her waist, and lifted her off the horse and onto his lap. She landed hard, but he managed to hold himself straight to stabilize her.

As soon as Midnight stopped, the lass turned to look at him. Before he could say anything she gave him an unbelievably hard shove, something he hadn't expected, and he tumbled off the horse, taking her with him. They landed at the top of a small knoll, his arms still wrapped around her, and they rolled down the bumpy incline until they finally stopped at the bottom, both on their sides looking at each other, panting.

He heard horses' hooves, and since he didn't yet know who they belonged to, he put his finger to her lips and said, "I'm a Scot, not a bloody Englishmen. I'm here to return you to your companions, but for now, you must be quiet. There are more reivers about, and we don't want them to catch sight of us here. You can yell at me afterward, if you must."

She stared at him a long moment before nodding.

Beautiful wasn't a strong enough word for this woman. Long dark hair the color of Midnight's mane had fallen out of her plait, the silky strands curling around her face. But it was her eyes that clutched at him.

They were dark blue, the color of a sapphire jewel he'd seen in the hilt of his grandsire's sword. He had two cousins who were blessed with blue eyes, but they were both a light blue. The eyes that stared at him were the color of a midnight sky. Mesmerizing. Even more so since they were set above high cheekbones and luscious red lips.

He took in every detail of that lovely face, noting the arch of her brow, the peak of her hairline, and the trembling of her lower lip. She was likely frightened, but she held still. In spite of her position at the bottom of the glen, she was as regal as any Scotswoman.

She was a Scotswoman, was she not? He'd assumed so, but perhaps he only wished to think it.

"My thanks to you, but please return me to my husband."

He was relieved to hear the deep burr in her throat, but that other word dampened his spirits. Husband. He heard another rustling, however, reminding him they were still in danger. "A few more minutes," he whispered.

Two horses passed by them, the riders' view concealed by clumps of bushes. The men traveled on past, one yelling at the other, "Hurry, those bastards fight too much. Get the hell out of here." He knew from the way they spoke they were English.

"Who were they?" she whispered, after they'd gone on by. Her lips tickled his ear, sending a jolt of energy through him. Then, in a very husky voice, she asked, "Who are *you*?"

———◆———

Emmalin was so struck by the man's looks that she could barely speak, but she forced herself because she had to know if he was a friend or enemy.

He wore a dark red plaid, though she didn't recognize it, and he had a Scottish lilt that warmed her heart. It was a voice that spoke of confidence, pride, and loyalty. All the characteristics of the kind of man she'd wished to marry someday, not the English dandy she'd been saddled with thanks to the King of England.

"I'm Alasdair Grant, and we would do best to wait until my cousins find us. Leave them to take care of the rest of your attackers."

Relief cascaded through her. The Grants had been her sire's allies. He'd been proud to call the great Alexander Grant his friend.

Alasdair's gaze locked on hers and she returned the stare. They lay so close together she could see the blue flecks in his gray eyes. He had long dark eyelashes and hair the color of night, almost black, long and untethered. He was definitely a Highlander, what the English would refer to as a savage Scot. A scar along his right jawline didn't detract from his appeal one bit—indeed, it enhanced his good looks, if that were possible.

Her father had always said a scar earned fighting as a Scot was one to wear with pride.

He stood and pulled her to her feet but kept her close enough that their noses nearly touched, something that happened simply because of the uneven terrain underfoot. Although she knew she should push him away—she was married, after all—she couldn't bring herself to do it. He smelled of the winds and the pines, and he was tall enough that he made her feel small, something that was rare for her. Without thinking, she reached forward and took his hand in hers, clasping it for warmth. Holding it, she felt safer than she had in a long time.

Thankfully, he allowed it.

Until the spell was broken.

———◆———

The meaning of her words struck him the very next moment. She was married, and thus off limits. He stepped away from her, against his own base desire.

He nodded and said, "I shall return you right away. What is your name?"

"Emmalin MacLintock. Nay, my pardon. I'm newly wed to Baron Langley Hawkinge. He is awaiting my return, I'm certain."

"Any relation to Finnean MacLintock, laird of MacLintock Castle?" His grandsire had spoken of the MacLintocks before—they were allies from the Lowlands, if he recalled correctly.

So why was she married to one of the enemy?

Sadness filled her eyes. "Aye, he was my sire. He passed on nearly a year ago. My marriage was arranged after his death, an arrangement forced on me by King Edward."

"But you're Scottish. You should marry a Scot."

She cast her gaze down, but that look of grief, of unhappiness, stayed with him. Was she sad because she'd lost her sire or because she wasn't happy with her new marriage?

He knew what Dyna would say—*none of your business, Alasdair.*

A whistle pierced through the air, Dyna's signal that all was well, so he helped Emmalin back up the knoll and over to his horse. Midnight had stood steadfast through all the chaos.

After helping her onto his horse and mounting behind her, he flicked the reins and headed back to where he'd left his cousins. There was plenty of tree cover around them, so he knew his other cousin was likely swinging from tree to tree with her bow at the ready.

She knew how to stay hidden.

He approached the group warily, scanning to be sure the attackers had all been killed or wounded. Many of the lasses' companions had dismounted. He knew immediately which of the group was her husband. A fair-haired man stood in the middle of the gathering, hands on his hips, bellowing at everyone around him. He certainly looked the part.

It was a small group, fortunately. King Edward's cavalry sometimes rode into Scotland in huge numbers. Hundreds or even thousands of men. His grandsire had advised all of them to stay far away from such large groups, which seemed bent on causing trouble and killing Scots.

Alasdair's two cousins, Elshander and Alick, were still on their horses, not far from the baron. As Midnight approached the group, Alick pointed to them and said, "There they are."

Elshander, whom they all called Els, said, "There she is, as we promised. Saved by our cousin."

Alasdair whispered in her ear, "Your husband doesn't look verra happy."

"He's probably worried," she said, pushing forward in the saddle so her back was a distance from him. Even so, he could feel her shiver, and he could not help but wonder why. Covered with her mantle in late summer, she shouldn't be cold. Was she afraid of her own husband?

Now his interest was piqued. The lads in Clan Grant were all taught to respect lasses and treat them right, a legacy enforced by his grandsire. But Alasdair knew that lasses were mistreated in other clans, and most certainly by the English.

"Get down from there. You should not be riding with a savage Scotsman," Hawkinge said, glaring at both of them as they approached.

The man reached for his wife, but Alasdair pulled Midnight back.

Langley Hawkinge, in true English style, clearly did not favor the Scots.

Which was fine by Alasdair—the Scots did not favor the English either.

Hawkinge's eyes narrowed, but he did not move. "Bring her to me." His clenched jaw told Alasdair everything he needed to know.

Baron or not, Langley Hawkinge was a bastard. And he was clearly no warrior or knight. If he'd made any effort to rescue his wife, it wasn't obvious from the look of him. His hair was fair and neatly coiffed, like a lady's should be.

Alasdair was tempted to say as much, but the lass turned to him with a frightened gaze that caught him.

"Please. Do not taunt him." Her mouth opened as if she wished to say more, but she kept quiet, casting her gaze downward.

He felt an odd compulsion to do whatever she asked of him. But that didn't mean he would allow Hawkinge to assist her off Midnight. Rather, he moved his horse forward and placed his hands around Emmalin's waist, lifting her up and then setting her down with the greatest of care. "No thanks for saving your wife?"

Langley gave him a brief nod. That was all the thanks he would get, he was sure of it. Alick wore a wide grin behind the brute, silently encouraging him to say more, but he did not.

He stopped his urge to teach the man a lesson only because of Emmalin. The baron struck him as the kind of man who would make her suffer for his anger. Whether it was the line of his jaw, the coldness in his eyes, or the clench of his fists that told him so, he wasn't sure. But he would not cause this woman any pain if he could help it.

The man stooped to kiss her cheek and whispered, "Did he harm you at all, my love?" The "whisper" could be heard by all.

"Nay, but who were those men, my lord?" she asked, staring up at her husband, who was pacing the ground, clearly still agitated.

He stopped and glared up at the Grant cousins. "Why are you still here? Begone. We do not need you."

"Are you sure about that? You didn't do a great

job of protecting your wife a few moments ago," Alasdair drawled.

"We would have handled the attack without your help. We'll handle everything from here. Take your leave. *Now*." His ten guards had fallen in around him. Some bore injuries from the battle, but all had survived.

Except for the two who'd gotten away, all of the reivers were dead.

Although Alasdair was tempted to argue with the man, the English knights outnumbered them. Perhaps it was best to stand aside and allow the group to continue on.

Alasdair nodded to Emmalin and said, "If you're ever in need of assistance, my lady, please send a message to Grant land. My name is Alasdair. I'll be glad to help you in any way I can, one Scot to another."

He was possessed by a sudden need to dismount and stand beside her, but he denied himself that pleasure, knowing it might inflame the baron. She was taller than most lasses, although Dyna—who still hid in the trees—stood nearly as tall as he did. Emmalin met his gaze, and they stared at each other for a long moment. A searing heat passed through him as if her gaze had just branded him.

He interpreted it in only one way.

Help me.

CHAPTER TWO

———

ALASDAIR GRANT WAS A NAME Emmalin wouldn't soon forget.

She stared up at the man as he spoke to her, taking in his long dark locks, his gray eyes, and his powerful shoulders. The scar across his jaw looked even more pronounced from a distance. The wound would likely have killed him had it been any lower, but it was impossible to imagine anyone besting this man. His raw power took her breath away. He seemed completely confident in his abilities as a man and a warrior.

And yet he'd set her down from his massive stallion with more tenderness than her husband had ever shown her.

Her sire, bless his departed soul, had often spoken of Clan Grant's strength, for they were known as the strongest and largest clan in the Highlands, but he'd also mentioned their honor and fierce loyalty. He'd told her once that if he could ever choose a husband for her, he would arrange a match with one of the Grants, but they lived far away and had many allies.

She knew he would never have chosen an Englishman for her.

The Scotsmen departed, and her husband's hands

squeezed her waist a bit harsher than normal as he tossed her up onto her horse. She had to grab the beast's mane to find her seat, but she managed. Her sire had insisted that she become an accomplished rider.

Staring at her with blazing eyes, the baron whispered, "May I remind you that your gaze belongs on your husband, not on a stranger."

She had no defense, so she said nothing. She merely watched as he stalked away and mounted his own horse. Soon, they were riding again as if nothing had happened, Emmalin following her husband's lead on the path toward her homeland in Strathblane in the Vale of Leven. The trembling began soon afterward. She'd been abducted, almost taken by a group of men who would have used her in an appalling manner.

How could she not shiver at that thought?

"You're trembling," Langley said. She had not even noticed that he'd slowed his horse to ride beside her. "Are you cold?"

"Nay, my lord," she said, shaking her head. "'Tis a delayed reaction to being abducted by those men. When I think of what could have been…"

"Do not think of it in that way. You are safe, my dear. I'll have you home in our bed by the end of the day." He winked as he said it.

She smiled, knowing that was what he would wish to see from her. On their wedding day six moons ago, she'd vowed to make the best of the marriage, to be obedient and cheerful.

If he loved her, perhaps he'd become more

pleasant.

It was the best she could hope for. After her father had died suddenly, she'd had no choice but to accept the English king's demand that she marry one of his barons, especially since the order had been delivered to her by King Edward. She'd decided it would be best for her people if she cooperated willingly. After all, everyone knew King Edward's cavalry frequently rode into the Borderlands, and even the Lowlands, to enforce his will. She did not have enough warriors to withstand a direct attack.

And so she'd married Baron Hawkinge.

In her heart, Emmalin was still a proud MacLintock, a proud Scot. She wouldn't give up her Scottish heritage for anything or anyone. Or the land that had been overseen by her family for decades. It might be the baron's by marriage, but it was hers by blood.

To her delight, MacLintock land came into view. How she loved the rolling hills, now green with the burst of summer, the trees full with the promise of more beauty to come in autumn. She didn't know which season she favored more, the warmth of summer or the brilliance of autumn colors. The sight of her land always made her smile, as if a soft whisper were welcoming her home.

Once they made it over the bridge, the stable lads rushed out to assist the group. Her steward, Gaufried, came out to greet her. He'd been acting second with her father for years. When the baron had taken over her castle, she'd insisted on retaining Gaufried, although he had become the steward of the castle instead of her second-in-command. That job had been given to one of Hawkinge's men.

"How was Edinburgh?" he asked.

"Lovely. My lord purchased several new gowns for me, and we stayed at a nice inn. The trip home could have been better," she replied as he helped her to dismount.

Besseta came out to greet her, seeing to her satchel and the packages that were hers. "I'll take care of everything, my lady." Bessie had been her personal maid for as far back as she could remember. Thank goodness, the baron hadn't argued about keeping her on. Emmalin had lost her mother before her father, and her maid was all the family she had left.

While she and Bessie would have normally taken time to chat upon her arrival, they had learned to hold their tongues until they were alone in her chamber. Langley had chastised her for being too friendly with the servants, something he did not believe in.

There were many things Langley didn't believe in. The truth was the man questioned everything she said, undermining her in front of the servants, even humiliating her in front of them, yelling at her over trifles. Once he'd insisted she kneel and beg for his forgiveness after she'd allowed the cook to make a Scottish delicacy for dinner.

"My lord, please excuse me as I see to the evening meal," Emmalin said, turning to the baron. "'Twill nearly be upon us," she said.

Langley grabbed her around the waist and snuggled her neck as a tease, leaning in to whisper,

"Do not forget what my favorites are, will you?"

"Of course not," she replied.

"And they are?" he asked, pulling back to stare at her.

"Boar meat, lamb, barley, and cabbage," she recited carefully.

"And?" He asked this question as he twisted her arm out of sight of the others. They could never accuse him of being abusive because no one ever saw what he did to her.

She hissed through her teeth at the pain and said, "Bread. Forgive me for forgetting."

"That's better, my dear. If you would just do your job, I'd never have to reprimand you. You know I don't like to."

"My fault, and many thanks for your patience, my lord," she said, each word smarting like a pulled tooth.

He leaned over to whisper in her ear again, "Very good, my dear. When you've finished that task, please see me abovestairs in my chamber. I have another task for you." He nipped her earlobe before he turned away from her.

"Aye, my lord."

She dug her fingers into her palms as she walked away. She knew exactly what that task was to be. Langley had a voracious sexual appetite.

Before she joined him, she would indulge herself by fantasizing about all the ways she could pay him back for his cruelty. She understood the way of the world, of course—fantasizing was all she could do. If she told a priest how her husband treated her, he would tell her that husbands had the right to discipline and oversee their wives. She'd be reminded that her job was to do as her husband asked, keep his castle the way he wished, and to become a quiet, obedient wife.

Her preference would be to take her sewing needle and stick it in his eye.

Or have someone bigger than she was do all the things he'd done to her—the pinching, the silent twisting, the taunting.

Bessie had told her some women enjoyed the marriage bed, but she doubted she would ever be one of them. Langley wished for her to be completely submissive to him, and everything inside her revolted at the thought.

However, she tried her best to meet his needs, knowing it was the way to get concessions from him, such as keeping Besseta and Gaufried and other servants.

She moved inside the keep, making her way through the great hall. It hurt too much to look at the cavernous space, which used to be warm and inviting, so she kept her eyes on the path in front of her.

Not at the missing red and black plaid on the cushions.

Not at the blank spot on the wall where her sire's best swords had hung.

Not at the missing tapestry her grandmother had made of the keep in winter.

The space was best described as empty and cold.

Her dear sire would have been devastated by

the changes. She vowed to see all of her family's precious things returned to their spots.

If only she knew how.

CHAPTER THREE

———◆———

ELSHANDER AND ALICK CONTINUED TO tease him as they rode through a meadow, moving slow enough to talk. Dyna joined in occasionally, her comments always as sharp as her arrows. She'd returned to the group as soon as they were a good distance from the baron's men.

They'd come upon the reivers on their way home from a mission to Edinburgh. Their co-chieftains and grandsire had sent the four of them there for the latest news on Scotland's ongoing battle for independence from England. The tidings had not been good. After his success in the Battle of Falkirk, Longshanks continued to subdue the Scottish rebellion. His men continued to push deeper and deeper into the country, encroaching on clans who'd lived there for centuries. They'd reached a truce two years ago, but Wallace remained free, his location a mystery, and many still pushed for Scottish freedom.

The Scots would not rest until they chose their own king, something Edward would never allow. With their grandsire's encouragement, the four cousins had decided to become active in the battle for independence.

Alexander Grant believed in knowing your

enemy, and he didn't trust King Edward, something that had been borne out in the king's devious actions.

What better example than that English dandy who'd been wed to a stunning Scottish beauty?

Dyna said, "He's an arse."

Alasdair smirked and glanced over his shoulder at her. It did not surprise him that she'd guessed at his thoughts. Dyna possessed abilities no one understood or discussed, mostly because it upset her.

The first occurrence he recalled was when they were five winters, and she'd been about three and a half. The cousins had stayed home with Grandpapa and Grandmama while their parents paid a visit to Clan Ramsay.

The three lads had gotten into an argument at the top of the stairs. Although Alasdair could no longer remember the substance of that argument, he'd never forget the way Dyna had stared up at them from the great hall. "Don't fight," she'd pronounced. "You'll be sorry." She'd then stalked off to find their grandparents in their chamber at the end of the hall.

The three had ignored her and continued to argue. Soon, they'd started shoving each other about, and then Els had tripped. Alick and Alasdair tried to pull him back before he fell down the stairs, except they'd gone down with him instead. Their grandparents had stepped out of their chamber just in time to see the three lads lose their footing and catapult down the steps. Grandmama had screamed, and the lads had done the same.

Alasdair remembered seeing nothing but arms and legs and steps flying past him as the three hurtled down the staircase. Servants came running, but as soon as they landed, everyone quieted, not speaking.

At the bottom of the staircase lay two thick cushions that had stopped them from being badly hurt. Grandmama just stared at the cushions, wondering who had moved them from their usual position by the hearth. She looked from one servant to the next, but they all shook their heads.

Dyna strolled back into the hall and said, "I told you that you would be sorry."

Grandpapa knelt in front of her. "Dyna, did you put those cushions there?"

She nodded.

"Why?"

"I knew they were going to fall, Grandpapa. I saw it." Then she toddled off to the kitchens. "I'm hungry."

The story hadn't been told to any of their mothers. Grandpapa had said it was to be their secret. But each of the cousins was well aware of Dyna's abilities. The main reason she was allowed to travel with them, despite the dangers, was because of her propensity to detect danger before it happened, to assess a person's character at a glance. Although the abilities were temperamental, they tended to be stronger when she was around her cousins. As a spy, she was invaluable—even more so because she was also a fantastic archer.

Dyna spoke again, wrenching him free of the memory. "Something is wrong with their marriage. I could tell from the way they stood together."

"I won't disagree with you," he said. In his mind, he could see the fear in Emmalin's eyes. "He is an arse. She should have been allowed to marry a Scot."

Els said, "I do believe he's smitten."

Alick chuckled and said, "I was waiting for him to ride off with her. 'Twould have taken her husband a while to notice the way he was carrying on."

Els laughed at that, and Alasdair couldn't help but smile, even though he was by far the most serious of the three of them. *Just like your father*, his grandpapa often said. People in their clan joked that each of the three Grant lads who'd been born on the same night, at the same time, carried the qualities of his sire. Alasdair tended to be more quiet and reserved than his cousins—but just like Jake Grant, he had the temper of an angry hornet if pushed. Els was a chatterbox, much like his father, Jaime, and Alick, son of Finlay, was a jester, though his red hair showed in his occasional bursts of temper.

Their grandsire had always told them the night of their birth was the most memorable occasion in his long life, and their aunt Jennie insisted there was some special meaning behind it.

Nineteen years later, they'd yet to learn exactly what it meant, although they all knew their bond was special—and that strange things sometimes happened when they were around one another. Although they would eventually have to meet their destiny, Alasdair wasn't ready. The past year had been the most challenging in his life, and it had heaped a great weight on his shoulder. He needed to figure out a way to shed that weight before he could do anything of significance.

"Nay, you have it wrong." Els said, picking up the joke where Alick had left off. "He was ready to kidnap her, spit on the baron, and take her straight to a kirk. Well, I suppose he'd have to kill the bastard first."

They waited for his response, but he gave them nothing. In truth, it peeved him a bit that they'd so easily picked up on his attraction to Emmalin. It was dangerous for a warrior to let his feelings show. If he did so in battle, it could mean the end of him.

He deliberately changed the subject to the one thing guaranteed to turn their jovial mood. "I've been thinking of the last battle after we joined the Forest." Using the name the Scots used for Selkirk forest where Wallace and his men had gone into hiding, many of them residing in the forest during the worst of the battles over the last seven years. "When Brechin Castle was lost." The Scots had fought hard, but Edward had overtaken the castle, defeating the Scots after a short battle.

Alick's whole demeanor changed in an instant. "I think of it every day. 'Twas just a short time ago. I'll never forget it."

They'd gone to stand for the Scots at various times, but the last battle at Brechin Castle had been the most frustrating, mostly because they'd been crushed by the English. All three had survived, to everyone's surprise. Many Scots had lost their lives that day. Even so, the confrontation had left a lasting mark on each of them. And as Grandsire reminded them, English curs lost their lives, too.

Although Alasdair had literally been marked in that battle, the memory of the wound he'd sustained was not what haunted him most. He'd killed a man, only to turn to find two more upon him. He'd killed one and Els had killed the other.

Both of the bodies had landed on him.

He'd never forget that feeling of being crushed.

He'd sought advice from his grandsire and both of the Grant lairds, hoping they'd help him wash the memory away, but nothing had helped.

Some nights, he woke up bathed in sweat, his sword arm swinging. A scream in his throat.

"It takes time, so my sire says," Els offered. "The power of the memory will remove its hold on you after a few moons, or even years."

He glanced at his cousin, arching his brow in question. He, Els, and Alick were as close as any cousins could be—as close as brothers, really—and it often seemed as if Dyna wasn't the only one capable of picking up on his thoughts.

Alick grinned. "Aye, we know what you're thinking some days. Mama says it's from all the days we were put in the cradle together. She said she knew what our traits would be even back then."

"I know, I know," Alasdair drawled. "We've all heard the tale a hundred times."

"Aye," Alick said. "Elshander turned back and forth to both of us, attempting to talk non-stop before he could say a word, I smiled at his babbling, and you? Well, you did you."

Alasdair let out a bark of laughter at his cousin's summation. He knew his part of the story. According to his mama, he used to get frustrated at his cousins' antics. He'd push them away until she came to lift him out of the cradle and hold him close.

His mother, Aline, had passed on from the fever about a year ago. Losing her had left a cavern in his heart. While Els and Alick had siblings, he'd been his parents' only bairn. It helped that he had such a big family, full of aunts and uncles and cousins, but he missed his mama something fierce.

"Aye, your mama spoiled you," Alick said.

His cousin had read his mind again. This time Alasdair just smiled.

They arrived at the gates of Grant Castle, the wind whistling through the pines as they galloped through the meadow. The portcullis opened as soon as they neared the entrance, the men on the curtain wall recognizing them instantly.

It was a sad testament that they kept the gates locked at all times. They never knew when or if the English would attack. The cousins dismounted once near the stables, and Alasdair tossed the reins to one of the stable lads and hastened toward the keep. He passed Aunt Gracie, Els's mother, who stopped to give him a hug before continuing on to greet her son.

"The lairds?" he asked.

"Off on a visit to our neighboring clans," she

said as she stepped away. "They'll be back in a few days."

A few moments later, his uncle Finlay, Alick's sire, called out to him from the lists. "He's in his usual spot awaiting your report."

"Thank you, Uncle!" he said, hurrying on toward the keep. Once there, he threw the door open, found the staircase, and took the steps two at a time until he reached the top floor. He then hurried down the hall to the end of the passageway and made his way up the final flight of stairs. When he reached the top, he opened the door carefully, always cautious around the old man.

Alexander Grant, his namesake, sat in his stone chair, built into the wall of the parapets, his favorite place in the world. At nearly seventy summers, the man was ancient, but his mind was as sharp as the tip of the sword he still polished every night.

"Greetings, Grandsire."

"Alasdair, I noticed your arrival. Tell me what you discovered. Anything new?"

"Nay. The English are bastards, but we already knew that. I fear Edward will not stop until he subdues all of the Scottish rebels. He thinks we've succumbed, given in to his rule. We all know better. Our quest for freedom will never die."

His grandfather stared off over the edge of the crenellations, something he often did when a memory came to him. They'd all been given strict instructions to let him be during those times, simply because it was probably something he relished.

By the look that crossed his face, however,

Alasdair guessed this memory was not one of the good ones. "Are you thinking of your first battle, Grandpapa?"

"Aye."

His grandsire had told him the story often, so much so he could probably recite the details, and yet he said, "Tell me more about it. Tell me about the lass."

"Why do you ask?" He brought his sharp gaze back to Alasdair, probing in his silent way, ready to pick up on any change in his demeanor. His many years had made him skilled at detecting behaviors before they appeared.

"May I tell you after?" Alasdair also liked to test the old man. He would do anything for him, including carrying him up here to his favorite spot on the parapets when he struggled. Grandpapa often cursed his old bones. Alasdair noticed the finely hewn piece of wood next to him, so he knew he'd been able to make it this time with the assistance of that wood support. Sometimes he made it on his own, but oftentimes he needed help from one of his children or grandchildren.

"I'll never forget it, as you know, nor the look in the eye of the lass. She looked so hopeless, so resigned to her fate. Her name was Sarah. My sire knew right away it was the English who'd done it. He said they had no honor, no morals. What they did to that poor lass..." He shook his head and stared off for a few moments.

Alasdair gave him the time he needed, leaning over the stone wall and peering out over Grant land. As a younger lad, he'd thought it stretched out forever, and indeed, the land was theirs almost as far as the eye could see. Hills, valleys, burns, the loch, and mountains. It wasn't the most fertile land, but they'd made good use of the soil they had.

"Your question, lad?"

"You often speak of the look in her eyes... I think I saw it on our journey. We happened upon a group of travelers being attacked by reivers. There was a woman who'd been abducted. I chased her kidnapper, pulled him off his horse, and brought her back to her husband."

His grandsire tipped his head back, a sign that he had his complete attention. "And?"

"She was a beautiful Scot, but she was married to an English fool, some baron. Not quite newlyweds anymore—they've not been married for long, I'd guess. I cannot explain it, but after watching him for a few moments, listening to his empty words, I knew he was a bastard."

"Trust your instincts. He probably is. Get on with the tale." That spark of wisdom and the beam of pride in his country flashed in the old man's gaze, something that always caught Alasdair.

"The look she gave me...it was like she was beseeching me to help her, but it passed so quickly. Almost as if I'd imagined it. Can you make any sense of it?" He was clearly worried about her, but something was not right.

"The marriage must have been forced on her. Which reminds me. I received a message from someone who believes a lass needs help. She's the daughter of a late Scottish laird who was an ally of mine. My friend is concerned about the lass's new husband."

"Who sent you the message?" He couldn't believe his grandsire still had any friends left at his age. To live seven decades was quite rare.

"The stablemaster."

"But Grandpapa, how can you trust something a stablemaster sends you? Don't you need a warrior's opinion?"

"Always trust a stablemaster's opinion. They know everything that takes place in the clan. It was a stablemaster who sent me a message about the mistreatment your grandmother was suffering. I have him to thank for all of this and all of you. He brought me to Maddie, bless her sweet soul."

His grandsire stopped speaking and looked down at his lap for a moment. Alasdair did not need to ask why. Alex Grant missed his wife every day, even though she'd been gone around five years.

But when he lifted his gaze again, he gave Alasdair the look of a fearless leader, a strong fighter.

Of a fierce Highlander who you would never dare question.

His long peppered gray locks blew in the wind, but he never touched them, and his gray eyes settled on Alasdair's matching eyes.

"Her name is Emmalin MacLintock and you must save her."

Alasdair nearly fell over the parapets in shock.

"That's the lass's name, Grandsire. She *is* in trouble. I knew it."

CHAPTER FOUR

TWO DAYS LATER, EMMALIN SAT beside her husband, who was selecting the food to offer her from their shared trencher, when the door flew open with a gust of wind behind it.

It was her steward, Gaufried, his face flushed. "My lady, there is a messenger here for your husband." He pointed to the dais and the messenger strode toward them, intent on delivering his message post haste.

The man gave them a slight bow.

"Speak. What is the message?" her husband barked.

"The message is from King Edward. He requests your immediate presence at his royal castle in Berwick."

Emmalin waited for her husband's response. Berwick was in the Borderlands, quite a distance from her property in the Lowlands. King Edward had ravaged the town not long ago and declared Berwick Castle an English castle, something the Scots hated. It was yet more evidence that their nation was under siege.

Her husband asked the messenger, "How long a journey was it?"

"It took me nearly two days, my lord." The lad

wiped the sweat from his brow. "I must convey that the matter is urgent. He requests your presence immediately."

The baron waved a hand at Tamsin, one of the serving lasses. "Feed the lad and find him an ale." Then, turning to his private steward, he said, "Assemble my things. I'll be leaving within the hour." He gave small instructions to a few other servants before he turned back to her.

"Do you wish me to travel with you, my lord?" she asked, praying he would say no. She would much prefer to stay at home alone.

"Nay, my dear," he said, leaning over to kiss her cheek. "Being that it's an urgent matter, I must insist on a punishing pace. I would not subject you to such a journey. I vow to be back as soon as possible. I have no idea why our king wishes to see me, but I suspect it has something to do with the savage Scots."

Her sire's voice rang out in her conscience. He'd always insisted she should always honor her ancestors. Her heritage. "But *I'm* a Scot, my lord."

He turned to look at her. "You *were* a Scot, now you're English. You've married an English baron and your sire's castle is now an English castle, as is your land." He ran his finger down her jawline, letting his nail graze her skin. "Please do not forget this, my sweet."

A sudden chill shot up her backbone. But the chill wasn't simply inside her—it was *in the air*. She felt certain her sire had heard the comment, the heresy.

Her husband strode over to speak with his second, and she stood, looking at the others in the hall. Did they feel the chill, too?

Aye, she saw others shivering. Mothers pulling mantles about their shoulders, children edging closer to their parents. She was not the only one.

Tamsin rushed to her side once she had delivered the food to the messenger. "What has happened, my lady? Why is he leaving? More battles?" Tamsin, Aunt Penne's personal maid, had been part of their household for two years. She was lovely, with long waves of hair a deep shade of chestnut brown, but Aunt Penne always insisted she wear it up. She had a slew of other rules besides, and Emmalin often felt a wee bit sorry for Tamsin, who was close to her in age. Whenever possible, she talked to her, trying to make her feel more at home. Bessie did the same. Of course, Aunt Penne put a stop to their efforts whenever she could, insisting there must be a separation between the family of the house and their servants.

Langley whole-heartedly agreed.

"I don't know, and we may not find out until he returns," she said, waving her on once she noticed Aunt Penne frowning at them, something she often did when she took the time to answer the servants. Tamsin nodded and continued her work without another word.

Ever since King Alexander III had died, all the Scots were unsettled, even the servants. This lass was no different. There was far more chatter amongst everyone in her clan ever since the baron had arrived.

And she'd bet none of them were any more pleased about it than she was.

Her father had made her repeat his favorite saying every day: *MacLintock Scots, always brave and forever strong.*

Always brave and forever strong.

She didn't feel so brave or strong at the moment.

Instead, her home, her mighty castle had been overtaken by a stranger, someone who didn't have a speck of Scots blood inside of him. Someone who disrespected the very people he lived among. Bearing that in mind, how could she expect Langley to love this land the way she did? To him, the soil they tilled was but a handful of dirt to be thrown into the wind; to her, it was the land her ancestors had fought for, land that had belonged to her clan for decades.

A place to bring up bairns to be happy, carefree, and productive.

As her sire's only child, she should have been laird, just like Diana Drummond had famously been laird of Drummond Castle. She knew it was what her sire had intended, for he'd told her so. He'd *trained* her for it. MacLintock Castle was to be her heritage, and she was to run it with pride. He'd even taught her to use a dagger, a last line of defense in case anyone managed to get past her guards and attack her.

Only her lairdship had been usurped by an English baron, one who hadn't needed to fight for the pleasure. While she still hoped to win him over, if only to make her life more palatable, she felt as if she were standing on one side of the moat and he on the other. Could they ever bridge that gap?

Did she want to?

She stood by the hearth as her husband prepared to leave, and after a time her dear companion Bessie appeared by her side, holding her mantle up for her. The garment was a beautiful dark blue wool, with a fur-trimmed hood and a wide pocket in the front where she could tuck both of her hands as protection against the cold Scottish winds. The hem nearly swept the ground.

Her aunt Penne, her sire's sister, came flying out from behind Bessie. "Your husband is leaving? Make sure you follow him out like a proper Scottish wife. All good wives must say farewell to their husbands, and then you must pray for his quick return."

"Of course." She leaned down to kiss the older woman's cheek, a necessity since she towered over the woman. Aunt Penne lost her husband in battle years ago after only a few short years of marriage. She'd lived in the castle ever since. Her age showed in her soft gray hair and widening hips, but she still liked to have a say in everything that happened.

Sometimes she wondered if Aunt Penne didn't envision herself as laird of the castle.

Bessie ignored the woman, probably a wee bit upset she'd been interrupted. She didn't always get along with Penne, who tended to treat the servants as if they were nothing more than hired help. She held out the garment for Emmalin. "'Tis fiercely cold in here, and you'll be expected outside soon enough," Bessie said, clucking her tongue. "'Tis important that our mistress be warm. Your boots are only so tall."

She thanked Bessie and her aunt, then made her way out of the hall. Her steward, Gaufried, already awaited her. Since it was proper for a wife to be at the gates whenever her husband was to leave, Emmalin always complied, simply because she always did what was proper. At least she had her own friends and allies within the house to support her.

Baron Hawkinge flew down the pathway to the stables, but he hastened to her side once he'd given his orders to his second. Another man she'd never met arrived, calling out to him, "Hawkinge, I'm here to escort you to Berwick. King's orders that we're to get you there safely as soon as possible."

She listened to their talk, hoping to get more information as to the urgent matter at hand, but they said nothing of importance. As she watched her husband, his outfit too pretty for travel, she found herself thinking of a fierce Highlander with dark wind-blown locks and intense gray eyes. Eyes that had been focused on *her*. Her memory even teased her with a growl—had he made such a sound?

Although her husband was an attractive man, she found she preferred the callused hands of a warrior to the baron's soft skin. She'd watched his ways for a long time now. He was exceptional at giving orders, but rarely did he take part in any activity that required physical exertion. His sword skills were barely passable compared to her sire's, and laughable when compared to the prowess of Alasdair Grant. He'd used his sword as if the weapon were an extension of his being. Heavy and large as it was, its movements had been as fluid as the twists and turns of a river.

The Grant warrior had been more skilled than her sire.

This man in front of her, her husband, was as far removed from a Highland warrior as any man she'd ever met. Even if she could make him love her, she knew she would never love him. She would always see him for what he was not.

"As soon as I'm done with my lovely wife, I'll be ready to leave," Langley said. "Tend to my bag first. My thanks for joining us, Sheriff de Savage." Then he gave his attention to her, reaching for her trembling hands.

"Sheriff?" Her husband was English yet this sheriff was Scottish. She wondered if that was significant.

"Aye, our esteemed king has gone out of his way to install more Scottish sheriffs. Since I am of noble rank, he would send a proper escort for me. A sheriff familiar with the area along with many knights is necessary. You don't know much about my station in nobility, do you?" He lifted his chin a notch and peered at her.

"I am unfamiliar with the English nobility rankings, my lord. We don't have many…I'm only…" He had her flustered, something that happened much too often. She did not feel comfortable around him. She did not feel capable of being herself. He'd ensured it was so.

"Nay, I'm unfamiliar with English rankings," she said. "We do have earls and barons, but chieftains carry noble blood in the Highlands. It carries over into the Lowlands."

He gave her a smile. "Forgive me. I know you had many adjustments to make when we married." He squeezed her hand. "For now, I must focus on the matter at hand. I'll be gone at least a sennight, possibly a fortnight depending on the reason I've been summoned."

Curiosity got the best of her. "Do you have any notion why you've been called away so urgently? You haven't done anything to anger the king, have you?"

"Of course not. I am one of his favored barons, which is why I was given your land, er…" It was his turn to be flustered. "Why I was given your hand in marriage. I am most pleased to have such a lovely wife to return to."

He gave her a brief kiss on the lips, then spun on his heel, barking orders as he strode away.

"Godspeed, my lord," she called out, though she doubted he was listening.

He mounted his horse and turned to give her a wave and a smile. "Gaufried will take good care of you, I'm sure."

Emmalin's heart lifted as she watched the group depart. She hoped he would be gone longer than he planned.

Or, better yet, that he would never return.

Alasdair sat at the table the next morn, finishing his third bowl of porridge. He reached for the honey, but Alick beat him to it.

"Did you tell Grandsire about the lass? Emma or whatever her name was?" Alick asked, focusing on making his porridge and honey mixture just so.

When had his cousin become so particular? He couldn't help but stare across the table at him, noticing how his hair was neatly combed, his beard trimmed just the way he liked it. Alasdair tipped his head to him. "When did you become so fussy about everything?"

Alick put the honey down and said, "Fussy? I'm not fussy."

"The hell you aren't. You didn't used to be that way."

Els, who sat beside Alasdair, said, "I have to agree with him, Alick. You've changed. Your hair is almost as fancy as that English baron's. Why?"

"Did you two eat some boar shite? Because 'tis all I'm hearing from you." Alick slammed his dagger down on the table. "Alasdair just wants to shift the subject from his lady."

"Mayhap so, but I'm ready to move on, as well," Els said. Turning to Alasdair, he asked, "What did Grandsire say about the king?"

"Not much. He is hoping the Bruce will become King of Scotland. He thinks Wallace is failing in his quest for the throne." Alasdair said, making a mess of his food as if to make a point.

Alick glared at him.

"And Grandsire said something else, too. You know how Edward himself has left Scotland for now?" he asked, not using the monarch's title as intentional disrespect, something he would only dare to do on Grant land, away from prying ears. Not recognizing Edward as the rightful King of England was considered traitorous.

The man had been known to hang men for less.

"Aye," Els said. "Does he think he'll try to come to the Highlands?"

"Nay, he said he has the men but not the provisions. Edward seems to think his victory at Stirling Castle established his dominance. And 'tis for the good of all that he stopped pushing forward, reinstated the Scottish sheriffs, and returned some land. But he's a fool for thinking this is over. Wallace and Bruce will never end their quest for Scottish independence."

Alick, looking more serious than usual, asked, "But what if someone agrees to give him food? Then what? Will they make it here? Will they go after our food stores?"

"Grandsire said the clans and magnates are having a meeting in the Highlands. Our lairds will be attending. We must band together to support the Bruce. Scotland must prevail, but we must be more careful."

They would *never* forget their heritage. Even as the thought crossed his mind, a pair of deep blue eyes surfaced in his memory. It hurt to think of the indignities suffered by Emmalin MacLintock, whose castle had been all but taken from her. The Scots were a proud people, and King Edward needed to recognize that.

They needed to prove it to him. The king had more than ten thousand men at his disposal, however, and the only way the Scots could win was for the strongest clans to band together. Not an easy task when so many men wished to claim the throne.

The door opened at the end of the hall, and their grandfather made his way through the door, slowly as if his legs pained him this morn. "We'll not speak of any of the details we heard in front of Grandsire," Alasdair said in an undertone. "He'll only get upset."

In a louder voice, he said, "Good morn to you, Grandsire." He saw a look of pain cross the man's face just before he crashed to the ground, his stick unable to hold his weight.

"Grandsire!" The cousins' voices rang out together as they raced to his side, joined by anyone else within hearing distance.

"Grandpapa, are you hale? Don't try to get up. We'll help you," Alasdair said, his stomach twisting in a way that made him wish to vomit. He'd already lost so much—he couldn't lose his grandfather.

Not yet—not ever!

Aunt Kyla and Uncle Finlay appeared on the balcony above. His aunt looked stricken when she saw her father on the floor. "What happened?" she shouted. "Papa!"

Alasdair scooped his grandsire up and headed

back toward his bedchamber, which had been moved down to the lower floor some years ago. He stopped when the old man grabbed his wrist. "Nay, I'll not go back in there to stare at the four walls. Move my bed into the hall," he said, his eyes fluttering closed.

Alasdair gave instructions to his cousins, who'd followed him. "Els, you and Alick move the bed out here while I hold him. Aunt Kyla, go for Aunt Gracie." His aunt had become the healer for their clan, though she did not yet have much experience.

Once they had him settled in his bed, arranged at the end of the hall, Aunt Gracie came in and hustled over to see to him. She assessed Grandsire's leg, which seemed to have buckled under him, but he couldn't seem to stay awake either.

Anxious to do something to help, Alasdair found a partition and moved it over to the bed to give the poor man some privacy.

He paced and paced, praying furiously, and scratched his head as though he had one thousand bugs in his hair.

"Stop scratching," Aunt Kyla said. "He'll be fine."

"Will he?" he asked, staring at his aunt as if she'd just kicked him in the belly.

She patted his shoulder, a movement he knew was an attempt to soothe him, but it wasn't working. He welcomed any words she would offer him.

"My father is the strongest man I know. This won't stop him." Aunt Kyla was the spitting image of his grandfather, except she had the piercing blue eyes of her mother. The years had done nothing to dim her beauty, but only a fool would underestimate her.

She was as tough as any man.

Aunt Gracie stepped out from behind the partition. She was shaking her head, a sight that instantly alarmed him.

"What the hell does that mean, Aunt Gracie?" Alasdair bellowed, blushing at his crudeness a moment later. "Sorry, Auntie. I shouldn't yell or curse. My thanks for coming so quickly."

"I understand your concern, Alasdair," she said, setting her hands on his towering shoulders. "I think he'll be fine, he just cannot move. I don't know what's wrong with his leg or hip. We need Jennie."

Aunt Jennie was his grandsire's youngest sister, one of the best healers in the land.

The two lairds were on patrol, so Alasdair made a decision. "Alick and Els, we must go after Aunt Jennie. We have to do everything we can for Grandsire."

A voice called out to them then, quiet but steady. "Alasdair?"

He hurried around the partition and knelt next to his grandfather's bed, pleased to see him awake. "Grandsire, is there something I can do for you? We're going to get Aunt Jennie. Aunt Gracie doesn't know how to help you."

"Let the other two go for Aunt Jennie. You must go after *her*." He closed his eyes and panted as if in severe pain. "Alasdair, please. This is just my old bones squawking at me like a hooded crow, naught to concern yourself with, but what I'll tell you is more important. I had a dream. You must go."

"Where? I'll do whatever you like."

"The lass from Clan MacLintock. You must help her. She's in grave danger. I don't know…" He paused and sucked in a deep breath, holding it before he let it out again. "I don't know what is happening, but you need to go to MacLintock land. Finnean came to me in my sleep and told me that his daughter needs our help. You must go at once." He wiped the sweat on his brow away with a sigh.

"Was there something else he said? You don't usually sweat like that, Grandsire."

The man closed his eyes in resignation, pausing for a few moments before he opened them again. "He said she's in danger. Someone means to kill her. You must go." He was silent for a moment longer, then he glanced over Alasdair's shoulder and smiled. "And you must take her."

When Alasdair glanced behind him, he saw his cousin Dyna, her nearly white hair pulled back in a tight plait, her light blue eyes filled with fear. "Grandsire? What's wrong? I heard you fell."

Their grandfather panted and held his breath again, his eyes fluttering as if he struggled to stay awake. Suddenly, they opened wide, and he said, "Promise me, Alasdair. Promise me you and Dyna will go to MacLintock land and save Emmalin." His voice slowed. "Promise. Let the others go for Jennie." His eyes fluttered shut again.

"Grandpapa!" Alasdair shouted, not caring if he

was bothering the man. When the old man opened his eyes again, he said, "I'll do it. I promise, but you must also promise me."

His grandsire met his gaze. "What?"

"Promise me you'll not die while I'm gone. Promise me! I am not ready to lose you. Not yet. It's too soon." He squeezed his grandfather's hand, doing his best to keep him alert. He'd never let on how important this was to him, but he needed his promise.

The sly old man shut his eyes for a long moment. When he opened them again, there was a twinkle in them. "Wise arse," he whispered. "Go."

Alasdair couldn't help but smile.

CHAPTER FIVE

EMMALIN SAVORED THE WIND AGAINST her face as she rode through the land outside the castle gates. Riding was her favorite pastime, not just because she adored her dear mare, but because it was the only time she ever felt *free*.

Free of everything English.

Free of others' expectations and the need to pretend.

When she rode her horse across the lovely Scottish countryside, it reminded her of her upbringing, of her sire and his pride for their clan, and of her mother. Her mother had died about four years ago in her sleep. She'd never been sick, so it had been a shock for all of them.

Her father had been shattered over the loss of his wife, but he'd done his best to stay strong for Emmalin, keeping her busy with different tasks. He'd taught her all he could about managing their estate—the keep, the village, and the many tenants who lived on MacLintock land.

She'd impressed him with her ability with numbers, so much that he'd had her do sums in her head to impress his steward and others. She'd blushed every time, but his pride had emboldened her. Although it was her papa who'd first taught her to use a dagger, she'd practiced on her own. Her skill with the weapon had grown into an obsession as the English continued to encroach into Scotland. Although it was foolish—a dagger could do little against a sword or an arrow—it made her feel less helpless. Her maid had sewn a pocket into every gown she had so she could always carry her dagger with her, though she hadn't taken it to Edinburgh with her.

It was there now, for all the good it would do her.

Heaving out a sigh, she leaned down to whisper into her mare's ear. "We've little enough freedom, don't we, sweet lassie? Let's fly. Take me over the outcropping there." Moments later, she sailed through the air on the graceful beast, her guards choosing to go around the boulders embedded in the ground.

She laughed at them. "Gaufried, why did you not even make an attempt? Your stallion could have made it." The feeling was as close to flying through the air as possible and she loved it, but when she glanced at Gaufried, her feeling of euphoria quickly disappeared.

Gaufried froze, drawing his weapon. She slowed her horse simply because of his expression. It took her a moment to realize what had put him on alert. His voice carried that low tone she dreaded because she knew immediately what it meant.

Gaufried was afraid for her. "Mistress, return to the keep at once. We will follow as soon as we determine the source of the noise. It sounds like horses to me."

How she prayed it wasn't more English. Her husband had left just over a sennight ago, so she doubted it would be him yet. She certainly hoped it wasn't. When the horses came into view a few moments later, she sighed with relief. The approaching men wore plaids, which meant they were definitely not English. She'd allow Gaufried to handle them. They could be bringing news or just seeking out a light repast.

She did as he advised and turned her horse around, sending the mare into a gallop toward the keep. When she was nearly at the gates, she glanced over her shoulder.

Gaufried was escorting two men toward her, while another four held back. She had a sudden burst of butterflies in her belly.

One of the men riding with Gaufried looked like Alasdair Grant, but why would he be here?

She moved across the bridge and inside the gates, bringing her horse to the stable lads, who helped her dismount. Rather than return to the castle, she decided to wait for her steward. In the interim, she couldn't stop herself from smoothing her riding skirts and tucking in the wild curls that had escaped her plait. She loved the feeling of the wind lifting her hair as she rode. In fact, her favorite way to ride used to be with her hair unbound, long and flowing behind her.

She hadn't done it since her wedding day. Langley had said it was conduct unbecoming of her station.

The stable lads moved out to grab the reins of the visitors' horses. The riders quickly dismounted and

moved to stand in front of her. She'd been right—
it *was* Alasdair. His black hair was askew, just as hers
had been, and he looked at her with fire in his eyes.

Gaufried said, "Mistress, the Grant contingency
have come for a visit. They are requesting an
overnight stay. What say you?"

She couldn't think of a better way to spend the
next day with her husband gone. "Of course, you're
welcome to stay." She hadn't taken her eyes from
Alasdair yet, but when she glanced at the other lad,
she was surprised to see him, or her as it appeared,
remove her head covering to reveal an abundance
of nearly white hair that fell to her hips. The lass
smiled and said, "My name is Dyna. Alasdair is my
cousin."

She vaguely remembered seeing her in the
background after she'd been attacked and met
Alasdair's group, but she hadn't seen her with her
hair down. Dyna was stunning and carried an air of
power uncommon in women, something she had
to admire. "I welcome both of you to MacLintock
Castle. Please join me for dinner. My husband is
away, so I look forward to having your company
for the evening meal." Shifting her head toward
Dyna, she asked, "Would you like to freshen up
in your chamber first? I have one at the ready for
you."

"Aye," she said, "that would please me."

Once inside, Emmalin showed Dyna to her
chamber, then sent a maid to bring fresh water and
linens for her use.

Dyna said, "I'll be down in an hour or so. Feel

free to start dinner without me. Alasdair can speak to you of our concerns."

"Your concerns?" she asked, wondering what they could possibly be.

Dyna intentionally leaned toward her and lowered her voice. "Alasdair will speak to you of it, but possibly you could arrange for a more private setting."

Nothing would please her more, but how appropriate would it be for a married woman to have a private meeting with a man who was not her husband? She suspected she knew all too well what Aunt Penne would say if she found out. As if reading her thoughts, Dyna whispered, "The meeting would be between two Scots, naught more. Or are you pleased to have the English in your sire's castle? My grandsire would guess not."

Struck speechless by the other lass's quick and accurate assessment, Emmalin nodded her agreement. "Your arrival pleases me more than you could know. I will do what I can."

She left, her curiosity more than piqued, and made her way to the kitchens to make arrangements for a private meal in her solar. The kitchen help originated from her clan, so she knew they would brook no argument. If anything, they would be immensely pleased to think she was strategizing with another Scot.

When she returned to the great hall from the kitchens, Alasdair stood by the hearth with a goblet of ale in his hand. Some of the villagers had come inside for the evening meal, though the guards wouldn't be in for a couple of hours.

She fussed over her hair one last time before she approached him, wondering why this man made her feel so uncertain. It wasn't a bad sort of uncertainty, however, but a sense of anticipation— as if something was about to happen.

He spun around and smiled at her. His smile was arresting, the white of his teeth a lovely contrast to his bronzed skin and dark hair.

"Your husband has left?" he asked.

"Aye. He was called to Berwick to meet with King Edward." She had an immediate attack of butterflies deep in her belly.

"Pardon my bold question," Alasdair said, drawing her focus again, "but did he share with you the reason for the visit?"

"Nay, he did not. A sheriff came to escort him, although I know not why. If you can shed any light on the circumstances, I'd be most appreciative."

Alasdair's gaze narrowed, but he didn't say anything, instead motioning for her to sit in front of the hearth. He joined her once she was settled.

"I don't have an answer for you." His gaze scanned the hall. "Your sire built a strong fortress."

"His sire had most of it built, but it doesn't look the same as it did when he was alive."

"Aye," he said softly. "It looks like you're missing some wall hangings."

Of course he'd noticed. "Aye," she said. "My grandmother's tapestries. My sire's weaponry. Even some of the silver has disappeared. What is next? King Edward told me I was to be a willing wife, or

I would give up my land. But I've basically given it up anyway. As you know, whether you look to Scottish law or English, a husband's rights rank above his wife's."

"Except in primogeniture. We do allow female heirs to lead their clan."

"That right was taken from me. I doubt I'll get it back."

"My lady…"

"Emmalin, please."

"Emmalin, my grandsire sent me here because he was friends with your sire. I have some questions for you. May we talk in private?"

She nodded, leading him into her solar off the back of the hall. How she wished he would have some good news about Scotland or at least a fond memory of her sire. Anything that would give her hope of a change in her present situation.

Once she closed the door and sat down at the table, she motioned him to a seat opposite her.

Alasdair sat and said, "I'll not mince words. Your sire came to him in a dream and told him you were in trouble. Do you know why that might be?" His gaze bored into hers.

"Because my sire knows I'm not happy? I sense his spirit. He's not happy with the English here. He wants his land, his heritage, to be restored to Scottish control." She folded her hands in front of her on the table simply because it would prevent her from reaching out to this man. Hearing the reason for his visit made her want to wrap her arms around him and never let go.

"Mayhap we can come up with a way for you to be free of Hawkinge. I cannot believe such a man would be satisfied living in Scotland. Has he gone back to England often?"

"This is the first trip without me."

"Do you get along? Forgive me if I'm too forward."

Emmalin stared at the man in front of her. How she wished to tell him the truth—that she'd prefer it if *he* were in her bed every night instead of her husband. That she prayed each night for a way out of her marriage. That she hated every mark the English had left on her beautiful castle. She played with the stray threads on her skirt for a moment, then looked up at Alasdair again. "Nay," she said at last, "we don't suit each other at all, although he pretends otherwise when it suits him. Still, he's my husband, legally and under the orders of King Edward. How can I undo this?"

"Perhaps we'll think of a way. If you come to us, we will protect you."

"I'll have to give this some serious consideration, and this is the best time since he is absent." She stared at her folded hands on top of the table. If it were this simple, to just walk away, she could picture herself leaving on the morrow. But then she'd be forfeiting all rights to this land. *Her* land.

"Is that mutton stew? It smells wonderful," he said, his gaze catching hers.

"It is. Forgive me for my rudeness." She got up and moved to the door. "I do have a wonderful cook, though she's been sorely tested by my new husband." She opened the door and waved to Tamsin. "Bring our guest a trencher of stew and a platter of whatever else you are serving with a goblet of ale, please."

The servant returned quickly before she could take her seat again, setting a large trencher in front of him along with a platter of bread and various cheeses. She thanked Tamsin and closed the door behind her.

He smiled as he looked at the trencher. "I have to agree you have a fine cook if the aroma is any indication. Pardon my question, but will you join me? At least have some bread or cheese?"

She didn't hesitate to nod. "It smells so good that I would like a taste of the stew if you don't mind." It was customary for a husband to feed his wife, although much less so for a guest to do so. Langley always seemed to feed her morsels she didn't care for, as if he hoped to change her mind. Or torment her. But the thought of this man feeding her made her belly do flip-flops. And since they were alone, what difference would it make?

"Your favorite part of the stew, lass?"

She did her best not to let her surprise show on her face, strictly because she'd never been asked that question before. "The vegetables, if you please, my lord."

He arched a brow at her.

"Alasdair," she corrected, watching as he speared a parsnip for her. He held it out for her instead of shoving it into her mouth. Touching her tongue to it to determine its temperature, she noticed

Alasdair's eyes darken. His own lips parted.

A burst of heat shot through her, settling in places she hadn't expected. She chewed her food carefully, not wishing to rush the pleasure of the meal, or of watching him as he took a piece of meat, his eyes never leaving hers. She knew it was wrong to savor this man's companionship, but her husband was cruel and dismissive. Part of her wanted to know what it would be like to be married to a powerful Highlander like the man sitting across from her.

Although she knew she was pushing the boundaries of acceptability, she took a deep breath and asked, "Have you ever noticed, Alasdair Grant, that some things can be quite sensual with one person and quite ordinary with another?"

His gray eyes darkened a bit more, if that were possible, and not a sound could be heard in the solar except for their breathing. His gaze dropped to her lips and he whispered, "I have noticed that with you. Would you like another bite?"

"Just a small piece, if you please." She leaned toward him and parted her lips, closing her eyes as she did so. Although she'd gotten out of the practice of trusting men, she knew in her heart Alasdair wouldn't hurt her or do anything cruel.

"I'll place it on your tongue and you must guess what it is."

She nodded slightly, her lips still open, her eyes still closed. A warm morsel landed on her tongue, although most of her attention was fixed on the warm breath that now feathered her cheek. He had leaned in close.

He whispered, "What type of vegetable is it?"

She savored the piece, letting out a small moan that she hadn't planned, and finished chewing before she said, "Carrot. A delicious carrot."

"One more. Do not open your eyes."

She leaned forward, offering him her tongue one more time. The tiniest tidbit landed on her tongue, something she hadn't had in a long time because her husband didn't care for them. "A pea. My favorite."

She opened her eyes and stared straight into those gray eyes that reached right down to her soul. His thumb came up and rubbed her bottom lip. "Gravy, you have a bit of gravy there."

Looking her in the eyes, he licked the salty liquid from his finger.

Emmalin swore she was about to pass out from a desire so foreign to her she didn't know how to handle it. Oh, if only things were different. If only this man were her husband instead of Langley. She knew that he would protect her and love her the way a woman was meant to be loved, with every part of his being. She imagined his every touch would feel like a caress to her soul. Her imagination and her desire were getting away from her.

She was married and this man was not her husband.

And she didn't care.

Fortunately, two serving maids knocked and came in, interrupting them with two fruit tarts.

The spell was broken, but she knew one thing.

Someday, she'd kiss Alasdair Grant.

To hell with Langley Hawkinge.

CHAPTER SIX

—————◆—————

THE NEXT DAY, AFTER THE cousins had taken their leave, Emmalin wandered around the courtyard, giving thought to all Alasdair and Dyna had said.

Would it be best if she just ran away?

Part of her rebelled at the thought. This was her land, MacLintock land, and she did not wish to leave it behind. And yet, she wasn't sure how much longer she could play pretend. Ultimately, she decided to give herself a few days to make a decision. Langley wouldn't be back for at least that long. If she ever made her mind up to go to Grant land, she didn't think it would prove difficult for her to get away.

Gaufried called out her name, jostling her from her thoughts, and when she turned toward him, she immediately noticed two things. He looked distressed, and he was with two men dressed as knights. Clearly they were English. These were the king's men, of that much she was certain. Were they here with some message from Langley?

They both bowed to her in tandem, then one said, "Your pardon, my lady, but we have bad news to report."

"Get on with it," she said, having no idea what

they would tell her. Her heart was in her throat.

"Your husband has passed on. He was found dead, I'm afraid. An animal attack." The man turned a bit green after this pronouncement.

The other man stepped forward and handed her a small bag. "These are his belongings. Our king wished for us to return them to you."

She froze, staring at them, unsure whether she'd heard correctly. "An animal? What kind of animal?" They had to be referring to someone else.

Dead? Langley was dead?

"A boar. Or rather several boars. No one knows for certain. But he is dead."

Emmalin stared at the two men as though they'd grown stalks of wheat out of the tops of their heads. They couldn't be telling the truth, could they? She'd wished for him never to come back, and now he wouldn't.

Could she somehow be at fault?

No, that was a foolish thought.

One of the men cleared his throat. "We're sorry for your loss, my lady. The king grants you a fortnight to mourn, then requests your presence at the royal castle in Berwick."

"She's had a terrible shock," Gaufried said, rushing over to stand at her side. Perhaps he worried her knees would buckle. They did indeed feel weak. "We must get her inside."

He attempted to spin her back toward the castle, but she didn't move, her gaze still on the messengers.

"Go about your business," Gaufried said to the

other guards standing around watching them. "I'll see her inside. I fear she could faint."

Turning back to the two knights, he said, "If you would like a light repast, I will arrange it for you inside."

They followed him along, which suited Emmalin just fine. At this point, she didn't wish to make conversation with anyone. Shock had silenced her tongue. But she felt no sadness, only relief and a hint of guilt because of it. Her marriage to the cruel baron was over.

She would have to go to the king in a fortnight, but for the next half a moon, she was free.

Free of judgment, snide remarks, and fits of violence.

Gaufried waved the knights toward a trestle table once they were inside the hall, but Emmalin barely noticed. What she did notice was that the people in the hall looked happier than they had of late. They looked *freer*. Had they already heard the news, or were they simply pleased the baron was away from home?

Gaufried waved to Bessie. "Take your mistress to her chamber. She's had quite a shock. Messengers from the king arrived and said the baron died from an animal attack."

Bessie's eyes widened with shock, and she rushed to Emmalin's side, taking her elbow.

"Oh my dear, I'll take her abovestairs, find her something warm to drink."

Gaufried whispered, "Water of life, get her some."

She climbed the stairs, dear Bessie right behind

her, urging her forward. The great hall began to fill up with her dear clan, whispers and gasps rising up to her.

If she had to say, some sounded quite pleased by the events of the morn.

When they reached her chamber, Bessie helped her into a chair by the hearth, then banked the fire. She disappeared for a moment and returned with a wee goblet of a golden liquid.

"Here now," she said, handing it to Emmalin. "Drink this."

Her sire's favorite beverage that he closely guarded.

She swallowed it down, the fire in her throat feeling oddly wonderful, then returned the goblet to Bessie.

"'Tis quite all right if you cry now, my lady," Bessie said, squeezing her shoulder. "No one will hear you. They'll not think worse of you, either." For a moment, all she could manage was a nod. Her maid started to bustle around the chamber, dusting and cleaning as she moved.

"Bessie?"

"What is it, my lady?" She hurried back to her, standing directly in front of her to do her bidding.

"I don't feel like crying."

There. She'd said it. Would her maid be shocked?

"It will come, I'm sure of it. For some, it takes a few days. The tears will come. You'll see."

Emmalin just shook her head. "But I was forced to marry him. I tried to do everything he asked of me like a good wife should, but he didn't love me."

"And you, my lady? Did you love him?" Bessie reached forward to stroke her cheek, her touch so very gentle.

She shook her head. "Nay, of course not," she said, but a tear fell from one of her eyes.

"Then why do you cry?"

"How awful it seems for someone so young to die and not be missed. Bessie, I wished that he wouldn't come back, and now he never will."

Bessie let out an unladylike snort. "Good riddance. If you'll pardon my frankness, that man only loved himself. He doesn't deserve to be mourned by anyone. Why, I'd throw a celebration if I could. Leaders should lead by example. That man was as shallow as they come and had no idea how to lead. He was naught more than a parasite." Then her maid's hand went to her mouth. "Dearest me, I shall learn to keep my tongue when speaking of the dead."

Emmalin burst into laughter, then got up and hugged her maid. "I do love you, Bessie. Do not concern yourself. Every word you speak is true, but we shall keep them between us. Whatever would I do without you and Gaufried?"

"Do not worry your pretty self. We'll take care of you. Now, did the king give you any decrees? Even though there was no love, he was still an English baron. You must be careful how you react and act devastated by his loss. Do whatever you are told to do."

"Aye, I must appear at Berwick Castle in a fortnight. I fear he'll wish to marry me to another baron. Mayhap a worse one." She found herself thinking of another man, a Highlander with fierce yet gentle gray eyes. "I have a thought," she said. "I'd like you to send a message to Alasdair Grant. They cannot be too far yet. I want him to be aware of what's happened."

Bessie squeezed her shoulder as she guided her back to a seat in front of the fire. "I'll take care of it. There's no use speculating, my dear. You have a fortnight to relax and enjoy yourself. You deserve it, my dear. You did a fine job holding up to your end of the marriage, but I'm glad to see it end. He'd have not made you happy."

Emmalin had to admit, truer words had never been spoken.

———◆———

Alasdair and Dyna were about three hours from MacLintock land when he motioned for them to stop. He had a sudden urge to turn around.

"Something's wrong," he said as he dismounted, motioning for his four guards to take a break. He found a copse of trees where they could find shelter while they decided what to do next.

"I agree. I feel it in the wind. It will be nightfall if we return to her castle," Dyna said. "A good time to creep about a strange castle." She'd plaited her hair back on top of her head in case she had to pretend to be a lad again. Dyna always did like a challenge.

"You already crept about, did you not?" he asked glibly.

Dyna grinned, bringing out a skin of ale and taking a swig before handing it to Alasdair. "I did. I searched the upstairs and the cellars while you were feasting."

He ignored her wee tease and asked, "And did you discover anything unusual?"

"Aye, I saw verra few valuables. Where were the swords on the walls? There were a few candlesticks, but I saw verra few decorations or heirlooms. You know how the Scots are about their castles. 'Tis a sense of pride."

"She mentioned that her husband had taken many of the things down."

"I wonder if he didn't take some of the items for himself. Think you he would sell their possessions?"

"From what little I know of him, he would sell his own brother." Alasdair took a swig and paused, thinking. His sire had always taught him to follow his instincts. Right now, he had a nagging feeling that something was happening at Emmalin's castle. Dyna hadn't sensed anything, but then again, her abilities had always been a wee bit temperamental. She didn't always know—but when she sensed something it was inevitably true. Besides which, Grandpapa had had that dream…

"Aye, I'd like to go back," he said. "You did a fine job of stopping the bastards who tried to kidnap Emmalin over a sennight ago, but I hope you won't need to shoot anyone this time." He broke out a couple of oatcakes and handed her one.

She took it, but before she took a bite, she paced around the area. He knew Dyna was ensuring they were indeed hidden, something she did without thinking.

Apparently satisfied, she broke off a piece of her meager meal and sat on a log, crossing her long legs straight out in front of her. She had on the same type of leggings Great Aunt Gwyneth, her archery teacher, had worn for years.

"We were lucky to stop those men," she said. "Had they not been such poor warriors, we may not have rescued her. Her husband didn't go to much of an effort to get her back, did he?"

"Nay, I thought the same. His every hair was still in place." He sat beside her, sighing as he did so.

"She said she was in an arranged marriage, aye?" she asked.

"Aye, a marriage arranged by King Edward, which means he conferred with no one other than his one baron. He's trying to take over Scotland in every way he can, and I don't like it. If he keeps stealing our Scottish lasses, all our land will be owned or managed by the English. She's too good for the English bastard." He stared up into the trees, noticing the flurry of birds in the area.

"Do you know what I hate, Alasdair? I hate that women are assumed to be ignorant. Incapable of leading. Who started that whole idea? I can think as quickly as most men. I'm quite certain Emmalin did not need the king to marry her off so someone else could control her land and people. She should lead like Diana Drummond does."

"I agree, and you know it. Forget what the world thinks. Your parents believe in you and your sisters.

They treat you the same as they do your brother. And Alick, Els, and I know you can out-strategize most men."

Casting him a sideways glance and a smirk, she said, "My thanks to you. All but Grandsire. No one can out-strategize him. He is a brilliant leader."

"That he is," he said wistfully, dreading the day they would lose him. Men and women lived into their seventh decade, so he hoped and prayed Grandpapa would live into his eighth. True, he was not the swordsman he once was, but his experience was invaluable.

She played with her plait and stared into the sky. "I also hate that I must hide whenever we encounter anyone on one of our journeys. Everyone is always so worried about my reputation. Well, I don't give a shite about my reputation. I travel about with my cousins, not a bunch of English rogues."

He grinned, loving to see her in a fury. "You don't like the English much, do you?" He knew the answer, of course, but he thought to bait her.

"Nay, I don't. They'd have me sitting on a settee primping my hair. I'll not do that and you know it. Thank goodness for my parents and Great Aunt Gwyneth. Aunt Ashlyn, too. I can protect myself thanks to them. I'd join the Norse before I'd join the English."

"Well, your mother *is* half Norse," he said, cocking his brow.

They shared a laugh, and Dyna gave him a fierce grin. "We'll help Emmalin, Alasdair. Don't you doubt it. I think you're right about going back. But we should go alone, just the two of us. If we bring the men, there'll be trouble."

He nodded, trusting her impulses better than his own. Although it seemed they'd be safer with the men than without, he knew Dyna's words carried weight.

Wanting to waste no more time, he quickly found the leader of the guards. "Bring the men back to Clan Grant. We'll follow on the morrow."

Although the guards were reluctant to leave them, they had little choice but to do as they'd been bidden.

Soon afterward Dyna and Alasdair began their ride, moving too fast to speak. Two hours into their journey, Alasdair froze, glancing up at the sky again as another flock of birds squawked overhead.

"What is it?" Dyna asked, reaching for her bow as she slowed her horse beside him.

"I'm not sure," he said, dismounting, "but we should take a look before we gallop onto her land on horseback. I suspect we're not alone." She got down, too, and tied up both horses. Alasdair listened for a moment before he moved over to a break in the trees to peek out, Dyna directly behind him.

"I feel it, too. Something is wrong, verra wrong," she whispered.

"Hellfire, 'tis a whole garrison…an English garrison. They don't look like a reputable bunch, do they?" he whispered, even though they were much too far away to be heard. Several knights led the charge. They carried no banners, which was highly suspicious in his mind. There were probably a hundred men, fifty on horseback and fifty on foot. "Emmalin only has about fifty men. 'Twas all I counted when we were there."

"Mayhap those are Hawkinge's men returning. Do you see him anywhere?"

"Nay. They are too quiet to be visiting. This is meant to be an attack, and the two of us are not going to stop them." They would have been able to confront the men if they'd brought their guards along, but Dyna's instinct had been to leave them. There had to be a reason for that. Perhaps a battle would have put Emmalin in too much danger. "We have to make a plan to get Emmalin and her maid out," he finished.

Dyna squinted at the men, attempting to see them better, then gave a nod full of self-assurance. "They look like a seedy group if I've ever seen one. My mother warned me about men like that."

"She did? What did she tell you?" Dyna's parents were both known for their quick-thinking and skills. Connor Grant had proven to be the son of Alexander who'd gained most of his sire's talents with a sword, and her mother was Norse, and according to Uncle Connor, one of the strongest women he'd ever met.

Dyna was proving to have the best talents from both of them.

"Not to trust them. She said they'll stab you in the back without thinking twice. We need to be careful. In my opinion, they look like sneaky arses who deserve to get their arses kicked."

Alasdair grinned. "Your mother knows best, and

if I remember correctly, she trusts no one outside Clan Grant. I was thinking of catching up to them to question one or two, mayhap use bird calls to get one of them alone."

"Don't do it," Dyna said adamantly. "You'll regret it. I say we sneak into the castle and find out what they want. 'Tis the only way because the English are also lying bastards. The mistress is Scottish but the chieftain is English, aye?"

"He's no chieftain. Only the Scots are chieftains in my mind. He's a bloody English baron." He spat off to the side to stress his point. "I'm going to sneak inside. She's seen me before, so if I show up in her bedchamber, she'll not scream…"

Her face contorted at that comment, though he didn't understand why. "What?"

She jerked her head. "You'll just appear in her bedchamber? And what if you catch them in the middle of…"

"I won't. Trust me. I need to talk to her. 'Tis the only way I'll know for sure whether she's in danger from those men. Grandpapa won't be satisfied unless I do. You know how he is about his dreams." He let go of the branches he'd been holding aside to give him a better view of the group. "This could be the exact reason he'd had his dream, the verra danger he feared. Her life could easily be in danger."

"Aye, you know his dreams do tend to come true. You must be careful. What about me?"

"Can you hide just outside the curtain wall and watch the activities inside the keep?"

"There's a moat, but I'm not interested in

swimming. I should be able to find a tree I can climb. Mayhap I'll dress as a lad and sneak inside."

"Just don't get caught," Alasdair warned.

Dyna just smirked.

"Never."

CHAPTER SEVEN

EMMALIN WAS SITTING IN FRONT of the hearth in the great hall when the door to the keep flew open. Gaufried hurried inside with one of his guards. The man had sweat pouring down the side of his face and looked liable to faint.

"What is it?" she asked, her heart leaping into her throat.

"My lady, a garrison of English soldiers is headed this way. What shall we do?"

She stood, her needlework falling to the floor. "What? Why? Are you sure they're coming here?"

"Aye." Gaufried kneaded his hands. Bessie approached them from where she'd been cleaning the table and preparing for dinner, her hands going to her mouth. Tamsin was behind Bessie, already close to crying. Aunt Penne came down the stairs, taking everything in.

"I was afraid this would happen," Gaufried said. "You've lost your husband. You have no one to protect you or your land, my lady."

"How many men have we?" She glanced about the hall, looking at all the maids and warriors gathered inside. The concern on their faces was evident.

"We sent half our forces with your husband. We

have less than fifty. They look to have more than twice that number."

"My lady, you must hide," Bessie said. "They'll come for you. Pardon me for being blunt, but the English are known for raping our women. Get away and take some valuables with you."

Aunt Penne whispered, "They'll rape us all. We must hide." Clearly stricken with fear, she froze, which didn't help her in the least.

Emmalin stood there for a moment, biting her lip, trying to absorb what had just happened, but she knew she couldn't afford to delay. Her father had trained her well for a moment like this. "I cannot believe they are coming for me. After all, our mourning banner is flying, and the king ordered me to come a fortnight after the baron's death. That is still several days away. And yet, we must still prepare as if they were. Bessie, have the ladies take our nice set of silver goblets and hide them in the cellars. Tamsin, you are to take Aunt Penne and hide her in the village until Gaufried comes for you. Gaufried, you and your guard are to find all of the silver candlesticks and the one remaining bowl and bury them out back. Don't bring anyone else with you."

Tamsin said to Penne, "Come, my lady. We must pack a bag for you quickly. Then we'll leave."

Once they'd all left to fulfill their duties, Emmalin addressed the other occupants of the hall. "Be brave, my warriors. You must prepare to defend our castle. Tell the others outside to do the same. The rest of you must go to the village and tell the women and children to hide. Bring them into the forest if it becomes necessary." Thankfully they all left to tend to their duty. She prayed that they would be all right, but there was no time to fret. She had to leave the castle through the tunnel, just as her sire had taught her.

Gaufried returned from the solar, some valuables in his hands. His guard carried the rest.

"How much time have we?" Emmalin asked.

"About an hour. We'll take care of the rest. You must go abovestairs now, my lady," Gaufried said. "Disguise yourself as a lad."

"I will go with you, my dear," Bessie said. When she opened her mouth to object—if those men were after anyone, they were after Emmalin, and Bessie would be in more danger if she stayed with her—her maid simply shook her head. "'Tis my duty and my wish."

"Change quickly, mistress, and go out the tunnel," Gaufried said. He referred to the hidden passageway accessible from her chamber. The chieftain's chamber. "Leave now, as soon as possible, and Bessie will follow you. Wait at the end of the tunnel in the trees. She'll find you and advise you of all that's transpired."

She glanced at the dear faces, loyal workers who had been with her family for years.

"You must hurry, lass," Bessie whispered.

She gave them each a swift hug and hurried abovestairs. After changing into some breeches she occasionally used for riding and a dark tunic with no identifying marks on it, she grabbed a scarf to cover her hair. Her disguise complete, she packed a small bag with the barest necessities and then pulled her mother's jewelry from the chest. She tucked the ruby ring in the pocket sewn inside her breeches and packed two silver necklaces inside her bag. One had a sapphire stone that was priceless, but she'd mostly chosen the pieces because they reminded her of her mother. Although her mother had never been as warm as Bessie, she'd been beautiful and regal, and Emmalin had wanted to be just like her.

Bessie knocked before stepping into the chamber behind her. "Go now," she said. "I'll place the chest in front of the entrance to the tunnel so you'll not be caught. Godspeed, my lady."

Emmalin grabbed a lit candle just before she entered the secret passageway, taking her time to climb down the staircase so she didn't fall.

Once her boots landed on the dirt floor, she slowed her progress. Her sire had taught her to move slowly at first, giving the creatures inside time to scatter from the sound of her steps. To her surprise, however, she could hear something overhead. A din she soon identified as swords clashing. How had chaos broken out so quickly?

The English had arrived before Gaufried had thought possible. She'd only just made it out in time. The sounds filtering down proved that this was not a friendly visit and they had no respect for the mourning flag. Or, apparently, for their king's summons to the castle's mistress.

She froze where she stood, knowing she should

be running with wild abandon, but all she could think of were all the people she'd left behind.

But before she could even consider racing back up the stairs to help, a hand snaked around her waist and another clapped over her mouth, keeping her from screaming. She squirmed and tried to kick and bite her attacker, but a voice in her ear stopped her.

"By the bloody saints above, stop kicking me, lass! 'Tis me, Alasdair."

She stopped her attack, still holding a death grip on the candle, and fell against him with a sigh of relief, the candlelight illuminating the handsome face peering over her shoulder. The warm hand he'd held over her mouth slipped around to her neck, massaging the knots there. He whispered in her ear, "I'll protect you. We're leaving through the tunnel. There are over a hundred men in the English garrison and they do not look friendly."

"I'm so grateful you're here," she said. "But we must move. I heard swords clashing in the great hall."

"I agree," he said as he released her. "Where is your husband? Has he returned yet?"

"He's dead," she said bluntly, leading him down the tunnel. No need to be circumspect. "I received a message from King Edward saying he was killed by an animal attack."

She glanced over her shoulder. Although she couldn't see him well, she suspected he was as surprised to learn about Langley's death as she had been.

"My sympathies…" he said after a moment.

She stopped in her tracks to turn to him. "I don't need anyone's sympathy. Although I'm sorry he died so young, he was not a kind man."

"So you are not a grieving widow?" he asked, his hand brushing her cheek.

"Nay, I'm not," she whispered. It felt strange to admit it out loud, to a near stranger, but Alasdair had never felt like a stranger.

To her surprise, he reached for her, tugging her close to face him, the warmth of his hands sending tingles through her.

"Good, then do I have your permission to kiss you? I've been wanting to for some time now, but with you being a married woman…"

Her answer was to snake her free around his neck and pull his lips to her. He gave a low growl and kissed her back, pressing against the seam of her lips until she opened for him. His tongue met hers and they danced until she was nearly breathless, feeling the hard planes of his body against her breasts.

He finally pulled away and planted a small kiss on her forehead. "We must go," he said, tracing the line of her cheek. "Much as I would love to kiss you here for hours, I'll not risk us getting caught."

She grinned at his declaration, pleased that he'd enjoyed their encounter as much as she had, but she knew he was right. Time was a luxury they did not have. As before, she led the way while he checked behind them.

"Have you any idea why your castle is being attacked?" Alasdair asked.

He took a step closer and she caught his scent, a pleasing aroma she recalled from their previous meeting. What was it? Pine? Mint leaves? Something else...

"You know as much as I do. As you've said, my steward told me 'twas a garrison of Englishmen. I know not what they're after."

"Or whom? My guess is they're here for you. We have to get the hell out of here if that's the case." He made a small inhalation, then said, "My apologies, Emmalin. I spend too much time around my cousins."

He was interrupted by the sound of a door opening at the top of the staircase she'd descended.

Acting quickly, she blew out the flame of her candle. "Now we really must get the hell out of here," she whispered, tugging him along faster.

A voice echoed down to them. "She's probably in the tunnel. We must go after her."

"I'm not going in that hole," another voice said. She didn't recognize either voice, but they were both men and their accents identified them as English.

"Then I'll find others who will." He bellowed some names, and he and the first man continued to bicker while they waited for the new recruits.

Taking the opportunity to get ahead, Emmalin and Alasdair hastened their travel. He stopped her once they were far enough not to be overheard. "If they follow us all the way until the end, they'll catch up with us," he said in an undertone. "The tunnel is too small for us to run hard, especially in the dark. Is there another way out or must we take it to the end?"

"The tunnel was designed with many curves so their light will not reveal us, my sire's idea. He also prepared another safety precaution. There's a chamber hidden near the end of the tunnel. We can hide in it if need be."

"Can you locate it easily without the candle?" he asked, turning around to check behind him again. The men hadn't started their pursuit yet, but it was only a matter of time. "They're not close. I'll lead. One never knows what's at the end of these tunnels."

She was glad for the switch, if just to settle her worry of creatures in front of her. "Aye, there are three rocks built into the wall to mark the location. I'll need to keep my hand along the side of the tunnel to locate them."

"Come, we must hurry." He took her free hand, and that small movement made her feel more protected than she'd ever felt since losing her sire. Alasdair was strong and fierce, but he was also a gentleman.

They sped along silently, while in the distance, three pairs of boots descended the stairs. No matter how quickly they moved, the men could be heard following behind them, and the soft light from the men's glowing candles lit the passageway enough for them to see.

Alasdair changed places with her, giving her the lead ahead of him. "They're getting closer. If I must, I'll fight. You continue on to the hidden chamber.

I'll find you once I've gotten rid of them."

She hurried ahead of him, but murmured, "There are three of them and one of you. I must be able to help in some way."

"Nay, you were almost kidnapped in front of me once, I'll not risk it happening again. You must go in front of me," he said, his hand lightly on her lower back. "Besides, three against one are the odds I prefer."

Again, she thought she saw a gleam in those gray eyes. How she wished the light from the candle was stronger.

The way he was touching her, gentle, protective, reminded her of the way her father had been with her mother. He'd always been so solicitous of her well-being. So caring. He'd keep a hand on her hip, her lower back, her shoulder.

Something that had definitely been lacking in her short marriage.

They traveled silently for another half hour before her hand hit the first stone in the wall. "There. 'Tis the first one. The hidden door is not far ahead."

"They're still coming, so do what you must to enter it."

She found the door hidden behind a rock at the bend in the passageway. It was a clever arrangement because no one who didn't know about it would ever think to look for it. She glanced over her shoulder at him as she pushed it open, and before she could enter, he pulled her back.

"Allow me to go first, please."

She did as he asked, suddenly powerfully aware of his presence. Once he finished checking, he moved into it, standing sideways, and tugged her in to stand in front of him, facing him. He positioned himself so he could use his sword arm as soon as the door was opened.

"Will we both fit?" she asked, doing her best to squeeze into the tight space. "I think it was designed for one person, or one person and a child."

"We'll fit," he said, "You will have to touch me. Trust me, I'll not do anything that would be considered taking advantage of you. My grandsire would have my arse if I did."

She peered up at him, and even in the dark she knew he was a handsome devil. Her eyes had adjusted to the darkness, but not to *him*.

His long dark hair, his scruffy whiskers, his piercing gaze, his strong cheekbones all called to her. And his body? She chose not to think about that. If she did, she wouldn't be able to stand in this small space, pressed against him.

She leaned against Alasdair, and he closed the door, sending them into total darkness. The slight amount of candlelight filtering down the passageway had made a difference.

The darkness forced her to *feel*. Her hand fell against his hard chest, as sculpted as if it were the side of a rocky ravine. If she could trace him with her hands, she knew what she'd find: a narrow waist and muscular thighs.

Muscular thighs. How did one get muscles like that in their thighs?

Horseback riding, she had to guess. He could probably command his horse merely by moving his legs. Or could it be from running? Or sword-fighting? Whatever it was, he'd done a fine job at his task because his thighs felt like stone, too.

She leaned her head against his chest and felt his warm breath against her ear—and something else. The erection she felt gave her a little smile. It pleased her that he wasn't unaffected by her presence, though she decided not to mention it given their close quarters.

As the sounds of boots came closer, she began to tremble. She hated that there was nothing more they could do but be as quiet as possible.

She hated that it had come to this, hiding in her own tunnel while her people were being attacked.

Willing her rapidly beating heart to slow down, she stared at the ceiling above them. Voices carried to them, but she did not recognize any of them.

A warm breath whispered in her ear, "Do not say a word."

The boots came closer. She gripped Alasdair's hand in a panic, the one settled on her waist. The other held his sword, ready to attack if need be, so she couldn't touch that side of him.

He gave her hand a squeeze and pulled her closer, encouraging her to lean into him again instead of standing so straight, her knees locked in fear.

What else could she do?"

The boots came closer.

"You two go to the end. I'll wait here." The man was short of breath from the exertion of the walk, if she were to guess. "I need to sit on one of these rocks."

"Don't move," another man said. "If we find her, we'll come get you." Two pairs of footsteps moved forward while the third man sat on a rock with a huff.

A moment later, one of the two returned. "Give us the torch," he insisted. "You don't need it." The man on the rock must have done so, because the sound of boots retreated.

She couldn't talk, wouldn't talk, no matter what. Closing her eyes, she inhaled the scent of her comrade, the pine, the bit of horse, and oats. He must have just eaten an oatcake. She dipped her head, willing herself to stay strong.

The two sets of boots returned and came closer. "There's no sign of them. We're heading back through the tunnel. Mayhap she was hiding in the castle, waiting for an opportunity to use the tunnel. We could run into her on our way back. And what if there's a hiding place along the way?"

"Hiding place. In a tunnel? I've never heard of such a thing."

"Well, I have, you daft fool. We have to check. It could be anywhere."

The boots moved and stopped directly in front of their door.

They'd both be dead if they found them.

CHAPTER EIGHT

ALASDAIR WOULD NOT BE ABLE to tolerate this much longer. The fools were arguing just outside their door. They were extremely vulnerable in this position, but they had no choice but to stand still and wait. At first, he'd been quite pleased to have her next to him, his traitorous arousal pressing against her in a way she couldn't ignore.

But then the truth of their situation had taken over.

And the closeness.

Sweat ran down the side of his face. He wished he could wipe it away, but Emmalin had a tight grip on his one hand and the other rested on the hilt of his sword.

The walls were too close, there wasn't enough air, and their bodies were pressed too tightly together. How he wished he could will his thoughts away and just focus on the fact that he had a stunningly beautiful woman in his arms, leaning against his chest, but he couldn't. He couldn't stop thinking of his last battle. Of the bodies that had fallen on him, the dead weight of them. He'd flailed to get them off, but their combined weight was too great— it had sucked the air out of him. He'd clawed at their skin, kicked and pushed until Els had finally managed to move one. With one moved from him, he had easily lifted the second dead man.

He felt that way again. Unable to breathe, to move.

What if the English bastards had moved the rock a wee bit and edged it in front of their door?

What if they were stuck in here for hours while the English continued to search the area, concentrating their efforts on the passageway?

What if the hours turned into days?

How long could they live without water?

He let out a breath as slowly as possible so as not to make a sound. The brutes stepped away to walk down the passageway again, all three if he were to guess from the sound, headed toward the end. He felt like a total failure. His fears, the ones he hated so, *dreaded* so, had taken over.

He closed his eyes, focusing on the sweet scent of flowers in front of him.

"Are you hale, Alasdair?" Emmalin whispered.

"Aye," he lied. "I'll be fine. I tend to panic in small spaces. I'd attack, but I fear one of them would grab you while the other two fight me, so I think it would be best if we wait for them to leave. Unfortunately, I'm not a patient man in most situations."

"Did something happen to give you this fear? Something in your past?"

Hellfire, something certainly had happened, but he couldn't talk about it. "Aye, but I cannot speak of it now. We must be careful. They could return and hear us."

As if sensing the extent of his discomfort, his fear, she pulled his left arm around to the front of her waist so it settled between them. Humming lightly, she rubbed her thumb in circles across the back of his arm.

Hell, but she was an angel from heaven. He tipped his head down until all he could smell was the scent of wildflowers in her hair. He focused on her scent, her touch, and her humming, and the looming panic slowly disappeared.

They stayed that way for a while, until all sounds of the Englishmen disappeared. Opening the door, he led with his sword arm. He moved her out but quickly stepped in front of her.

"They're gone, I think." He grabbed her hand behind him and held it fast. "How much longer is the tunnel? I was in such a hurry when I first came through that I didn't pay enough attention. We need to get away before they come back or send someone else." He waited for his eyes to adjust to the darkness. Although the intruders' light no longer penetrated the darkness, a small pinprick of light came from the door at the end.

"But where will we go?" she asked, resting her hand on his upper arm.

"Do you have family anywhere else?"

"Nay," she whispered. "This is my home." Her tone was such that he guessed tears would be next, but he didn't hear any sniffling.

"Until we can figure out what is going on with your land, I'll take you to Grant land. Our lairds should have information on what the English are doing now."

"Whose side are you on? The Bruce or the English?"

He snorted. "I told you I'm a Scot. That should answer your question."

"Some Scots think the Bruce shouldn't be our king."

"And they are fools. I know there are others who wish to be King of Scotland, but we must unite behind one man. We must stand beside the Bruce or we have no chance at defeating the English. We must unite. John Balliol was tossed aside by the king, and Wallace is making foolish mistakes. The Bruce has the best chance of pressuring Edward to install him as King of Scotland. And if that happens, most of our troubles will be over. He certainly wouldn't allow Edward to force you into another marriage to a foul Englishman."

She didn't say anything, so he was uncertain of her reaction to his words. Did she agree with him? He wished he could see her face, read her feelings in her expression.

"I'll go to your clan with you. 'Tis not safe here. I just pray my aunt, my maids, and my steward will be spared."

"Many times the English will spare the help because if they plan to occupy your castle, they'll need maids and cooks. Your aunt could be used against you. Where is she?"

"I sent her with one of my maids to be hidden in the village or possibly the forest. Was I wrong? Should I have brought her along?"

"Nay, probably not. 'Tis a long tunnel and if she's older, she may not have made it to the end. The garrison will have no idea who she is. If they are after you, they'll search and leave. Edward is not giving the order to massacre at present."

"I'll pray that no harm comes to anyone."

"We'll not be much help to them if we stay, but they may survive. You've reason to hope. We can talk later. For now, we must go. You realize you are now the laird of this castle, so your safety is my priority." He didn't wait for a response, but instead wished to remind her what was most paramount when going against the English.

They headed down the passageway, and when they reached the end, he leaned forward and placed his ear against the door, listening to the sounds on the other side. Finally satisfied that all was quiet, he opened the door slowly.

He needed to retrieve Midnight and find Dyna—if she didn't find him first. He and Alick and Els hadn't always loved spending time with their younger cousin. In fact, they'd occasionally attempted to leave her behind. Once, they'd caught sight of a cave that looked to be a perfect fort. They'd gone inside, intent on keeping their newfound secret, only to find Dyna sitting on a log in the back.

Elshander had gone daft. "How the hell did you know we were coming here? We didn't even know!"

Dyna had smirked, shrugged her shoulders, and said, "I'm magical." She'd winked at Els and strolled out the mouth of the cave. Her parting words had upset Els even more. "And I'm smarter than you. Don't ever doubt me."

They'd all learned the truth of those words. Dyna's talents were undeniable, and he hoped beyond hope they would assist her now. They needed to escape as quickly as possible.

Emmalin had a tight grip on his hand as they crept out into the night. He took four deep breaths to satisfy his need for fresh air after spending so much time in the tunnel. It was exactly what he needed to calm his pulsating blood. All was quiet, so he pointed back toward the castle wall. "This should be the quickest way to my horse."

"Something moved," she whispered, stopping him and pointing into the distance near some bushes.

Three men on foot came at them. He guessed them to be the same ones who'd walked up and down the passageway searching for them, although he could have sworn they'd talked about going back up the tunnel. Pushing Emmalin behind him, he swung his sword in an arc twice to attempt to frighten them off. Two hung back, but their companion lunged at him with a roar. They parried three times before he caught the man in the belly and he collapsed onto the ground. The last two finally got the gumption to attack, coming at him with a bellow.

Emmalin reached for a rock and lifted it overhead, ready to hurl it at one of them. Fear nearly choked him. She was much too close to danger. "Get back,

Emmalin. I can handle two of them."

Rather than step back, she heaved the rock at one of the men, hitting him on the back of his neck, which threw his focus off and allowed Alasdair to slice him deep in his leg. He swung again, cutting the third man's sword arm and forcing him to drop his weapon.

The two men stared at him, their eyes full of murder as if they were trying to decide what to do next, when two arrows sluiced through the air, killing them both before they could wonder what had struck them. Emmalin ran to Alasdair and attempted to tug him behind two trees, but Alasdair knew better.

They were in no danger from this archer.

"Dyna, where are you?"

His cousin dropped out of a tree, landing not far from him, a wide smile on her face. "I was beginning to think I'd have to come in after you."

"Nay, we were delayed, but Emmalin has decided to go to Grant land with us." He turned to Emmalin, who still had a strong grasp on his hand. "Emmalin, you remember my cousin Dyna?"

"Greetings to you," she said. Although she had to be surprised, she'd recovered quickly. "Where did you learn to shoot like that?"

"Many people, but primarily Gwyneth Ramsay. Would you like to learn? I'd be happy to teach you someday."

Emmalin turned to look at him before she answered, a small grin appearing on her face. "I'd prefer to learn how to fight with a sword. My sire taught me how to use a dagger, but I'd like to try a larger weapon."

Alasdair arched his brow at that.

"I'd be pleased to teach you, lass. There's no better place to learn than Grant land."

CHAPTER NINE

EVEN AFTER TWO DAYS OF riding, Emmalin's mind continued to fret over everything that had happened. Two thoughts recurred the most:

Her husband was dead.

Her castle, her sire's beloved castle, was presently occupied by the English.

One thought made her wish to jump for joy while the other made her wish to sob her heart out. Her sire would be devastated, but he wouldn't blame her. She wouldn't give up, either. If she could reclaim her home, she would. Was it foolish to hope it was possible?

"Lass," Alasdair said, tugging her back against him on his horse. "Do not make yourself daft thinking of the past. You cannot change it."

She glanced at him over her shoulder. "How could you tell?"

"The wrinkles in your forehead." He gave her a sly grin as he said it.

"I don't have wrinkles on my forehead," she said, her fingers brushing against the skin there. At least, she didn't feel any yet.

"Made you forget your thoughts, though, did I not?"

"Aye, you did." When they came into a meadow,

she saw it for the first time—an enormous castle rose up in the distance, the kind she'd thought only existed in England. "Is that Grant Castle? So large this far into the Highlands?"

Dyna rode up on the other side of her. "It's quite a castle, is it not? And the inside is just as beautiful. I'm so glad we live here. Mama talks about visiting the Norse, but I'd hate to be that far away from Grandpapa. I fear he'd pass while I was gone."

She could feel the pride emanating from him as he nodded. "My grandsire loves the land. He was born here, and he's doubled the size of the keep to handle all of our clan. He did not want any of his bairns to live elsewhere. We're nearly all here."

As they drew closer, she squeezed his hand, which was presently wrapped around her middle. "I love the flowers at the entrance. Who tends them?"

"That would be Aunt Elizabeth and Aunt Kyla. Grandpapa expects them every year. Grandmama planted many of the ones that return, which is why he doesn't consider it summer without some wildflowers. But they also plant more once autumn comes."

"My mother loved flowers. We spent many hours planting in her gardens. Those are cherished memories."

"You've lost your mother?"

"Aye, about four years ago, my sire a year ago."

"I lost my mother a year ago."

"I'm sorry to hear that. 'Tis verra hard to lose a parent." She wished to ask him more questions, but a group of horses came flying out the gates, two lads in the lead.

The sight of them made him grin. "You've m[...] these fools before. They're my cousins, and we were all three of us born on the same day. 'Twas a cold day in February." He waved as they rode toward them.

They did look familiar, although it struck her that the lads didn't look at all alike. All had different coloring, even Dyna. "But you are all so different."

"Aye." He waited until they were close enough, then introduced them. "My cousin Elshander is the fair-haired and Alick is flame-haired."

"Greetings to you both," she said, nodding her head.

"She was in danger after all?" Els asked.

"Aye, we'll explain inside. Grandpapa? How is he?" he asked, turning his head to Emmalin to explain. "He took a fall before we left."

"Strong as ever, but he has a more exaggerated limp when he walks," Els explained. "Aunt Jennie had to stay for a while to keep him from moving about so much. He's a stubborn man, but she said he'll be fine in another moon."

Emmalin stayed quiet for the remainder of the ride, soaking in the sights and the warmth of the clan. Several people rode out to greet them, smiles on their faces. She enjoyed visiting different clans, for it oft made her think about how she could make her own clan better or improve their keep.

But was it still her keep?

Would it ever be Scottish land again?

Alasdair set her down near the stables. Dyna,

ınted, smiled at her. "I'll see you
ments. If you need anything at

.hough she hadn't spent much
..ıı Dyna, she quite admired her. Tall
..e, her skills at archery would put many a
..ıan's skills to shame.

Alasdair's other cousins vied for his attention, but he just shook his head. "Someone wishes to meet her. We'll be down for some food once I take her to visit with Grandpapa."

He whisked her away from a flurry of greetings and welcoming smiles.

"You have such a large, warm clan."

He gave her a wide smile, something she didn't see often from him. A serious man, usually, but these were serious times. "I do love my clan. I don't appreciate them as much as I should. Or I should say, I do appreciate them, but I'm not good at letting them know. I'm just used to being surrounded by a crowd."

"You are verra lucky. My clan is much smaller."

"You'll get your castle back."

He said it with such certainty, as if it were a promise. A pledge. Her heart leapt into her throat.

"I hope you're right," she said. "I fear the English will get their way about everything. They're certainly accustomed to it."

He led her inside the keep, but a lovely dark-haired lady caught him by the arm before he could start up the steps. "He's in his chamber. He's not feeling well today."

"Thank you, Aunt Kyla," he said, introducing Emmalin before they moved away. She could tell his aunt's tidings had left a mark on him, for his smile slipped away as he led Emmalin through the great hall. Servants were bustling about, putting torches in brackets around the walls and getting ready for the evening meal. Alasdair and Emmalin walked past them, to a chamber at the end of the hall. It had a wide doorway, much wider than she'd ever seen.

He noticed her stare and explained, "It was built as a healing chamber. The doorway was widened to make it easier to carry people inside. I have two aunts who are renowned healers and many cousins who are learning. We'll step in to see if he's still awake."

As soon as they entered the chamber, a booming voice called out, "I'm here by the fire, waiting for you."

Alasdair took Emmalin by the hand and led her to the small hearth on the outside wall. An older man sat in a chair with a fur across his lap, a long stick resting on the floor next to him. "Grandsire, this is Emmalin of Clan MacLintock."

"Come near the fire so I can see you, lass."

She moved closer to greet him, reaching for his hand to give it a squeeze. His strong grip surprised her. After hearing the story of the man's fall, she'd thought to see a decrepit old man with a grizzled beard, but this man was anything but decrepit.

Perhaps she shouldn't be surprised. Everyone had heard tales of the legendary swordsman and chieftain.

"Alex Grant. I was a friend of your sire's. He was a fine man. I'm sorry you lost him."

"My thanks," she mumbled, not sure what else to say to him.

"Sit down, please." He motioned to one of the empty chairs beside him. She sat, taking in the great man's presence. Her father had loved to tell the tale of how the great Alexander Grant had come to their rescue many years ago. A neighboring clan had threatened the MacLintocks without just cause, and the famous leader had come to help them, along with warriors who had upper arms three times the size of MacLintock soldiers and unrivaled fighting skills. They'd made quick work of their attackers, sending them off in a fright. The two men had remained in occasional contact ever since. Her sire had respected the man more than most.

"Grandsire, you are better after your fall?" Alasdair asked. "I was worried about you."

"Don't worry about me. When my time comes, I'll go gladly to see my dear Maddie again. 'Twas just another mishap with my knee."

Even at nearly seventy summers, an age hardly anyone achieved, the man had a commanding presence and keen eyes that followed everything in the chamber. "Tell me all," Alex said. "I hear your husband is dead. Should I give my apologies, or are you glad to be free of the English cur?"

She couldn't help but smile at his quick assessment of her situation. "I feel sorry for my husband…"

"But?"

"But not for myself. We never quite suited, but I felt I had no choice but to wed him. My sire told me to go along with Longshanks to keep everything peaceful." Knowing where the Grants' loyalties lay, she felt comfortable using King Edward's nickname.

"But 'twas not all your papa said."

"Aye," she said, pausing to gather her control. "He said I was to do as instructed by Edward, hope for the best, but if the worst came to pass, I should contact you or your sons. And if my land became a war zone, I was to disguise myself and get to Grant Castle."

Pride crossed the old man's features, a look she'd seen in her father's eyes on occasion. She could tell he was grateful for her sire's belief in him. Grateful to still be of use to his fellow Scots. The look passed and his quick mind pressed on in its quest for information.

"Which I see that you have done. Your sire visited me in a dream, you know, full of concern for you. What happened, my dear?"

"A garrison of English soldiers was sent to take over my castle. My steward notified me when they were an hour away. I took a few valuables and descended into our hidden tunnel. That's where I met your grandson." She fussed with her hands in her lap. The intense scrutiny in the man's gaze was a bit unnerving. "He had come back, you see, after leaving that morn. He had sensed something was wrong."

"And you brought her here without any fighting, Alasdair?"

"Aye. We only had to battle three, and with Dyna's assistance, we easily made it to our horses."

The man nodded and scratched his jawline, then said, "But I doubt Longshanks would leave you be. If I know the bastard well enough, he must have summoned you to England, probably to use you as another pawn. How long did he give you?"

Shocked again at the accuracy of the man's assessment, she didn't hesitate to tell him everything. "I was told to report to King Edward at Berwick Castle within a fortnight. The order was delivered a sennight ago."

Alex Grant leaned back in his chair, grinned, and said, "You'll be leaving before then. We have to get there before they have the chance to hide their lies."

Anxious to find out what the wise old man thought of her situation, she asked, "Why is he commanding me to go to Berwick? I'm supposed to be in mourning. I thought he'd leave me be for a while."

"King Edward will do what he must to subdue the Scots and stay in control. Make no mistake about it, Edward's ultimate goal is to become king of both England and Scotland. The more land he hands over to his English barons, the easier it will be for him. He'll do aught he can to subdue our people. What I'm unsure of is why he'd send a garrison of soldiers to overtake your land while you're in mourning. It would benefit him more to marry you off to another baron."

He thought for a moment before he continued, "My guess is that they weren't acting on Longshanks's orders. Another nobleman might be trying to force you into marriage with him. Tell me, where were your husband's estates?"

"I'm not sure of all of them. I know he owns one in London, but he also owns a manor in Berwick."

"And that's where the king said you are to report to him?"

She nodded.

Alex leaned back in his chair and said, "I don't like that. Something is afoot. Alasdair, you and your cousins will have to uncover the truth. Mayhap the information will be helpful to the Bruce." He reached for his goblet and held it up to both of them. "To Robert the Bruce and the Scots."

Alasdair and Emmalin both held their goblets up and said, "Long live our king."

CHAPTER TEN

———

EMMALIN LEANED OVER THE PARAPETS, breathing in the fresh night air. She could see forever up here, or at least it appeared so in the dark. It was a rare clear night, and the stars were out overhead, sparkling as if to say things would get better.

She shivered in the cold but had no desire to go back inside. One of the mistresses of the castle, Gracie, had led her to a lovely chamber. There was a warm fire in the hearth, two chairs pulled up in front of it, and plenty of furs piled on the soft bed. Sleep would be an appealing prospect, but her insides were still in a turmoil.

The screams she'd heard the other day had penetrated deep into her consciousness. Those had been her people's screams, and she didn't know what had happened to any of them.

The door opened, and she expected she would have to go back down the steps to her chamber, but to her surprise, Alasdair stepped out. She could tell by his reaction that she'd startled him as much as he had startled her.

"Lass, I was not expecting to see you here. Are you not cold in the night breeze?"

"A wee bit, but 'tis refreshing. You need not call

me lass since I am now a widow. Lasses are usually unmarried."

He stood next to her and leaned his elbows against the crenellation, looking over the vast courtyard of Grant Castle. "You were forced into the marriage, and you were wed for less than a year. You're still a lass in my eyes."

She nodded but didn't say anything. What could she say? "How many years wise are you, Alasdair Grant?"

"Nine and ten. And you?"

"Twenty. But you seem to have much more worldly experience than I do. I have never ventured far from my clan."

"I have gone many places," he said, his expression thoughtful. "Most of the time I respect and appreciate the experiences, good and bad, because they make me stronger, but other times, I regret them."

"Why? You can learn so much from travel." She leaned over the parapets with him, staring at the courtyard below. It was still early enough that quite a few people were milling about.

"Because some things have happened that I wish to forget."

"I understand that. I do," she said, swiping a lone tear that fell from the corner of her eye.

He stood and set his finger under her chin, turning it gently until their eyes met. In a very quiet voice, he said, "But the experiences I would sooner forget happened in battle. What made you feel this way? Is it something that happened during your time as a wife?"

Her hand shook as she pulled his finger away from her chin. "Aye, but I know so little about marriage. My mother was not here to advise me of my duties, so I know not if 'tis what any wife is asked to do."

"I'm not a woman…"

"Clearly…" She smiled but didn't wish to distract him from his thought.

He rolled his eyes, but continued, "and I've never been married, but I have many close kin who *are* married. I think I would know whether 'tis unusual. If you're willing to confide in me."

She sniffled, as she stared up at the sky.

"If you tell me what happened, I'll share one of my battle memories. We can trade secrets."

"All right." She swallowed, making the decision to confess one small truth to see what he thought. "My husband thought I was too bold. That my sire had cossetted me and made me too independent."

Alasdair's brows arched, but he said nothing.

"He told me I needed to learn my place."

"And what was your place?" His jaw had clenched, but she sensed his anger was for the dead man, not for her.

Too embarrassed to tell him the entire truth, she told him just enough until she could gauge his reaction. "I was bound for a day until I learned my place."

He still said nothing, but she could see the fury building in his gaze. "Your *place*?"

"My place was to do as I was told. I was not to

question him. And that built a fear in me I hadn't known I was capable of harboring."

He reached for her hand and ran his thumb back and forth across the back, a tender caress that sent warmth shooting up her arm.

"The fear of being married to a bastard?" he asked. "Because you were. Any man who would tie his wife up to teach her a lesson is a bastard. If he weren't dead, I'd kill him for you. And that is not a threat said lightly."

She gazed into his eyes, surprised to see the emotion there. It was clear he meant every word. Her respect for him grew to the size of the mountaintops nearby. "Nay, the fear of being tied up, unable to move. It was the closest form of torture I've ever experienced."

"And it didn't bother you being confined in that small space with me in the tunnel?" he asked, incredulous.

It hadn't, much as it had surprised her. "Not with you there," she said. "You made me feel safe. You always make me feel so safe and protected."

He ran a finger down the line of her jaw, and although it was the merest of touches, her body reacted more than it ever had to anyone. She found herself taking a small step toward him.

She trusted Alasdair Grant after a few days of knowing him, more so than she'd trusted her husband after months.

"I'm sorry you had to deal with that," he whispered, his lips so close to hers that she felt the wisp of his breath.

Anxious to shift the conversation away from her, she said, "Your turn. I told you something, now you must reveal a secret of your own."

He leaned back a touch, the moment between them gone. She had changed the air about them, simply because she was unsure how to act around a man like Alasdair. He made her feel as if she was, once again, losing control, only in a completely different way.

He let go of her hand and leaned against the parapet again. "Aye, I'll share one secret but only because of our agreement."

He stared into the dark night, a slight breeze ruffling his dark locks. She kept quiet, giving him the time he needed to gather his thoughts.

"My cousins and I fought at a recent battle in the Borderlands with Wallace. It was one of many I'd participated in, and this one gave me lasting memories I wish to forget, though I was fortunate to survive to tell our story. My cousins and I all survived."

"Be more specific please…" she pushed.

He shifted his gaze back to hers. "I'm so attached to my cousins that I found myself searching them out instead of focusing on my own fight. My grandsire warned me about it." He pointed to the scar along his jawline. "Earned me this."

He turned his head at an angle so she could see it in the moonlight. "I noticed it when I first met you. Had it been a wee bit lower, you may not have survived." She reached her finger up to touch it, but then held back, afraid he would refuse her.

He whispered, "You may."

"Does it hurt?"

"Nay."

She touched it softly, then traced it down to the edge in his neck. "I can't imagine feeling something so painful."

He took a step closer and set his hand on her hip. "I don't even recall it. There are other memories from that battle that haunt me more."

"Secret?" she whispered.

"Not to you. Two dead bodies fell on me and I couldn't breathe. I thought I would die there if not for Els who pulled them from me."

She nodded. "I understand your feeling in the tunnel. If I were to guess, it took a great strength for you to come after me through that enclosed space."

He stared up at the night sky. "True, but I never considered not coming after you."

She didn't step away, instead basking in the simple pleasure of his closeness. "Why have you never married?" she asked, dropping her hand from his scar to his shoulder.

"Fear."

She gave him a puzzled look. Then, unable to stop herself, she ran her finger across his bottom lip, exploring him, touching him in a very different way than she'd ever touched her husband. There was one major difference.

She'd only touched her husband when she was forced into it.

Alasdair she touched because she *wanted* to

touch him, to feel him, to explore his maleness, the hardness of his body. Already, she knew he would never use his strength against a woman, only *for* her.

"What are you afraid of, Alasdair Grant?"

His other hand settled on her hip and he pulled her a wee bit closer, his gaze now on her lips. "Falling in love and losing the woman I love."

The earnestness in his voice was unexpected. She had the oddest feeling he had just bared his soul to her, shared his deepest, darkest secret.

His voice turned husky as he continued to stare at her lips. "I'm willing to overlook the fact that you are in mourning, my lady, but only if you are willing, also."

She dipped her head, tearing her gaze from his. It would be impossible to look at him as she gave her answer. "I'll trade another secret with you."

"Agreed." He tucked a stray hair behind her ear.

"I'll emphasize a truth I've already told. I'm not mourning my husband at all. Now your secret?"

"I'll emphasize my own truth. I want to kiss you more than I've ever wanted to kiss a woman, but you must ask me. I want to see your boldness, not quell it."

She would be more than happy to oblige him. Cupping his face with both hands, she said, "Kiss me, Alasdair Grant. Please."

———◆———

He enveloped her in his arms with a low growl, his lips meeting hers in the moonlight. She parted her lips, and before he could delve inside with his tongue, she did so to him. She would be a passionate one in bed if he had to wager.

She tasted as sweet as he'd expected, her body melding to him as it had in that underground room. He slanted his mouth over hers, their tongues dueling in the oldest ritual in the world, yet it seemed fresh with Emmalin.

She was beautiful, warm, intelligent, and bold. Aye, he liked her boldness. He savored it.

Her husband had been a fool.

He ended the kiss, the wind now howling in a manner that cautioned a storm was on the horizon. He kissed her forehead and tucked her in close against the wind. She shivered, and he thought to remove her from the cold elements around them.

"You're cold. I'll escort you to your chamber."

"Nay, a few moments more, then I'll sleep better."

"I'll gladly hold you for as long as you like."

He meant every word. Holding her soothed him unlike anything ever had. It made him forget, for a moment, the experiences that had scarred him more than the battle had injured his face.

"Alasdair, will you teach me how to use a sword sometime? Do you have a small one I could use?"

"Aye," he agreed at once. "I know exactly where to get you one. I'll make sure it fits you perfectly."

They stayed like that, wrapped around each other, until a cold rain started.

"I'm ready," she said, turning in his embrace.

He moved behind her to protect her from the weather, then followed her down the dark staircase.

She led him to her chamber, then turned to him and said, "My thanks for listening to me."

He kissed her quickly and said, "I look forward to sharing more secrets."

He left her and headed down the stairs, the sudden need to see his grandfather overpowering him. The hall had quieted, and no one stopped him as he made his way to the chamber at the end. To his surprise, his grandsire's door was open. He knocked on the wall beside it and stepped inside. "Grandsire?"

"I've been waiting for you."

His grandfather sat in front of the hearth, just as he had before, and motioned for him to take the seat beside him. "How did you know I was coming back?"

"You've been chatting with a lass, have you not?" The old man gave him a sly grin. Hell, his grandsire knew him too well.

"How would you know that? We were on the parapets."

"'Tis my job to know what my bairns and grandbairns are thinking and doing. Now that Maddie is gone, you are all my priority. Besides, I made a promise to her long ago, and I intend to keep it."

"To watch over us?"

"Aye," he said, his eyes sparkling. "Enough about me. You've met a lass you're drawn to finally?"

He considered lying to his grandsire, but he couldn't bring himself to do it. "I *am* drawn to her."

"And you fear it could become a problem?"

He shrugged his shoulders. In order to answer the man honestly, he'd have to ask him some hard questions. Perhaps, given everything his grandsire had been through in the past several days, this was not the right time for those questions.

"Why not ask me now?"

He scowled, turning his head quickly to stare at the dear man. How the hell did he always know his thoughts? "All right, I'll ask. I'm not sure I wish to get so attached to someone. I saw how awful it was for you after Grandmama passed on, and for Papa after he lost Mama. I don't know if I could handle that kind of pain. I don't want to fall in love with a woman only to have her leave me."

Shocked at the dampness around his eyes, he swiped under them to keep tears from falling. His memories of watching the men he most admired grieve, while he grieved, too, pained him worse than that awful memory from the battle near the Borderlands.

Alasdair was an only child, so he'd witnessed every bitter minute of his sire's grief. He'd seen the private pains that had not been shared with anyone else.

"It's too painful, Grandpapa. How did you handle losing Grandmama?"

"Alasdair, aye, it was painful, but I want you to think on this. What would my life be if not for Maddie? You would not be here with me now, nor would I have Aunt Kyla, Aunt Eliza, and Aunt Maeve to help me."

He took his gaze from the dancing flames in the

hearth to stare at the beloved man next to him, someone he knew he would lose, too, someday.

But age had given his grandsire wisdom more valuable than any amount of coin.

The deep voice of wisdom continued, "You'd have no cousins, lad. No aunts or uncles. Obviously you wouldn't exist either, but you do understand what I'm trying to tell you?"

He nodded, because this man had given him an important insight.

"Maddie enriched my life in so many ways, and as painful as it was to lose her, it was my honor to hold her in my arms and ease her passing. She'd done so much for me over the years, given me children, grandchildren, loved me with all my faults. She gave me a reason to come home from battle, son. And everyone needs that."

Alex Grant paused, gathering his thoughts before he put an end to the conversation.

"As do you, Alasdair. Don't send her away because you're afraid to feel. It's what gives your life meaning and passion. Scotland is headed into a dark time, and you will need someone, possibly Emmalin, possibly someone else, to carry you through."

Alasdair had no words to say to his grandsire, and so he simply listened.

"Someday, lad, you'll learn to savor those things, because they are the moments you'll always remember."

CHAPTER ELEVEN

———◆———

THE NEXT MORNING, ALASDAIR CAME
in from the lists wiping the sweat from his
brow, hoping to grab something quick to eat but
surprised to see Emmalin bolt to her feet as soon as
he entered. She wore leggings and a tunic, and she
had the brightest smile he'd ever seen.

She was a far sight better to look at in the
morning than Elshander and Alick. Mayhap his
grandsire had a good point, something for him to
ponder a bit more.

"Good morn to you, lass. Did you sleep well?"
They were the only ones in the hall at the moment,
other than a couple of servants busy at the other
end of the cavernous space, so he didn't hesitate to
lean over and give her a quick kiss.

"Aye, but I was most anxious to see you this
morn. I'm eager to do as we planned."

Alasdair paused for a moment. Had they made a
plan? Surely he would have remembered.

Fortunately, she assisted his foggy mind. "The
sword? You said you would help me find one that
would fit me and then give me a few lessons. You
have not changed your mind, have you?"

Hellfire, how could he forgotten that? "Nay, I
will gladly help you. Shall we go now? Judging by

the clothes you're wearing, you're ready. You wear those leggings well, by the way," he said, grinning at her.

She took his elbow and yanked it, pulling him toward the door. "Never mind that. Find me a sword. Please."

Chuckling, he snagged her hand and held it, and they walked out of the keep together. "We have an excellent smithy," he said.

"Does he make many swords for women? I couldn't lift yours, I'm certain of it."

"He makes smaller swords, mostly for young lads. I think I was given my first real sword at the age of six winters."

"Six?" she said, squeezing his hand. "Did you not hurt someone with it?"

"The three of us received our weapons at the same time, but we were only allowed to use them if one of our sires was available to train us." His mouth tugged into a grin. "Or so they thought. Grandpapa used to take us out to our own area to practice. He called it the trio's lists. We loved having our own place to practice because we believed it made us important. Before that, I practiced with a wooden sword, working with it every day to make my sire and grandsire proud. I'm sure we can find one that suits you. You'll just need to practice as much as you can to build your arm strength."

"Being a woman, will it work?" she asked.

"I have many female cousins and aunts who have proven they are capable of doing anything as well as or better than a man. Dyna's archery is a good example. I can't beat her in archery. Most people can't."

She nodded, apparently mulling over whether she could make it work for her.

"Who taught you the most?" she asked.

He thought for a moment, but he didn't have to think long. "My sire and my grandsire, without a doubt."

When they arrived at the smithy's hut, he guided her inside and introduced her. "Isaac, this is a friend visiting from Clan MacLintock. She would like to find a sword to fit her grasp."

If the rugged blond smithy was surprised to see a lass, he didn't say so. After they exchanged greetings, Isaac rubbed his hands together and said, "Come with me." He led her over to a special case that sat atop a large chest, filled with an array of swords of different sizes. "I think several of these would suit you, but I know not if they are...sweet enough for you?"

"Sweet enough?" she asked, unsure of his meaning.

Isaac cast a nervous glance at Alasdair. "Do you not want one that has a feminine-looking hilt? Or some gems embedded in it?"

The edge of Emmalin's mouth quirked, as if she were fighting a smile. "Nay, I don't want it to be recognized as something belonging to a lass. I want it to look just like any lad's weapon."

Alasdair met her gaze, smiling a little himself, and said, "I think 'tis a wise choice. Isaac, the English have been encroaching on her land, and I promised to show her how to use a sword, just the basics, to protect herself."

"The English?" the smithy said with a scowl. He strode over to the door, opened it, and spat outside. "Say no more," he added, slamming it behind him. "They are bastards, pardon me, my lady, but 'struth. I'll give you one of the finest blades, a sharp one, with a solid sheath to go with it. If you strike them, you wish for them to be dead." He stood back, picked up a sword from the middle of the table, and held it in front of him.

Alasdair knew what was coming next, so he put his arm in front of Emmalin, pushing her back a wee bit. Isaac loved to test his creations himself. He swung it three times and said, "Och, this one will serve you well." He brandished it through the air one more time, then held it out for her to take, handle first. "Here, my lady, try it for yourself."

She gripped the hilt of the sword, getting a feel for it. "'Tis comfortable," she said, nodding slightly.

"Try holding it over your head," Alasdair suggested, "see if it feels too heavy." He stepped back to give her the room she needed. "You can use both hands."

She did as he suggested, then sliced the sword through the empty air in front of her, her eyes gleaming with excitement over the swish of the blade through the air.

The sight made Alasdair grin. "Isaac, you've made a sale. Please find a sheath for the lady's sword. I must take her to the practice field before she loses that smile."

"To the lists," she asked, her expression full of hope.

"Nay, I don't wish for any of our men to cut off their own hands. You are too beautiful to move amongst them."

Isaac found a suitable sheath and fitted the sword inside, showing Emmalin how to wear it, if she so desired. When he finished, he gave a slight bow and said, "Godspeed be with you whenever you use my blade, but remember 'tis meant as a powerful weapon."

Alasdair whispered to Isaac that he'd compensate him later, and as soon as they stepped outside, he took Emmalin's hand. "My gift to you," he said.

She squeezed his hand back, her eyes gleaming again, and he stared at her for a moment, wanting to soak up the happiness he felt. But he knew how eager she was to get started, so he led her into the woods and found a private clearing where they could practice away from prying eyes.

Alasdair began the lesson by instructing her on how to hold the sword. He then stood behind her, setting his hands over hers on the hilt of the blade, and they practiced swinging it back and forth in front of them. "First of all, never take your eyes from your opponent or you may end up with a facial scar like I have. Never try to swing the sword unless you have complete control. When you do lose control, drop the weapon. You can hurt yourself as much as others."

He had her practice alone until she had a good feel for the weapon. Once she was ready, he stepped behind her again, leaning into her until he held the weapon with her, ready to teach her how to use her weight to control the blade and put more force behind it.

Only that wasn't what happened. Not exactly.

She froze and pushed back against him. His throbbing erection had caught her notice, he was certain of it, but instead of moving away from him, she moved closer. Heat passed through her to him, igniting a flame of lust that he fought to control. If he had his way, he would settle her on the ground and make her his, but he surely couldn't do that here on Grant land.

Not days after she'd lost her husband.

Not when she was the daughter of one of his grandfather's good friends.

"Lass," he whispered, asking for mercy.

"Nay, Alasdair," she said, "please give me just one moment to imagine what might have been, if my sire hadn't died, if the English weren't so bent on creating havoc, if I were truly free. Give me a moment to draw strength from you. Please."

He tightened his grip around her, realizing every word she'd uttered was true. This was a moment out of time, for him and for her. It felt wonderful to pretend that the rest of the world had fallen away and that they could simply be together.

But the moment ended, as all moments do. He heard Els and Alick approaching them through the trees, joking and teasing each other as they went, and he stepped away.

He immediately missed the warmth of her.

———◆———

Emmalin changed for dinner and made her way down to the great hall. Surprised at how much her muscles hurt from her first few lessons, she vowed to continue to make her sword skills stronger, if not to make Alasdair proud of her, but in the hope her sire was watching from the heavens above. She sat at one of the trestle tables with Alasdair and Alex Grant that evening. His three cousins were also present, Elshander, Alick, and Dyna, along with her mother, Sela Grant.

"Tell me again what the messengers told you about your husband," Alex said.

"They informed me of my husband's death and said I needed to meet the king at Berwick in a fortnight."

"And how did he die?" Sela asked.

"An attack of boars." She was glad the fair-haired woman had spoken because it offered her the chance to look at her. Sela Grant had an ethereal quality, a powerful aura, something she had to admire. The similarities between mother and daughter were arresting, and they both acted as though they were unaware of their beauty.

Alasdair said, "Given what we know about Longshanks, I suspect he has a plan. As belligerent as he has proven when it comes to the Scots, I doubt he'll have much sympathy for you. His only concern will be what he can gain from the baron's death."

Her stomach did the familiar sinking whenever

the king's name was mentioned. It was inherently bad news for her whenever King Edward was involved. "Aye, and as we discussed the other day, I suspect his plan is to marry me off to someone else." The thought of marrying another stranger made her ill. Especially since she would much prefer to explore her new feelings for Alasdair.

"You are but a pawn in the eyes of the king," Alex said. "Longshanks gives land to his favored barons, so they're always seeking to add to their holdings," Alex said. "There could be several barons who will seek you out once word gets around about your husband's death. I'm sorry the truth is not better for you. I wish he would give you a mourning season, but I have my doubts that he is considerate of any Scot, even a woman. He will choose whomever he feels he owes the most."

Emmalin nodded again. "And suppose one of those barons is disgruntled that the king chose another…"

"Aye, and he decided to take what he wanted by force, bypassing the king's approval. Once a marriage is sanctioned by the church, even the king will not argue."

"But the plan didn't work," Dyna said. "So several men could still be looking for Emmalin."

Alex nodded. "I would hope not several, but more than one."

Emmalin had heard enough. Her entire life had been uprooted within the last year, and here it was happening again. It seemed any glimmer of happiness would be stolen from her. She would be controlled and dominated again, her land taken from her. "Forgive me, but I would like to go to my chamber. I still have a few days before I must report to Berwick, and I need my rest."

Alasdair and his two cousins all rose as soon as she stood from her chair. Dyna was chatting with her mother, so neither of them moved. The others sat down again, but he followed her. She stopped him at the bottom of the staircase. "Please, you need not escort me to my chamber. 'Tis not far and you should stay and discuss matters with your cousins."

"Are you sure you're hale?"

She smiled, doing everything in her power to hold back tears. If she gave in, they'd flood her cheeks and she'd probably fall against this handsome man and sob her heart out. Unfortunately, the curtain of darkness that had fallen over her at the possibility of being forced to marry another like Langley was too much. Suddenly exhausted, she needed to be alone.

Her dignity prevented that from transpiring. "I'll be fine, Alasdair. As I said, I am just tired." She grabbed her heavy skirts and lifted them so as not to trip on the steps. Although she'd seen the disappointment in his eyes, she would not turn back. She would not allow him to see her fall apart this eve after all he'd done for her.

She'd gladly do it in her chamber where no one could bear witness.

Once inside, she closed the door and fell against it, the tears finally falling from her eyes. She cried until she had no more. How she wished her dear sire would show up at the door to tell her what to do.

She was lost.

Should she trust the Grants? Trust the English king?

Or should she run away and hide in the forest somewhere?

Perhaps running away was the only way she could be truly free, but it wouldn't suit her. She wanted to go back to her land. It was part of her.

Nay, none of the possible solutions suited her.

An hour later, her tears spent, she thought about poor Alasdair and how she'd dismissed him. The kind thing to do would be to apologize for her abrupt behavior. She freshened up a wee bit with the basin in her chamber, then opened the door to leave.

Before she could step out into the passageway, she heard the booming voice of Alex Grant, echoing off the rafters. "You cannot risk all of your lives for one person. I want you all to agree to my proposal about this venture."

The four cousins each agreed with the proposal. This must have put an end to the conversation, for the next thing she heard was the screech of chair legs scraping across the stone floor. She stepped into the passageway and moved to the balcony so she'd be seen. While she had eavesdropped, it hadn't been deliberate, and she didn't know what to make of what she'd heard. Was *she* the one person they were risking their lives for? Alex Grant had seemed happy to see her—would he really have advised his grandchildren not to help her?

Alasdair bounded up the stairs and stopped in front of her. "You are better?"

"Aye," was the only word she could get out.

"You look like you've seen a ghost. Is everything to your liking in the chamber? Would you like another?" He kissed her cheek, but she still could not move. Her hands gripped his upper arms as if she were afraid he would disappear.

"The chamber is fine. I..."

Dyna called up to him from below, "She probably overheard Grandpapa's words and misinterpreted them."

Emmalin stared into Alasdair's eyes as he absorbed his cousin's words. Not for the first time, it struck her that Dyna was remarkably intuitive.

"Grandpapa tends to worry," he said at once. "He was warning the four of us not to go up against a garrison of fifty knights. Alick and I both have tempers, at times, especially toward the English, and he's always afraid we'll allow anger to get the best of us and bring us into an argument we cannot win. Els has had to play peacemaker before. Grandpapa wasn't telling us not to protect you. We will."

She still stared at him, her exhaustion now taking its toll on her.

He whispered in her ear, his warm breath soothing her. "*I* will. Do not worry yourself. I will always protect you. Besides, it was my grandsire who sent me to your land, remember? He knew you were in trouble."

Emmalin glanced over the balcony railing and looked straight into the eyes of Alex Grant.

"I don't wish to be a burden to any of you. Alasdair, I must practice with my sword on the morrow. I have much need to improve."

Alexander Grant was a man of mystery. Was he glad she was here because of his friendship with her sire?

Or did his concern for his grandbairns override everything else?

CHAPTER TWELVE

A LASDAIR PACED OUTSIDE THE STABLES, waiting for his grandsire to awaken. He'd stayed up later than usual to speak with them, to plan with them, and in his advanced age, he sometimes slept in after late nights. He wished to be on the road before the sun was highest, and they only had about an hour to make it happen.

They'd agreed last eve that the cousins would travel to Berwick to see what they could uncover about the king and MacLintock Castle. The big question was whether or not to take Emmalin. Grandpapa had wanted them to leave her behind, fearing her presence would put them at greater risk of being discovered. He also didn't think the lass would be safe in Berwick.

Alasdair wanted her to go with them, because he believed it was the best way to protect her. In truth, he did not trust anyone else to see to her protection the way he would. Selfishly, he also wanted to be with her.

He knew their conversation last eve had discomfited her. She feared she'd be married off again, but he would never let that happen against her will. Neither would his grandpapa. She'd misunderstood what she'd overheard last eve, something he needed to make her understand. As soon as they finalized their plan, he'd talk with her.

He'd made his tenth circle of the stables when he saw two horses surging toward the gates, one carrying an older woman. She looked frantic as she bolted off her horse and raced toward the guards. Alasdair hurried over, sensing she brought news. Urgent news, from the look of it.

"My mistress, Emmalin MacLintock. She is here, is she not?"

The guards looked confused, but Alasdair snapped to attention and hurried out of the gates to uncover her purpose.

"What know you of MacLintock land?" he asked, doing his best to be vague.

"My mistress," she stopped, panting to catch her breath.

One of her companions jumped down from his horse. "Please pardon Besseta. We're all worried about our mistress. We seek Emmalin MacLintock, daughter of the former laird of MacLintock Castle. We have come to warn her. I am one of her guards and she is her personal maid. The English whoresons who attacked the castle are heading this way. Someone there saw your plaid and told them. We fear for her life."

Alasdair stared at the man, doing his best to imitate his grandsire's intimidating glare. He waited for further information, needing to know were who they claimed to be.

Besseta joined the guard and clasped his shoulder. "We pushed her into the tunnel. I closed the door behind her. She never would have gotten away if not for the tunnel."

Alasdair nodded, although he was not yet ready to let them in. "Go find our guest," he said to one of the guards. "Bring her to the steps and see if she knows these people."

The man disappeared, and the next time the door opened, Emmalin stepped outside with a squeal. Running despite her heavy skirts, she launched herself at the older woman. "Bessie!" The maid was so thin Alasdair feared Emmalin might knock her over.

He cleared his throat and said, "If you know and trust them, invite them in, Emmalin."

"Aye, my manners. Forgive me. Alasdair, this is my dear maid, Besseta. She has been with me forever. And these are two MacLintock guards." She quickly turned her attention back to her Bessie. "What about the others? Gaufried and his men? Tamsin, Aunt Penne?"

"We have not seen or heard anything about Tamsin or Penne. Many villagers disappeared, mayhap they did, also," one man said. "They ran. Gaufried went on the attack and there was a battle, but his body was never found. I hope he got away."

Aunt Kyla emerged from the other side of the gate and offered an official welcome. "We welcome you to Grant Castle. Please come inside for a brief repast. You can tell Emmalin all that has transpired, and my sire would also like to hear your account."

Once inside, they settled around the trestle table where Alasdair's grandsire sat in his large chair. The others piled onto the bench. Alasdair made the introductions, then said, "Please tell us what else happened. Why have you come? You seem upset."

"I am," Besseta said, patting Emmalin's hand. "Though I feel much better now that I've seen you with my own eyes. I was so worried. Forgive me for sitting with you, my lord. I am but a lady's maid. I will take my proper place if you'll guide me to one of your maids. I had to see her with my own eyes. I promised her dear mother…" She stopped to mop her eyes with a well-used linen square.

Alex leaned forward and said, "My wife's maid was her finest protector, my lady. You'll stay where you are as you have earned the right to be by Emmalin's side. I knew her sire well, and he would not have had his daughter in your care if he did not trust you implicitly.

She nodded and took a sip from the goblet of mead she'd been served.

"Go ahead," Alasdair said, tired of waiting. He admonished himself to do better about learning his grandsire's art of patience. Although, as Alex himself had reminded him, it was the work of a lifetime, not a day.

"The man leading the garrison was named Sheriff de Savage. He came for you. A baron hired him to lead the men to your castle and overtake it. Once it was done, the baron was to bring you to Berwick."

"But I would have to agree to go with him, and I never would."

"They have their ways," his grandsire said.

"Which baron?"

Besseta shook her head. "We don't know, but as we said, they know you are at Grant Castle. We came upon another group of warriors headed in this direction. They asked if we knew of your whereabouts. Said we were to instruct you to go immediately to King Edward's castle in Berwick."

"You did not tell them anything, did you?" Alasdair asked.

"They would never give me up," Emmalin responded at once. "They are the most loyal in our clan."

Alex nodded. "I believe you. Did you hear any names?"

"Just de Fry. I've never met him before."

At this, the wise old man sighed. "Both de Savage and de Fry are Scottish sheriffs, but they're being bribed by different barons. Of that much I'm certain. Many of the sheriffs are easily brought to task with a bit of coin. But we don't know which barons are in play."

They all paused while the serving lasses brought more food for the travelers. Alasdair wondered if this would change their plan at all.

They didn't need to wait to find out.

"Emmalin, pack your things," his grandfather said. "I will meet with the cousins in my solar while she packs, since they will be your escorts to Berwick."

"You're sending me to marry the baron the king chooses for me?" Emmalin asked, her voice tight.

"Nay, I'm sending you and my grandbairns to

speak with King Edward. They will gain your
freedom, if they can. But it's most important
that you are protected from the rampant barons
searching for you. They know you're here. It's best
for you to leave."

———————

Why did she feel as though she were about to be
put in the dungeon? She knew her face had paled
at that declaration, but she didn't know how to
deny him. Her father had trusted Alexander Grant
more than any other, but could she?

Emmalin nearly choked at the elder's command.
Surely she'd be safest behind the curtain wall of the
massive Grant Castle.

Was Alex Grant just trying to protect his family?
Had Alasdair made up his explanation of the fifty
knights to protect her from the truth?

She blindly moved one foot in front of the other
and headed upstairs. Bessie followed her, rushing
ahead of her to pack her things. "You must have
a disguise at the ready, my lady. What if you're
captured? Perhaps you should wear a gown with
breeches beneath it, just in case. I thought you'd
be safer staying here, but the old man wants you to
leave. Do you understand it? I suppose he knows
better than I do."

Her dear Bessie had a tendency to ramble
whenever she was anxious about something.
Clearly, she didn't look forward to this visit to
Berwick any more than she did. They had to make
the best of it. She kept hold of her wits for long

enough to pack her things, but then her strength fled her and she collapsed into one of the chairs in a heap.

"Mistress! What is it?"

She glanced up at her dear friend. "I'm so grateful you've come, Bessie, but I don't know what is happening."

Bessie rushed over and clasped her hands. "Do you trust the Grants?"

"Aye, I do. Or I did."

"Did? Why not now? You've only been here for a short time."

"I didn't think they'd send me away." Tears fought to spill down her cheeks, but she held them in, wanting to hold strong in front of her maid.

"If you trusted them before, you should trust them now. I recall your papa saying Alexander Grant was the fiercest and most honorable Highlander of all. He may be old, but I doubt that has changed. You must have faith."

She patted her maid's hand. "Thank you, Bessie. I needed to hear those words."

"And I will go wherever you go. I must believe this old chieftain knows what's best for you. Who did your father tell you would assist you, no matter the problem?"

"Alexander Grant," she said, acknowledging the point. The old warrior also claimed her sire had visited him in a dream. Surely her papa would only have done so if he believed with all his heart that the eldest Grant would help her.

"And he's sending how many of his grandbairns

with you? How many warriors?"

"Many, I'm sure."

A knock sounded at the door, signaling the time had come, so she gathered her things, and she and Bessie left. Alasdair's aunt, Kyla, waited for them beyond the door.

She led them down the stairs, and when they reached the bottom, she said, "My sire wishes to speak with you before you go." She motioned her toward the spot where he sat in front of the hearth.

He shifted as they approached but did not get up. "Forgive me, ladies, for not greeting you properly. My knees don't always accommodate me."

"We thank you for your hospitality," Emmalin said, "and there is no reason for you to get up."

"Emmalin," he said, leaning back in his chair. "I knew your sire for many long years, and we agreed on one thing."

"What was that, my lord?"

"We Scots don't run from trouble. We stand up for our rights. Your father was bold yet protective of what was his, so I think we should honor those values by acting the same way."

His use of the word "bold" truly struck a chord with her—it was the very word that her husband had used to describe her worst attribute.

Perhaps it was her best. Strong and brave...and *bold*.

She took a moment to absorb his words, then said, "'Tis exactly what my sire would say."

"Understand that I send the Grant's strongest and best warriors with you, my four grandbairns.

Trust them to make the right decisions with you, although you may not be aware initially of the reasons for their actions. They will fight for your land to remain in MacLintock hands. Running and hiding will not solve the problem. You came to us for help, and we intend to give it. Understand that we will not rest until all is set to rights." The man's gaze never left hers, and she felt immensely better.

Besseta must have felt the same because she settled her hand on Emmalin's shoulder and gave her a wee squeeze.

"Many thanks to you, my lord," Emmalin said, meaning every word. "I hope to see you again soon."

"Next time, you will bring me good news."

"Aye," she said, "I hope I shall." She and Besseta thanked Kyla for the hospitality and left the keep.

To Emmalin's surprise, the group was already assembled at the stables. Alasdair, Alick, Els, and Dyna were there, along with ten additional Grant guards. Alasdair helped her onto her horse, and they left with little discussion.

They traveled the rest of the day without speaking, and her belly was in a turmoil because of it. She wanted to spend time with him, to see if they would suit, but how would that be possible when they were in a group? Besides which, they were riding to Berwick, where the king intended to marry her off to yet another Englishmen.

They found a clearing that night, and Els and Alasdair started to set up a single tent. Alasdair motioned for her to join them.

She came to his side and said, "I don't wish to have special treatment."

"This tent is for you, your maid, and Dyna. Believe me, 'tis best if you are away from the guards."

"And why is that?"

Alasdair hid a smirk, she could tell. She also heard Bessie clear her throat behind her. Oh. It was a matter of propriety, then. Alasdair finished with the tent, covered the ground in furs, and leaned over to kiss her cheek. "'Tis better this way," he whispered.

He started to walk away, but she stopped him. "Alasdair, may we talk privately?" She could tell her request surprised him, but he did not deny her. Taking her hand, he led her away from the others into a copse of trees.

"You are hale? Is there a problem?" he asked when he stopped and turned to face her.

"Nay, I was just wondering…" The discussion she'd had with Alex Grant had given her some reassurance, but she still hadn't fully talked the plan through with Alasdair. And while she sensed Alex had been honest with her, she also suspected they hadn't shared their full strategy with her. After all, the king was unlikely to see reason. What was to stop him from marrying her off as soon as she stepped into Berwick Castle? "I'm wondering why everyone seems so certain we should go to Berwick. I thought it might be safer back at Clan Grant."

He took both of her hands and looked her in the eye, his gaze unwavering. "Based on what your people told us, at least two groups are searching for you. After you went abovestairs, a couple of our patrols reported back with similar news. Several people are attempting to find you, it seems, and they all knew you were on Grant land. They were seeking ways to steal you."

"But didn't we just make it easier for me to be kidnapped?"

"Nay," he said, pausing to gather his thoughts. "All of these barons will continue to seek you out until King Edward puts a stop to it. If we report to him directly, he may call the barons away from you. Cooperating with him, for the moment, might buy us time."

"I don't understand. Why should we trust the king?"

"Trust him, nay," he scoffed. "We'll never trust him, but we may be able to use him to our advantage. If we answer his summons and show up in Berwick as requested, even earlier than requested, we may have a chance of changing his mind. He may insist on betrothing you to another man, but there's reason to hope he'll grant you a delay of a moon or two because you are in mourning. This would keep the other barons at bay, and there's a chance that King Edward will lose interest in the matter entirely. Regardless, we'll have time to form another plan. 'Tis what we need."

"But if he denies my request and gives me to another baron immediately?" she asked.

He kissed the tip of each finger on one hand. "I promise you I won't let that happen. We must concede to the English king's demand for an audience so we might win other concessions. It may appear we are not pursuing your wishes, but we are."

He set her fingers down and kissed her lips, but he pulled back when she didn't kiss him back with her usual fervor.

"What is bothering you?"

She considered not responding, but she could not ignore the entreaty in his eyes. "I'm afraid," she admitted. "I've already lost so much, and what am I to do if he wishes to take more from me? What am I to do if you leave me? I know 'twould be easier for you all if you did."

He stared at her, tracing his finger down her jawline. "We're not going to take you there and desert you."

She did not want him to see the tears in her eyes, so she leaned forward and wrapped her arms around his neck, whispering, "Please don't desert me."

CHAPTER THIRTEEN

A LASDAIR WISHED HE COULD CONVINCE Emmalin to believe him before they left the next morn, but he couldn't reveal exactly what his grandsire had instructed them to do. Still a masterful strategist, Alex Grant had a wonderful way of proposing different scenarios they might encounter and helping them hone a strategy for each one.

Dealing with the King of England would be delicate, no matter what came to pass, and Alex had cautioned them to keep some of their plans secret from Emmalin in case she was taken prisoner and the king forced her to talk.

Alasdair did not like withholding the truth from her, but he trusted his grandsire's wisdom.

Just then, he caught sight of a garrison of English soldiers riding toward them, carrying the banner of a baron. Several knights led the group.

This was something his grandsire had predicted, although that fact didn't make it any more welcome.

"Halt your progress," one of the knights shouted. "King Edward's orders."

Els, in the front, held up his hand, indicating that the others should stop. Els said, "But we are headed to Berwick on *his* orders."

"What orders?" barked the knight.

Another knight, in line behind the speaker, said, "Your orders do not matter. We are here by direction of our king and the Baron of Cockham to escort Langley Hawkinge's widow to Berwick."

"Which is what we are doing," Els answered. "We are not running from you but going toward you."

"Relinquish the lady to us. We will escort her."

"To Berwick or to the baron's estate?" Els asked, raising an eyebrow.

"She must go to the king's castle first. He is expected to be in attendance within a few days. Relinquish her now or we will attack."

Els glanced over his shoulder at Alasdair and Alick. Dyna had already slid behind them and taken out her bow. Her aim was perfect and deadly, but the numbers were against them. Fifty English soldiers versus the eighteen people in their party, and he suspected Bessie was not much of a fighter.

Alasdair turned to Emmalin, who rode beside him, and said, "Do you trust me?"

She nodded, the motion imperceptible to anyone else.

"Remember what I said," he mumbled. Then he turned to the group and said, "She has brought her personal maid and two of her own guards. You will escort them, as well."

"We will accept the lady and her maid only. Turn them over or else…" Ten men moved out to the periphery, drawing their bows and aiming arrows at all of them.

"We turn them over to you."

The expression on Emmalin's face nearly crushed him, but he whispered, "Secrets. We'll trade them again someday. Believe."

He took the reins of her horse and led the animal over to the garrison, motioning for Besseta to go with her. Within moments, the garrison had turned around and was heading south, Emmalin staring back at him as they left.

The expression on her face, one of total defeat, would never leave him.

As soon as the garrison rode off, Alick said, "You didn't tell her our plan, did you?"

They were all still mounted, staring at the road ahead, although naught could be seen of the other group but dust.

"Nay. You heard grandsire. He said not to in case she's questioned."

Els drawled, "That explains why she looked as if she were about to face a squad of archers."

"She *was* facing a squad of archers, Els. We all were. I'm sorry, Alasdair," Dyna said, bringing her horse closer to him. "It must have been hard for you to send her away. I wanted to tell her not to worry. That we were expecting this."

Alasdair said, "I know she looked terribly upset, but I did warn her that things may not go as she expected. I told her we would not desert her under any circumstance."

"I'm not sure she believed you," Dyna said, blunt as always.

"Aye, well, she'll discover the truth soon enough," Els said. "It happened just as Grandsire predicted.

Time for us to do our part. First we'll turn around to convince them we've left, then we'll follow." Els motioned for the other guards to turn their horses around.

"I can't wait to uncover what this is all about," Alasdair said. "There are too many inconsistencies." His gut told him the group was lying about their plans for her. But was it the king who lied or this new baron? His grandsire had thought it unusual that the king would request her presence so soon after her husband's death. Someone had an agenda for Emmalin.

He needed to find out who it was and what they wanted.

———◆———

A day and a half later, they arrived in Berwick. Riding up to the castle, perched atop the hill, gave Emmalin a sick feeling deep in her belly. It was an imposing structure, seemingly towering over every part of Berwick. The curtain wall took up a huge area, traveling all the way down to the water, appearing to disappear into the sea.

The gates were massive, with many guards standing about chatting. How she wished she dared to speak with Besseta. She'd do anything to release some of the fear traveling from her toes up her spine to the back of her neck.

Something was not right.

She'd never been to this castle before, but she would expect that the royal castle would have guards far more attentive than these men. They seemed completely relaxed, as if they hadn't a care in the world, until her retinue appeared in their line of sight. They all straightened as if on cue, and every last one of them stared at her.

Uneasy was not adequate enough to describe the feeling clawing at the inside of her belly. The only person who could alleviate that condition, along with all her fears, was Alasdair Grant. But he was nowhere to be seen.

She had barely dismounted when a young man flew out of the castle to greet her. "My lady," he said. "Our king is ready to see you now."

Bessie placed a hand on her shoulder, a silent request to join her. "My maid may go with me?" Emmalin asked.

"Of course." He bowed slightly and led the way into the keep, down the steps into the great hall, which was three times the size of the Grant hall, and on to the end where a set of large double doors stood open. Her gaze was drawn to the elaborately carved wooden furniture, the floor coverings, which were unlike anything she'd ever seen, and the paintings on the wall. While she'd met the tall, cruel king known as Longshanks, she hadn't been in his royal castle before. Everywhere she looked was proof of the value of the building and all it contained. "Right this way, my lady."

Emmalin stepped inside the chamber, surprised to see only four people inside.

But King Edward was not one of them. One of the men, more richly dressed than the others, turned to look at her. "Take her to her chamber," he said loftily. "The king will see her later."

Now she understood her gut feeling. This was all a ruse. The king had not sent for her, if she were to guess. One of the English barons had likely devised this plan to get her alone.

Did King Edward even know her husband was dead?

Surprising herself with her boldness, she said, "Where is King Edward? I was summoned to see him."

"Do as you're told, my lady," the richly dressed man scoffed, "and do not bother men while they are planning for all of England." He crossed his arms, his nostrils flaring, and it struck her that he looked much like King Edward. Was this a relation?

"But I was told my husband was dead. Is this true?"

"Aye, your husband's body was identified, but you'll not wish to see him yourself as proof. Were you told about the attack?"

"The boars? Aye, 'twas what I was told."

"It is true. Horrific though it may be, the boars tore much of your husband's skin, making him nearly unidentifiable. We had to go by the guards who found him, his clothing, and some of his possessions. He must have imbibed too much and wandered away from camp. My sympathies for your loss."

"If you please, I would prefer to go to our manor. 'Tis not far from here, and I would be comforted by going through his things at our home. I can return on the morrow." She lifted her chin, praying he would agree with her. It would be a much better place for her to await Alasdair's arrival. Between the four of the cousins, they would be able to find Langley's home.

The well-dressed man waved his hand to a nearby servant, who hastened to do his bidding. "Escort her to her husband's manor. Send her with a basket of fruit, bread, and cheese." Then he leaned closer to her, sending a shiver down her spine. "You will not leave that estate. Are we understood? I will send men with orders for you on the morrow."

She nodded, afraid her voice would betray her true feelings.

"Aye, my lord, I hasten to do your bidding," the servant said as he bowed. The gentleman sitting in the chair laughed, which made the one who looked like King Edward smile, and Emmalin and Bessie were dismissed.

They followed the footman down the hall and into another passageway, then out the front door. "You will wait for us here," the servant said. "We shall not be long."

Bessie squeezed her hand once they were alone. "Do you recall how to get to his manor?"

"Aye, I do." Then, in an undertone, she whispered, "I pray the Grants will find us soon."

A short time later, they arrived at Langley's manor, accompanied by a contingent of guards. She'd expected the men to stay, but they made a quick departure, promising to be back for them in the morn. It was a relief to be left alone, even though it was obvious they couldn't go anywhere.

If they did, they'd be found, and their reception at the castle would be far chillier.

Emmalin had been to the manor on one previous occasion. At the time, she and Langley had not yet been wed, so they'd slept in separate bedrooms. Because she did not wish to be reminded of her husband she decided to sleep in the chamber she'd stayed in before. Located on the second floor, it had a huge four-poster bed draped with silk fabric and a large shuttered window, something she hadn't noticed before. She looked out the window, surprised to see it gave her a view of the front of Berwick Castle.

The view did not please her.

"What shall we do, my lady?" Bessie asked, her tone fretful as she let herself into the room.

Emmalin sat on the bed, on the cusp of tears again, but she focused on her anger instead. "I don't think the king had anything to do with summoning me, Bessie. He's not even in residence. I don't know who that man was, but we must pray the Grants arrive before he sends for us on the morrow."

"Do you think one of the barons may have brought us here?" Bessie whispered. "But how would they have even learned of Langley's death?"

Emmalin got up to pace, going to the window again. "Perhaps I should search for the Grants."

"Oh, my lady. Please do not cause trouble. We were told not to leave. Did the Grants not say they would speak with the king on your behalf? Surely they can convince him to leave you be. They're still the most powerful force in the Highlands. Even

King Edward will be careful in his dealings with them."

"But what if King Edward has been in London this whole time? What if the barons summoned me here for their own purposes?"

"He can still intervene."

"I think that could have been the king's son we met," she said, feeling defeated. "I suppose he'll report everything to his sire, but I haven't a clue what's happening. I do know we can trust the Grants. Alasdair said things might not go the way I expected, but he would never desert me. I must be patient, Bessie, but 'tis so hard."

"They may not come as a group, my lady," Bessie said, clasping her shoulder from behind, "but I believe they will come."

Emmalin turned to look at her friend, thinking about the kiss she and Alasdair had shared, about the secrets they'd whispered to each other that evening on the parapets. That reminded her of his parting comment. He'd promised they'd share secrets again. She had to trust him. "As do I, but we can't risk waiting long, Bessie. I won't marry another stranger. I'll run away first."

CHAPTER FOURTEEN

A LASDAIR HELD HIS HAND UP to indicate for the others to stop. "I don't wish to retreat any farther. I don't want to lose the bastards."

"I don't wish to be seen either," Alick said.

"I agree," Els said. "We need to wait a bit longer."

Dyna had been shaking her head since Alick's comment. "Nay, we don't," she said. "We follow or lose them. Must I always have the biggest bollocks in the group?" She pursed her lips and glared from one to the next. "Sorry, Alasdair. You have some. The other two, nay. Let's allow these lassies to stay back while we go ahead."

"Actually, I think it *would* be a good idea for us to split up," Alasdair said. "The guards can stay with you and hold back. We can get closer if 'tis only two of us. Dyna, shall we?"

Dyna grinned and turned her horse around. The other lads shrugged their agreement.

"Where do we meet?" Els said.

"Meet us at that inn my father always speaks of," Dyna said. "'Tis right near the castle. My parents stayed there years ago. I think it's The Buck's Inn."

They separated, and Alasdair said, "My thanks for agreeing with me. Who knows where they are taking her? 'Tis probably Berwick Castle, but you heard what Grandpapa said. 'Tis possible the summons did not come from the king at all. We've all heard talk of his activities in the Borderlands and the Lowlands. If he's as busy as they say, he is not in Berwick."

"Aye. 'Tis mighty suspicious. We mustn't trust anyone we meet."

They arrived at Berwick before nightfall. They tied up their horses next to a burn and approached the town on foot. Dyna wore a cap to hide her white-blonde hair and dressed in a tunic and leggings. They'd agreed she would refer to herself as Alasdair's squire, because her stature made her look much like a lad.

Her face lit up as they moved along. "There's The Buck's Inn, at the end of this road. It's exactly as Papa said. It's on the corner of two roads, and if you take the other one it leads straight past the back curtain wall of the castle. Should we arrange to stay the night?"

"Aye. We'd best do so now. We may not be back until late."

The Buck's Inn was one of the northernmost inns in Berwick, so they did not have to pass through much of the town to get to it, but they saw enough for Alasdair to notice the place had an eerie feeling. The townspeople had always considered themselves Scottish, but now their home was presided over by King Edward and flocked with English soldiers. The people they passed looked down as they walked, seemingly avoiding eye contact. They seemed defeated.

The Buck's Inn was larger than most of the inns Alasdair had encountered in his travels. It looked commodious enough for twenty guests, something not seen often in the Highlands. He and Dyna stepped inside to a common room where ale was being served along with a thick, fragrant stew. Three men ate at one table, and the innkeeper motioned to them from behind a table at the back. Alasdair approached the counter alone while Dyna stood back and said nothing. This was typical when she was disguised as a boy—her melodious voice would reveal her.

The inn was mostly full, and the innkeeper said they only had one chamber left.

"My squire and I can use the same chamber," Alasdair said, "and we'll have two servings of whatever stew you have."

"My lord, 'tis the large chamber we have for nobility. It has two chambers for sleeping with four pallets in one chamber, beds in the other for the ladies, plus a common room with a table and chairs. Do you have the coin for such a chamber?" The man lifted his chin as if he doubted their ability to pay for such luxury.

Alasdair tipped his head to Dyna, who produced a coin that made the innkeeper's eyes widen just before his mouth stretched into a cat-like smile. "The chamber is yours, my lord."

"Two more people will be joining us here. We will stay for a few nights, though our companions may not arrive until the morrow." He purposefully avoided telling the man more than was needed, not knowing where his loyalties lay.

"I'll have my best ale sent along with the stew, my lord."

They settled in at one of the trestle tables in the inn's small hall and ate silently, not wanting to be overheard. They made their way up to the chamber, which was quite acceptable, then left the inn.

"We'll make our way toward the taverns in case we're being watched," Alasdair said, "then sneak down toward the castle. See what we can uncover."

About an hour later, they headed toward the castle wall, wandering amongst the drunks and the peasants begging for coin. After some time, Dyna whispered, "There's a woman following us."

Alasdair continued on his way without looking back, not wanting to alert their pursuer. "I thought the same. Red-haired lass? Young and quite a beauty? She appears to be drawing the attention of every man walking by."

"Aye, and she's coming closer. We'll see if she approaches us or not."

"Let's hope she's not brandishing a dagger she's about to stick into my side."

To his surprise, the red-headed lass bumped right into him not ten seconds later. "My pardon, please forgive me. I must have had too much to drink. Can you help me over to those trees?"

He quickly grabbed her and pulled her off to the side, away from the drunks and passersby. She grabbed her belly, groaning, as he led her over to forest to heave. Dyna followed.

She gave a great imitation of someone losing

their insides, but then she stood up with a smile, glancing over her shoulder. "My pardon, but I needed to get you far away from the crowd."

"We're far enough away that you needn't have demonstrated your lie so forcefully," he drawled, his hand on his hip.

"I prefer to be certain no one is suspicious. I do whatever I must."

Alasdair crossed his arms and stared at her. "You have one minute to tell me and my squire what you want."

She arched a brow and said, "Your squire? I doubt it with an arse like that."

Dyna glared at her. She took it as a personal offense when people saw through her disguises. "Who are you and what the hell do you want?"

The flame-haired lass glanced back over her shoulder and asked, "Are you not Scots? From Clan Grant?"

"What know you of Clan Grant?" Alasdair asked. "I'm not wearing any colors." He did his best to hide his shock. How could she possibly know what clan he was from unless she was a spy or something, someone who'd followed him from a distance, or… someone who'd found his horse?

Hellfire. Sloppy.

"Mayhap not, but I snuck a look at the plaid in your saddlebag when you went inside the inn." She crossed her arms and tilted her head. "Looked like Clan Grant colors to me. Nay?"

"What do you want?"

"Are you here to support King Edward?" she

asked boldly.

Dyna snorted, while Alasdair smirked. "What think you?"

"I think you're here to find out what's happening at the castle, and I'm guessing it has something to do with the new woman who was brought here recently. I'm also guessing you want to break into the castle to find her, but I have important information for you, something you'll want to know before you break in."

Alasdair said, "Get to the point. Do you have information we can use? Is King Edward in residence?" He had another twelve questions he could fire off rapidly if she answered the first ones correctly, but he had to see if she was half as good as he hoped she would be.

"King Edward is not in residence and the beautiful dark-haired woman was there, but she left."

Alasdair looked at Dyna, who shrugged her shoulders. "And why should we trust you?"

The woman tipped her head as she looked at him, as if scrutinizing whether *he* was trustworthy. "I need one question answered before I tell all my secrets. Are you from Clan Grant? You're clearly a Scot, so who do you support as King of Scotland?"

He gave her the slightest of nods, and she let out the breath she had been holding in a loud whoosh. "Good. I am a messenger for the Bruce, and you know what that means. I must keep my identity a secret, but I know the Grants stand behind us. If you need to find the woman, I can help you."

"You're a spy for the Bruce?" Dyna whispered, her eyes large.

"Please never repeat that again, but I do what I can for the Scots. Occasionally, I learn information that I send north."

"Your name?"

"Joya. 'Tis all you need to know."

"And what exactly do you do to get your information so easily?" Alasdair asked, still not entirely certain whether they should trust her.

She gave him a saucy look and said, "I bring joy to the soldiers through dance. I entertain the men who are in residence so they don't bother the king. They'll tell me anything I want to know."

"Is he truly not in residence at present?" Dyna asked. "We were told he was."

"Nay, he is not," she said. Alasdair's hands formed fists. This was what he'd expected, but he was even more eager to get Emmalin out of Berwick if the king had not ordered her return. He didn't dare leave her here longer than necessary.

"His son is there," Joya continued, "but I rarely see him. From what I've heard and observed, he isn't concerned with the visitor. In fact, she left shortly after her arrival."

Dyna gave her a pointed look. "And do you know where she is?"

She crossed her arms. "First answer me. Do you want in or not?"

"Aye, we're on the same side. Now tell me what you know of the visitor," Alasdair said.

"Verra little, except the king did not request her

presence. 'Twas a façade arranged by one of the barons. Quite audacious of the man, really."

"She is being kept somewhere?"

"Aye, and I know where. She's being guarded until the morrow, but I can take you there."

"Shite. If we don't get her away soon, she'll be forced to marry another Englishman. The Scots need that castle. We cannot allow the Vale of Leven to fall to English control."

Nor could he allow another man to force Emmalin to marry against her will.

"Meet me in three hours under the largest oak tree at the back of the castle wall. When I'm finished with my duties, I'll take you to the manor where the lass is being held. If there are guards, I'll distract them long enough for you to get inside to see her."

He nodded. "We'll be there."

"Only one of you," Joya said, her tone unequivocal. "Your choice."

Dyna looked at Alasdair and said, "You go. I'll stand guard with my bow. 'Tis the only way I can assist you."

Alasdair smiled and gave a slight bow to Joya, "Many thanks to you."

He was going to see Emmalin very soon.

He had a feeling inside his chest he hadn't felt in a long time—hope.

Seasoned with something stronger.

CHAPTER FIFTEEN

EMMALIN AWAKENED IN THE MIDDLE of the night, now frantically needing the garderobe that was in the back of the manor. She and Besseta had been using the chamber pot, not wanting to wander Langley's manor, but it was nearly full. As soon as she moved, Bessie popped up from the floor, eyes alert and alarmed.

"Bessie, you were to sleep on the other side of the bed. 'Tis plenty big enough for both of us."

"I will be fine right here, my lady. I have many pillows and furs. Do not concern yourself, but what has you up?"

"I have to..." She had to get out because the smell of the full chamber pot was making her ill.

Hurrying over to the door, she whispered, "I think there is a garderobe at the end of the passageway, I'll look and return as quickly as I can."

Bessie said, "Why are you whispering, my lady?"

Emmalin shrugged her shoulders. "This whole situation has me in knots. I'll return in a few moments." She opened the door and hurried out into the passageway.

She'd almost made it to the end when she stopped abruptly, her eyes wide.

Voices, clear as a bell, carried up the staircase

to her from the hall. Two men, arguing heatedly. At first she assumed the guards must have stayed after all, but then she recognized the voices. One sounded like the sheriff who'd come to the castle to fetch Langley, and the other sounded exactly like her departed husband.

Shock gripped her throat. The king's man had told her Langley was dead. Had it all been a ruse to get her here? But whose ruse?

She leaned closer to the sound, trying her best to understand what was being said.

"It was your fault in the beginning for hiring a garrison of men who couldn't follow simple orders," said the voice that sounded like Langley's. "Your mission was quite simple. Storm the castle and force the woman to hand over her jewels. How could your men have bumbled such an easy mission?"

The sheriff said, "She snuck out through the tunnel. We can still take care of the problem, but I want my share of the jewels at the end of this. Coin isn't enough."

Emmalin's reaction was to take two steps backward so quickly she nearly fell. They'd attacked her castle for her jewels? Was the man she'd married even crueler than she'd thought? This went far beyond anything she'd imagined.

"But it won't do if we're caught at this game," the sheriff cautioned.

"Nothing will happen to me. They all believe I'm dead. You're the only one who must worry. If anyone sees me, they'll think I'm a ghost."

"The king wanted you in charge at MacLintock Castle. He won't be happy when he learns of your 'death' and the effect it is having on all his barons."

"I still can't fathom why you left MacLintock Castle," Langley barked. "My dear wife might have escaped, but I assured you she would follow the king's summons. You should have stayed to look for the jewels."

"I searched the entire castle for them, but I could not find anything."

"I know you'll find this hard to believe, but my wife is not an imbecile. You can be certain she has them well hidden. But you should have stayed and kept looking. They cannot remain hidden forever. What did you tell your men? They cannot know of my façade."

"I only told them the king wants the castle in his hands before the Bruce returns to take it for the Scots. They believed me. Everything is about the English against the Scots. No one will ever suspect the true cause of all of this upheaval." The sheriff stopped pacing, and she couldn't help but fear they'd come upstairs and discover her.

She held her breath, waiting for their next move.

"You've left me with no choice," Langley said. "I'll just have to find her myself and force her compliance. And I would guess she carries some of those jewels with her."

The sheriff said, "I must say, that was a brilliant ploy to find a dead body and put it in a pen with the wild pigs. They chewed the hell out of that face, didn't they?" He chuckled, but then the sound of something banging on a desk interrupted his tirade.

Emmalin's mind was still stuck on what she'd learned about Langley's character. The extent of his cruelty and malice was far beyond anything she could have imagined.

"Can we focus on what's important before I'm uncovered? We have to find her soon. I want to leave this place as soon as possible. You need to remember that you were complicit in this. If they hang me, you'll be strung up right next to me."

"Never mind," the sheriff said. "Finding her will not be a problem. She'll likely be at the castle. The more pressing question is what we should do about her after she gives you the valuables. I cannot just kill the daughter of a laird in Berwick."

"Just find her and bring her to me. I'll handle the rest," her husband said.

"I'll start my search immediately. Where will you go?"

"I'm going to wear a dark mantle and search the city for my wife. We'll meet back here tomorrow evening. Do not return without information," Langley said, although it seemed to pain him to admit it. "Fear not. We'll find her jewels. I must end this soon, even if it means killing her." Her hand flew to her mouth. She no longer felt like going to the garderobe so she spun around and headed back into the corridor to return to her chamber. Thank goodness Langley's chamber was on the other side of the manor. She and Bessie had brought all of their things upstairs, not wanting to make themselves too comfortable. If anything had been left belowstairs, they'd probably already be dead. They would have to get out, but she knew not how. They certainly couldn't risk going down the stairs.

Back inside the guest chamber, she sat down on the bed and stared off into space.

Bessie grabbed both of her hands once she made it back inside, closing the door quietly behind her. "My lady," she said. "You look like you've seen a ghost."

"I have," she whispered. "Well, not exactly. I heard a ghost and I'm certain 'twas him."

"Who?"

"Langley!" she whispered. "My husband is alive. He's belowstairs with the sheriff."

She stared straight into the eyes of her shocked maid, making a statement so unlike her that she even surprised herself.

"I'm going to kill him."

———◆———

Alasdair stood in a copse of trees not far from the back curtain wall, waiting to hear a whistle from Joya. After meeting her, they'd walked through Berwick, listening as best they could. One of the largest ports in the area, it was also one of the closest points in England to Europe. It was a bustling harbor for goods, both honest and stolen.

They'd arrived outside the castle exactly three hours later, having learned little about Langley. No one knew of his death or whether he'd been in town, although it was mighty suspicious that he'd been called to Berwick to attend to a king who was not in residence. Dyna leaned against a tree, waiting patiently. Alasdair was not quite so patient. He hadn't realized how fond he'd grown of Emmalin until those men had taken her.

"I'm going to punch something if she doesn't hurry," he said.

"And that will help you how?" Dyna asked flatly.

He just shrugged his shoulders. She was right—he was overreacting.

"I'm certain she is busy *entertaining*."

Alasdair paced in a circle and ran his hand through his long locks. "All right," he groaned. "I'll be patient, but what is taking so long?"

Dyna gave him a sharp glance, one he'd become quite familiar with these last few years. It meant that she wanted him to shut up.

"What the hell?" he murmured to himself, kicking at the dirt a wee bit as he paced.

Dyna heaved out a sigh. "Aye, you're right. Joya should have ignored her duties and roamed about the castle, checking every chamber," she drawled, her favorite tone of late. But she turned serious the next moment. "She'll be here as soon as she's able. I trust her and so should you."

"I know, but the king's not in residence," he said sharply, "so she shouldn't have had much to do."

"So we think. Do you trust King Edward and any of his men? Because I sure as hell don't. That's another lesson I learned from my mother—men in power are almost always lying. You have no way of knowing what's going on inside that castle. They say he's not here, and yet he could be."

"You're right," he sputtered, hating that she usually was. At least she didn't feel the need to remind him of it often, unlike Alick or Els would. He glanced up at the clouds moving quickly across the moon, wishing them away. They'd need as much light as possible to find their way safely to the manor. "I suppose I thought Joya might be here early," he admitted.

"Nay, she's probably a woman of her word. Let's hope so, anyway."

"How do you suppose she can uncover so much information if she's merely a dancer in the castle?" he asked. "Why wouldn't the spy be a man?"

"Because most men think women are foolish, below suspicion. And…while you may not agree with me, women are smarter than most men. 'Tis why Aunt Gwyneth was so good at spying." Their great aunt, Dyna's mentor, had spied for the Scottish Crown, as had her husband.

"I'll agree with your first statement," Alasdair said, ignoring what she'd said about women being smarter. "Mayhap 'tis why the Bruce chose her."

"I'm sure there are men in the same position, but it would be harder for them to gain access. And a woman moving around the castle might be ignored—a man wouldn't be."

"Are you sure you don't wish to go with me?" Alasdair asked. Her perspective was always useful on a mission, as was her intelligence. He also valued her for her abilities, of course, but those only showed themselves occasionally, like the sun peeking through the clouds.

"Didn't you listen to Joya? She'll only take one of us. I must admit, being this close to Berwick Castle makes me think of my mother and my sister Claray. They both went through hell. I'm glad Joya didn't ask us to go inside because I promised my mother that I wouldn't go near the castle."

"She lived there with your sister for a time, did she not?"

"Aye. Although 'twould be more accurate to say they were prisoners. Mama says the castle is infested with spiders. That was all she needed to say to convince me. She's so daft around spiders she makes me afraid of them. Da and I have to kill any spider we see for her and Claray."

A whistle stopped their conversation.

"'Tis her, I'm certain," he said, looking around the corner of the curtain wall. His cousin was already climbing the tree she'd been leaning against just to scan the area.

Joya was dressed in dark clothing, her distinctive red hair covered with a scarf. "Hurry. I don't wish to dawdle. She's in her husband's manor. I don't think there are any guards there at the moment, but two men just left on horseback. They could be on their way there."

"Shite. Can you lead me there?"

"Aye, if you'll promise me one thing. Now, come around the corner so we won't be overheard."

"What is it?" he asked, following her, Dyna trailing after them.

"If someone enters, you must promise me to hide until they're gone. If we fight, I'll be discovered and I need to stay useful to the Bruce. If you want a battle with someone, you'll have to do it after I've gone. Agreed?"

"Agreed, but what if you get caught?"

"I willnae. I can get you in through the back staircase, but you may need to leave through the chute if those guards show up."

"Chute?" Alasdair asked. "What chute?"

"There's a secret chute built into the back of many manors in Berwick, an exit to be used in case of emergencies. 'Tis a common design because so many battles have been fought in the Borderlands. The chute will be your quickest way out, especially if you're discovered. There's a ladder inside with rungs for your feet."

"Agreed," Alasdair said. "We must hurry before the sun rises." He guessed the sun would rise in another hour or two. All should be asleep inside.

Alasdair's heart felt as if it would pound through his chest as he followed Joya down the road to Langley's manor, Dyna next to him. They walked their horses to an area far enough away not to be seen. Once they were close, Dyna climbed a tree in the front to keep watch and Joya led him around back.

Joya said, "Check inside to see if anyone is here. I only see two horses. I hope they belong to Emmalin and her maid, but we must be sure before we sneak inside."

"Where do you see the horses? The stables look

empty."

"If you turn your attention to the end of that path," she said, pointing in the opposite direction from which they'd come. "You'll see two horses hidden. I say good for her that she knew enough to hide them. I'll return quickly, but I must make sure there's no one else inside."

"She's an intelligent lass, for certes," he said in wonder. "Go ahead. We'll wait."

Joya returned quickly and motioned Alasdair behind her. They entered the manor as quietly as possible and climbed up a back staircase used by the housemaids. Joya peeked into the passageway and pointed to a chamber at the end.

"'Tis where she's staying. The chute is down that way." She pointed in the opposite direction. "It must be after the first two doors on the right. I noticed the outside door so it must be in that section."

"Got it. I don't see any guards," Alasdair whispered back.

"Nay, but I'll keep an eye out for you," Joya said, pursing her lips. "I'll go back and tell Dyna you'll be out in half the hour. No longer."

"Don't get caught," Alasdair said, although he suspected she didn't need advice from him on that account. Sneaking around was an art for her.

As soon as Joya left, Alasdair hastened to the door, tried it, slipped inside, and closed it behind him.

Waiting for his eyes to adjust, he snuck in next to the bed, tripping on something. Something that yelped. Bessie jumped up as Emmalin sat up in bed.

"Who…what?"

"Emmalin, 'tis me," he said. "I'm here just as I promised."

She launched herself at him and nearly knocked him over.

"You are hale?"

"Aye, but you'll not believe what we've learned. My husband is alive."

Nothing could have prepared him for that answer.

CHAPTER SIXTEEN

E MMALIN CUPPED HIS FACE, LOOKING into his eyes. She saw the emotions pass through them—disappointment, anger, the need for vengeance—even in the near dark.

"The bastard is alive? Truly? You're certain 'tis him?" he whispered.

"I heard his voice, Alasdair. I listened to him talk about how he'd planned the entire event. He's the one who sent the garrison after me. In fact...he wants my jewels so badly that he is willing to kill me to get them."

His eyes widened, but he said nothing. "Why? Is the man not wealthy enough?"

The fury was there, of that she was certain. "Alasdair, help me, please."

"'Tis why I'm here. I told you I'd protect you and I will," he said, kissing her lips quickly.

Emmalin squealed even though a small part of her knew she shouldn't, but he silenced her with another kiss. Melding her curves against the hard planes of his body, she parted her lips to give him what he wanted so she could taste him and ingrain it in her mind forever. She was in a thin night rail, something most inappropriate, but these were desperate times. If something separated them, she wished to remember the man who'd made her hope again.

Someone coughed lightly behind them. Bessie. Sweet Bessie.

Alasdair ended the kiss and smiled at her. "I guess this means you'll come with me?"

"Aye, please get me out of here. I have so much to tell you, but first we must get away." She moved away from him and donned the breeches she'd worn under her gown. After helping her dress, Bessie quickly pulled on her own gown, fussing with a sack at the same time.

"We must hurry," Alasdair said as Bessie fussed with Emmalin's boots. "We have to climb down a chute or the back staircase. I have a friend watching for any of the king's guards in case they return."

He stopped, frozen in place because of a sound he heard. "Someone is belowstairs in the kitchens. If we go down the back way, they'll hear us. We'll have to go out the chute. 'Tis safer."

"My husband told me he had one put in after the massacre. One can hide inside it, too. 'Tis down the passageway toward the other end."

"You'll go first, Bessie, and Emmalin will follow. I'll be last. Do not speak when you're inside because we may be passing occupied chambers.

Once they finished dressing, Bessie grabbed a small sack of Emmalin's belongings, and the three entered the corridor, Alasdair in the lead. They made their way down the hall, moving as silently as possible, until they reached an odd-shaped door. Alasdair pulled on the handle, opening it wide so he could peer inside. She waited for it to creak, but it did not.

"Alasdair, does it look safe? Will we fit?"

After giving it a quick inspection, he nodded. "'Tis wide enough and there are rungs on the right side. Grab ahold of it with one hand before you step inside."

He opened the chute and helped Bessie inside, the sack now tied around her waist. Emmalin went next, closing her eyes. Heights sometimes bothered her, but she had to be strong. Alasdair was facing one of his fears too, was he not? She remembered what he'd said about hating small areas. They'd face their fears together.

It felt like they'd climbed down an endless number of rungs by the time she heard Bessie lightly drop to the ground. She heard her exchange a few quiet words with someone, and then footsteps moved away from the chute. Emmalin took that as a good sign because if Bessie had been caught by one of the guards, she would have screamed for certain.

Help awaited them below, and they were nearly at the ground. She was no longer worried about her own slight fear, but she wondered how he was doing and glanced above her head. Alasdair hadn't been so lucky. The chute had narrowed as they moved toward the ground. His breathing had sped up, a sure sign of nerves, and then he simply stopped moving. She wanted to talk to him, but they'd agreed not to speak within the chute for fear of being overheard. There had to be some other way of helping him get through this tight space. When she looked up, she saw him staring straight ahead, his arms in front of him, his hands locked on the wide rungs.

With no other recourse, she climbed back up. He furiously shook his head at her, but she wouldn't leave him like this. Even in the dark she could see the crazed look in his eyes and the heavy sweat pouring down his face.

He was in a state of panic.

She moved up, noticing there was enough space on the rung he stood on for her to put one foot next to his. Ducking under his arms, she pressed her face to his cheek. "Don't let go, Alasdair," she whispered furiously. "We can do this together."

He shook his head.

"Aye, you must help me. I'm afraid of heights. You can help me and I'll help you."

If she acted as if she needed help, perhaps it would distract him from his own fear.

"Nay, go on down. I know you'll be fine."

She shook her head. "Nay, help me, please."

With those words, he finally loosened his grip on the rung and moved his foot down. She moved with him.

"If you climb down four more steps, you can jump the rest of the way," she said. "We don't have far to go. Four more rungs and I won't have to look down anymore. We'll be that close."

He squeezed his eyes shut and moved with her, slowly but steadily. Once they made it down the four rungs, she kissed him lightly on the mouth. He opened his eyes and said, "My thanks."

"Give me two minutes to get myself down, then you can drop the rest of the way."

"And if I don't fit?"

"You will. I can see it."

"Go."

She moved down the remaining couple of rungs, and someone reached into the chute from outside, motioning for her to come out into the cool night. Pleased to see it was Alasdair's cousin Dyna, Emmalin said, "Step back. He's going to jump the rest of the way."

"His fear got to him, did it not?"

She simply nodded.

"Well done getting him out of there."

The next moment, Alasdair dropped to his feet. She turned around to see how he looked, and he grinned at her, the sweat now gone from his brow. Relief coursed through her: he was back to himself. He wrapped an arm around her shoulders and squeezed. "We must hurry," he whispered. "The sun is coming up."

They followed Dyna and Joya across the back gardens, weaving in and out of paths until they reached the place they'd left the horses, pleased to see Bessie awaited them. Dyna mounted and found a different path to get onto the main road back to the center of the village. The roads were nearly empty, and the only two people they ran into were sound asleep, apparently wherever they'd landed in their drunken state. They parted ways with the red-haired woman, and Emmalin couldn't help but wonder who she was and how she ended up with them.

Once they were in the safety of their chambers at the inn, Emmalin threw her arms around Alasdair and kissed him. Although she normally wouldn't be so openly affectionate around Dyna, she couldn't bring herself to care about such small matters of propriety. Pulling back, she said, "I'm so furious. I cannot believe that bastard Langley is still alive. I'm so grateful I'm not carrying his bairn."

Dyna arched a brow at her but said nothing.

"Aye, I know I'm not. Thank God for that." She stared at the ground for a moment and said, "Imagine if I'd had feelings for him. How could you do that to someone?"

"Power and greed. Some men will do anything for power." Dyna pulled a chair out for her at the table and said, "Sit. Here's an ale for you. Methinks you need it."

Alasdair sat down beside Emmalin, clasping her hand as if he didn't wish to let it go, and Dyna sat opposite them.

"Tell us what you remember," Alasdair said, squeezing her hand. "Everything."

"Langley is alive. I swear 'twas his voice." The fury inside her built again, but she took a deep breath and willed herself to keep calm. "I overheard men talking about my castle. They blamed the men they had sent for letting me escape." She paused, gathering herself, then said, "Those men did not come to MacLintock Castle because some baron wished to marry me. Langley sent them to steal from me and kill me, if necessary."

The back of her hand went to her mouth as she thought of what had very nearly happened. "I owe you both for saving my life, although he still intends to murder me. He said he would take care of it after his meeting with someone on the morrow. And according to the sheriff, they faked his death by putting a dead body in a pen of pigs and they chewed the man's face enough that they passed him off as Langley. My husband helped him plan the ridiculous stunt."

"Where are they meeting and at what time?" Alasdair asked, his thumb rubbing the skin of the hand he was holding. "Try to remember every last thing he said."

"He said the morrow, but that would be late today. 'Twas arranged for sundown at the manor home. Whatever he plans, he needs my mother's jewels to accomplish it."

"Do you still have them or are they back at the castle?"

"I brought them with me. They are my mother's and they are hidden. I refuse to give him any of them," she said, crossing her arms in a fury.

"He's planning to return to his manor, the one we were just in?" Dyna asked.

"I believe so," Emmalin said. "I'm not aware of any others he owns, so it has to be there. Now I understand why he never told me much about his life. Everything about him was a secret. I was so foolish," she said, pursing her lips.

"Do not put any of the blame on your shoulders," Alasdair said. "'Twas Langley's plan from the start."

"He's the bastard," Dyna said. "You thought you had no choice but to marry him."

Emmalin said, "Please help me stay away, although I'd gladly use my new sword on the bastard. My land isn't enough for them. They're planning to expand their holdings though I know not where. He must be planning to buy more land. They won't be happy until all of Scotland is under their thumb."

Alasdair stood from his chair so fast that he nearly knocked it over.

"What's wrong?"

"We have family not far from you in West Lothian. I'll send the Ramsays a messenger to make them aware."

"If they go after the Ramsays, it will be war," Dyna said.

Alasdair said with a smirk, "And the English will lose."

———◆———

After they broke their fast with porridge, they made a plan for the day. They would sleep until high sun, then Alasdair and Dyna would go after Joya, with the hope that she would assist them in their return to Langley's manor. They hoped she could give them new information about the barons and their plans.

Emmalin and Bessie were to stay in the chamber at the inn. Emmalin had balked, but she was so exhausted she could barely stand on her own without her knees buckling. Bessie wasn't much better. He hated to leave them alone, but he felt they were safest hidden away and he needed Dyna's help. She was better at finding people, listening in on conversations.

While they wove through the town, walking from path to path, Dyna said, "I think the best solution to our problem should have occurred to you by now."

"What solution? We're going to Langley's manor tonight, and if I have to take the bastard out, I will. He's already supposed to be dead, so I certainly couldn't be blamed for killing him."

They wound their way through the streets, between the vendor stalls and the inns, hoping to see any sign of Langley or Joya. They traveled down to the water, amid the crews hustling to load their ships before departing. Watching the activity, searching for familiar faces, gave Alasdair time to think on what Dyna meant, though he was quite certain he knew what she would suggest.

He knew what she would say because the possibility *had* occurred to him, he just wasn't ready to seriously entertain it. Although his grandsire had caused him to rethink his fear of love, he still did not feel ready for marriage. Even to Emmalin. He scratched his rough whiskers, which he was letting grow because they were traveling.

"Do not play the fool with me," said Dyna. "You two obviously have feelings for one another, so why not marry her yourself?"

"Because she's married, for one reason. Her husband is alive."

And that was the only reason he needed at present.

"I doubt he'll be around for long. A man like that will pay the price for tangling with the wrong people, be it you or someone else. With him out of the way, she'll be a widow in truth. Why not marry her?"

"When that time comes, I'll consider it," he said.

"Cousin, mayhap 'tis time for you to accept all that has happened in the last year. The battle, losing your…"

"I'd rather not talk about it, especially here, Dyna. There are too many ears. We're Scots in an English port, and Highlanders, too. Many of the people here would be all too happy to listen in on our conversation. I'll not draw attention to us."

"Fine. Keep pushing your feelings away, and the memories will continue to eat at you." She cast him a sideways glare, but he ignored her.

He had to. It was the only way he could manage. It would do no good to dredge up the most painful events of his life, though she clearly believed the opposite.

"You continue to push all your troubles away, as if they'll disappear if you ignore them."

"What the hell does that mean?" He had no idea what she was talking about. True, he had a hard time leaving that battle behind, but it didn't affect what he was doing here.

"Must I be blunt? You almost got jammed up in that chute. If Emmalin hadn't been there to assist you, you could have taken a bad enough fall to break a leg. But you know as well as I do that the battle is only a piece of your problem. You've had a terrible year. When are you going to talk about it?"

"For what? Talking about it won't change anything." He continued to stare straight ahead, confident they'd find Joya soon and the uncomfortable conversation would come to an end. If not, he'd duck into a tavern to quench his thirst.

"You can't continue to let it tear you apart."

"There is naught tearing me apart except for the English. I hate them." Even as he said it, he knew it was not quite true, but he couldn't bear to continue the discussion. If she wished to save him pain, then she would desist her prodding.

They passed a tavern, and he swore he saw Joya's red hair popping in and out of one of the market stalls ahead of them. The color and style were distinctive. "There. I think 'tis her."

"I agree. Hurry."

Fortunately, his cousin did not attempt to keep him talking as they hastened to catch up with Joya. They stopped at the vendor booth where they'd seen her, and she gave them a look that clearly communicated they were not to talk to her. She had a dark green wool gown on, cut very low to show off her considerable assets, with a golden shawl tossed over her shoulders. Joya was skilled at displaying her best features—the way she'd wrapped the shawl around her waist and her upper body was enticing on its own.

Several men called out to her. She winked at a

few of them, but they all moved along after making flirtatious comments. They likely had ships to get back to, if he were to guess.

Alasdair and Dyna stayed nearby, watching, and after the spy purchased her food and left the market, she glanced over her shoulder to indicate they should follow her.

She led them down an alley and through a door at the back of a building large enough to be an inn. After checking to make sure no one followed them, something she accomplished with a wee tilt of her head, she led them down a passageway with a finger to her lips.

She unlocked a door with a key and let them inside a small complex. It looked like the interior of one of the cottages outside their bailey, though he'd never seen such an arrangement inside a larger building other than a castle. A partition within the space marked off a bedchamber. The main living area had a large hearth built into the outside wall, a chest for storage, and a table with four chairs. After pointing them toward the chairs, Joya busied herself with pouring three goblets of ale.

"You did not get caught last eve, did you, lass?" Alasdair asked as he and Dyna took their seats.

"Nay. I returned to the castle and danced for the guards to keep them distracted," Joya said, giving them their drinks before she sat down across from Alasdair. "No one commented on Emmalin's disappearance, but I overheard a conversation among a few barons the other day. They were discussing which of them would get the prize. I had no idea who or what they were talking about, but now I suspect they were talking about Emmalin."

"And what was the tone of the discussion?" Dyna asked.

Joya replied, "'Twas not a conversation you would wish to hear about your daughter. They spoke of a beautiful widow who needed containment."

Dyna snorted. "I'll contain those bastards, see how they like being ordered around." She shook her head and growled out, "Men." Then she patted Alasdair's forearm. "Of course, I would never speak of any Grant or Ramsay man in such a disparaging tone."

He nodded and turned to Joya. "We owe you a debt of gratitude. We could not have saved Emmalin without your assistance."

"You're welcome." She held up her goblet of ale, waving for them to do the same. "To the Bruce, King of the Scots."

Alasdair set his drink down and asked, "Would you recognize Baron Hawkinge if you saw him?"

"Nay, I've never met him. I've heard conflicting reports about him. Some say he is alive, some say he is dead."

"He is still alive, unfortunately, and he returned to the manor last night with his associate. Emmalin overheard them talking."

Her eyes widened. "Tell me more."

"'Twas Hawkinge and one of the sheriffs. The man helped him stage his own death with another's body. We don't know why the baron felt the need to fake his death, but his goal now is to gain Emmalin's jewels. We have to stop him. From what Emmalin overheard, we know Hawkinge is meeting the sheriff at his manor this eve. We've decided to pay them a visit."

"Wait a moment," Joya said, snapping her fingers. "I might know something about this. About a fortnight ago, I overheard a discussion in the royal castle. Someone in the Vale of Leven was caught with counterfeit coins. The king's men were to retrieve him so he could be tried for treason. Could it be Hawkinge?"

Her words sent a jolt through Alasdair, and he looked at Dyna, whose eyes had gone wide. "Aye, Emmalin's keep is in the Vale of Leven," he said.

"It explains everything," his cousin whispered, grinning back at him. "That's why he feigned his own death. He was going to be tried for treason. Now he has to hide or he'll be hung. This works in our favor."

"Exactly," Alasdair said. "This is verra helpful. Now we know what drives him. He needs the jewels to run away, yet he cannot show his face anywhere. It also explains why that garrison attacked Emmalin's castle."

"He sent someone to find her jewels, even if they had to threaten or possibly hurt her to get them," Dyna said. "But they couldn't find them, so now he has to find another way to get to Emmalin."

"I doubt Hawkinge has many friends among the barons," Joya said. "I suspect none of them know he's still alive. They seemed quite pleased about the traitor's possible hanging."

"Aye," Alasdair said. "They care naught about him. They are after her, but in the background is a desperate man accused of treason who must go into hiding. He's strictly after her jewels. The other barons want her hand in marriage and her land."

Dyna whistled, grinning again. "This could get verra complicated, but we have an easy threat against Hawkinge now."

"Aye," Alasdair agreed. "If we threaten to reveal his presence, he'll do whatever we ask. Leave or die by hanging. I cannot wait to tell him we know all about his troubles." He wished to spit to the side in disgust, but he didn't because they were inside. "So many of the English have no honor. We owe you, Joya. What can we do for you? Anything?"

"Kill as many English as you can," she said in a low whisper. "Get them before they get us."

CHAPTER SEVENTEEN

EMMALIN PACED THE SMALL CHAMBER in the inn before returning to the window. She felt restless, haunted by what she'd heard. Her husband meant to kill her for her jewels. She understood that, as many people were motivated by wealth. What she didn't understand was why he'd pretended to be dead. What would motivate him to do such a thing?

She could only think of one reason. His death ended their marriage. While she hadn't been in love with the man, she couldn't comprehend why he would have gone to such lengths just to be free of her.

Langley must truly hate her.

Though she had no warm feelings for her husband, the truth hurt. She couldn't fathom hating someone enough to do what he had done. Now he would chase her until he obtained her jewels, all while the other English barons pursued her for her land.

What hope did she have?

Only one. If she told the king the truth, that Langley was alive, he'd be forced to stay in the marriage.

Is that what she wanted? Did she wish to spend

all her days worrying about when her husband would find a way to eliminate her?

Never. She could never live such a life. She would much sooner remarry, which the king would surely order her to do once he returned. As she'd been told by many of her people, she was a pawn in a nasty game. If she refused the king, he might just take her land from her and hand it over to an Englishman. The land that her clan had spent years working and tilling, the castle her grandsire and his grandsire before him had spent years building.

She leaned her head against the window sash as the competing emotions warred inside her. Sadness. Anger. Hatred toward King Edward. Disgust toward the husband who'd slept in her bed. They were all such dark emotions.

But in her heart bloomed one lovely flower amidst a field of brambles: gratitude toward Alasdair and his clan. What would she have done without him?

If she had her way, she'd marry a man like Alasdair and reclaim her castle. Was such a dream possible?

She started when she heard bootsteps coming down the hall. Two people, if she were to guess. Moving over to the door, she waited for the triple knock they'd agreed to use. A relieved sigh popped out of her when it came, and she opened the door for Alasdair and Dyna. Bessie trailed in behind them with freshly-washed clothing in her hands, now ready to be hung to dry.

"Come in," she said. As soon as Bessie closed the door behind them, giving them relative privacy, she asked, "What have you learned? Did you find Joya?"

"Aye," Alasdair said, "and she had some important insights about your husband. Sit down and we'll explain."

"Aye, please. I've thought of little else while you were gone. I wish to travel with you this eve, to hear what treachery he is proposing with my own ears. Please do not consider leaving me behind." She ran her hands down the only gown she had, doing her best to smooth the wrinkles. Dear Bessie had done well to grab the most important one before they left her husband's manor. The most valuable jewels he so desired were hidden in the pockets. The other gowns and a necklace had been left behind in a sack, well-hidden in her chamber.

Alasdair moved to stand in front of her. "I would like you with us. Perhaps you'll recognize some of his accomplices."

"Good. 'Tis settled," Emmalin said at once. She hated feeling so helpless. If she did something, if she assisted in their efforts, perhaps it would feel as if she'd regained some of her power.

He grinned at her, and the warmth in his expression made her feel like she was sitting in front of a toasty hearth. Moving to the table to grab a drink, he said, "I'm starving. I need something to eat. Anyone else?"

"I'll go down and speak with the innkeeper," Dyna said. "No need for anyone else to come with me. I'll use my deepest voice." She shot her cousin a look and then added, "You two ought to stay and talk." Neither of them had the chance to object, not that Emmalin would, before she left the room. Bessie bustled about, taking care of her chores and paying them no mind.

Emmalin sat at the table, gesturing for Alasdair to join her. "I am ready. Tell me what you've learned about the bastard I married."

He took the seat next to her and cocooned her hands in his own. "Joya overheard talk of a man accused of making counterfeit coins. He was to be brought here to be tried and hanged for treason."

She gasped. "Langley? You truly think 'tis Langley? I thought he'd feigned his death to be rid of me."

"Nay," he said at once, "no man would be fool enough. The traitor lived in the Vale of Leven, and the king sent a sheriff to bring him to Berwick to be tried for his crime. This happened about a fortnight ago." He waited, giving her time to absorb all he'd said. "He did what he did to avoid being hanged for treason. Counterfeiting is a serious crime."

Suddenly, it all made sense. Except... "The boars. If they made the body unidentifiable, why did anyone think 'twas him?"

"He must have an accomplice. Someone he is paying to assist him."

She pushed her chair back from the table with a sigh, a weight lifting off her shoulders. "This wasn't about me at all. He cares only about wealth, and my land wasn't enough, nor the coin we earned from the hard work of our tenants. He wanted more."

"Aye, and he somehow made more coin. He was caught, and his attempt to hide his death is an admission of guilt. 'Tis something we can use against him. But he needs your jewels more than ever because he needs to escape to another country to avoid hanging." He stood and moved in front of her. "Do not take this threat lightly. He will kill you for your jewels. The desire for wealth is the only thing keeping him in Scotland, and he'll not allow you to stand in his way."

"Bessie and I left some of my things at the manor," she blurted out, thinking about the hiding place they'd chosen. Would it be good enough? "I have the largest jewels, but there is another there, though well hidden."

He moved closer and set his hands on her shoulders. "We will get them tonight. I know this must have come as quite a shock."

"I'm scared, if you wish to know the truth of it. Langley wishes to kill me, and the king will probably try to marry me off to another baron."

He gazed into her eyes and brushed his thumb across her cheek, then down her jawline. "Your strength amazes me. We will do everything we can to keep you safe and get you your land back. Do not give up."

Emmalin peered into his eyes—so intense yet so warm—and wondered if she had the nerve to tell him what their future would look like if she had any say. Women did not propose to men. And yet, she recalled one of her father's favorite sayings: *no knife is sharper than regret.* So she took a deep breath and forged ahead. "I have a question for you. 'Tis verra forward of me, but I am desperate. Would you ever consider marrying me if my husband were not an issue? I don't know exactly how it would take place, given he truly is not dead, but King Edward believes he is dead. I like you, and I think you like me. I know my sire would have been pleased with such a match, and in truth, so would I. We could share the lairdship in some way. Of course…"

Her words trailed off when she looked at him. He looked startled, which wasn't surprising given the unconventionality of her request, but he didn't step back from her either. She waited, giving him a moment to gather his thoughts.

He caressed her cheek again, slowly, sweetly. "I think we suit fine, and if I were ready to take a wife, I would be happy to marry you."

"But?"

"But you are a few days away from your husband's supposed death, your life is at risk, and we are in the middle of a precarious situation at the moment. It may not be the best time to speak of marriage. If we both make it away from here safely, would you allow me to court you?"

She nodded, chastising herself for having spoken so boldly. Women should not be so forward. It simply was not done. Her aunt would faint if she ever found out.

Then Alasdair flashed her a brilliant smile. "And if I wish to marry a woman, I will ask her in my own way. I've always said 'twould be special."

Something warmed inside of her—hope

blooming again.

"I understand," she said, taking a step back, "and I apologize for being so forward. Do not think on it again."

The door opened and Dyna stepped inside with a tray of meat pies. "Food for all," she said, holding the plate up.

Alasdair came from behind Emmalin, leaned into her and reached over her shoulder, his other hand giving her waist a small squeeze.

The squeeze went straight to her heart. That small move gave her the hope she so desperately needed.

———————

The three stood across the road from the large manor that belonged to Langley Hawkinge, tucked behind a couple of large trees and a stand of brush. They'd tied up their horses at a slight distance and approached on foot, stopping as soon as they had a good view of the manor. They'd been there for some time without observing anything of note, but a burst of horse hooves down the road told Alasdair it wouldn't be quiet for long. He reached for Emmalin and tugged her back to keep her out of the line of sight while Dyna climbed one of the trees.

Four horses galloped down the dusty path. They turned onto the path that took them to the small stables behind the manor, dismounted, and all four went inside.

Dyna dropped down from the tree moments

later. "I recognized two of them. One was definitely your husband. I don't know the name of the other, but I've seen him before. One of the sheriffs."

"I'm going closer so I can listen to their conversation," Alasdair said. "I can hide in the bushes in front of the house. Dyna? What do you want to do?"

"I'll stay in the trees, but there are so many next to the building that I think I can move closer. I'll have a better chance of hitting the bastard that way. I can get a shot with my dagger aimed directly into the front chamber. Let's hope they stay there."

"If chaos erupts, you should definitely be closer," Alasdair reminded her. "Mayhap we should have waited for Els and Alick to show up at the inn."

"I left a missive for them with the innkeeper. They'll know where to find us if they arrive in time."

Nodding to his cousin, he took Emmalin's hand and led her across to the front of the house. He'd given her a dagger to carry in the pocket of the men's breeches she wore, and her other hand was tucked inside, wrapped around the hilt if he had to guess. The sight gave him a painful feeling in his chest—she clearly feared they might be attacked at any moment.

He knew he'd hurt her with his words earlier. He'd known it the moment they left his mouth. And yet, he'd been right to tell her how he felt. Something deep inside him told him this wasn't the right time to consider marriage. He liked Emmalin very much, but her life was in chaos at the moment.

Not the best time to make important decisions. They could talk after this situation was more settled.

Voices got heated, bringing him back to the present moment, and he motioned Emmalin toward a group of bushes at the corner of the manor. They ducked into the middle of the arrangement, something that hid them well in the dark. A rustling in the trees overhead indicated Dyna had moved, too.

Alasdair crouched down next to Emmalin, putting his hand over hers, and listened intently. He made out Hawkinge's voice easily. His conversation was chiefly with another man he called Sheriff de Savage, but there was one other man just standing inside, his hand on the hilt of his small sword.

Toys compared to his massive Highland sword. He had no idea where the fourth man was at the moment.

"Look, Sheriff," Langley shouted. "I need to find my wife and those jewels."

"Baron, as you well know, you risk your life staying here. *Especially* if she finds a large clan to support her. The Bruce would like to see the Vale stay in the hands of the Scots. If he hears you are dead, he'll send a larger contingency to assist her, possibly more of Clan Grant. You need to get her to come to you and find the jewels. We cannot wait."

"Aye," Hawkinge said. "You'll get no argument from me. She needs to give me what I want."

"Since she's been brought here by one of the barons, you need to kidnap her and make her turn over the jewels. Then you'll have to kill her or she'll tell the king of the ruse. This cannot wait. For all we know, she could be at a kirk being married to another baron as we speak. Since you were declared dead, it might be deemed legal."

Alasdair wrapped his arm around Emmalin and tucked her close. Her whole body shivered, likely the effect of listening to two men casually discussing ending her life.

"I suspect she'll be here soon," Langley said with a wicked grin. He scanned the area as if searching for something. "Where are you, my dear? We've business to settle."

To Alasdair's surprise, Emmalin pushed away from his grasp. He let her go, thinking perhaps she had a cramp, but she crept away from the window. She moved quietly, gracefully, and yet her action sparked something. Three men came out of the bushes quickly, surrounding them. Alasdair attempted to fight them off, but his worry for Emmalin distracted him, and although he likely could have taken the three guards by himself, two more exited the house with Langley and the sheriff. He was outnumbered. Soon he found himself with a sword at his throat and two at his back.

"Well, there she is, my dear, dear wife," Langley said, a sardonic twist to his grin as he reached for his wife. "Where have you been, my love?" She spat at him, but he only laughed as he wiped it off. Alasdair cursed himself for not having waited for the arrival of his two cousins and their guards. His impatience had cost them.

Hawkinge wrapped his arm around Emmalin's waist, nuzzling her neck. "What? You did not miss me, my dear?" he asked.

"How did you know we were here?" she asked, her voice hard.

Hawkinge smirked as he whispered something into her ear, but Alasdair was too far away to hear.

"How did you get away from the men I sent to *my* castle, my sweet?" the baron asked in a louder voice. "Who helped you?" He turned to Alasdair, still holding Emmalin in front of him as if to shield himself. "Was it this ugly bastard?"

Alasdair's fingers itched to drive a blade into the man's black heart. He made another attempt to wrench himself free of his captors' grip and earned a fist to his back for it.

The baron gave him a condescending look down his nose and said, "Grant. Why don't you take your leave? If you drop your weapon and walk away, we'll let you live."

"And if you harm a hair on her head, you'll have a thousand of my comrades, the fiercest of the savage Scots you speak of, looking for you. Clan Grant will annihilate you and yours. The Bruce will support us."

Hawkinge spat off to the side. "You think I fear Robert the Bruce? We'll do the same to him that King Edward has done to so many of your comrades. Did you not learn anything at the Battle of Falkirk?"

Alasdair laughed. "Brave talk. King Edward thinks you're dead. I would wager he would love to hear that you are still alive. I'd come to watch your hanging, wouldn't you, Emmalin? Or is counterfeiting no longer considered treason?"

The bastard's face grew red, but he stayed where he was, behind his wife. "Emmalin, I'm going to ignore the fool you came with. Here's what you need to know. I want your mother's jewels. All of them. I know you brought them with you. You are to bring them to me by the morrow or your aunt Penne will die."

Alasdair bit back a curse. The baron was a wily man, and he knew he could use Emmalin's heart against her. He looked at Emmalin to see how upset she was by this declaration. While he could tell she fought to hide her emotions, the mention of her aunt had hit its mark. The look of sheer fear crossed her face before she was able to hide it.

"And your aunt's silly maid. I'll skewer them both if I don't have your jewels by sundown on the morrow." The daft fool had the audacity to look smug over this declaration.

A few of the guards chuckled at his comment. Which was when Alasdair finally heard the bird call he'd been praying for.

His cousins had arrived. They must have received Dyna's missive at Buck's Inn. He knew what his people would have to do next, and he gave Emmalin a hard look, praying she would understand. After a count of ten, he shouted, "Drop to the ground!" and drew his sword.

Emmalin stomped on her husband's instep, which loosened his grasp enough for her to fall to the ground just as a barrage of arrows sluiced through the air, taking three men out before they could even understand what was happening. She pulled the dagger out of the hidden pocket in her gown and spun around, ready to protect herself if necessary.

Alasdair lunged after the baron, who'd taken an arrow to his side, but a guard stepped between them. The coward took the opening and hastened into the house with the sheriff. Another group of guards appeared out of nowhere while the bastard got away, preventing Alasdair from following him.

Els, Alick, and the Grant guards rushed in with their swords. Alasdair fought harder than he'd ever fought before, driving his sword against the English guards' relatively weak swords, finding bone, ripping flesh apart. The thought of Emmalin drove him on, though he couldn't see her at present. If he did not hurry, he feared someone else would get to her first. An Englishman.

But then something strange happened. The hilt of his sword warmed in his hand—an unnatural kind of warmth, almost as if it had been stuck in the fire. He almost dropped it out of shock, but someone came at him and he sliced it through the air on instinct. A single swipe of the sword brought the man to the ground. It almost seemed as if it had become more powerful. He glanced at Alick, who had a wicked grin on his face as he swung his sword easily through the air. Part of him wanted to ask his cousin right now, in the midst of the fight, if the same thing had happened to him, but he couldn't be distracted from Emmalin. She was in danger, and he'd lost sight of her.

When he caught sight of her again, he was shocked to see she had a sword in hand, one she'd picked up from one of the fallen guards. It shocked him even more when he saw her slash the arm of one of Langley's guards—the one who was currently battling with Els. Though not a mortal wound, it shocked Langley's guard enough for him to be caught by Els's sword.

"Behind you, Dair!" Alick shouted.

Alasdair turned just in time to keep himself from being leveled, swinging his weapon up from the side with all his might to block the sword strike. He caught his opponent's shoulder, sending his sword flying, but it sliced Alasdair's leg on the way to the ground, his trews now damp with blood.

He turned around as two more arrows sluiced down, each meeting its mark. The battle had shifted enough so that a win was certain. Only three Englishmen were left standing against Els, Alick, and two Grant guards. The other Grant guards had to be searching the grounds for Langley and his conspirator.

Emmalin took a step back, her gaze now fixed on the blood on the sword. Her expression was as forlorn as if she'd wounded herself with the blade. If he were to guess, it was probably the first time she'd ever injured anyone. Assured of their win, he sheathed his weapon and raced over to her.

"Lass, 'tis me." He reached for her wrist, wrapping his hand around the hilt of the weapon and drawing it out of her grip. "Do not think of the harm you did. You could have saved my cousin's life by distracting that guard." He cleaned the sword on the ground and handed it back to her. "Carry it for now. You did a fine job."

She did as he said, then searched his gaze as if he were a stranger speaking an odd tongue.

"'Tis over, Emmalin," he said softly. "They'll not hurt you again."

A flash of recognition entered her eyes, and she threw herself at him, wrapping her arms around his neck. He held her close, whispering sweet words to her until she pushed away.

"You're wet," she mumbled, staring down at the bottom of her trews, now covered with his blood. "Alasdair, you're hurt!"

"'Tis just a scratch. Do not fash yourself." He reached down, surprised to see how much blood was there. Els and Alick came up behind him, both staring at his wound. The battle had ended.

"Push on it," Alick said. "Aunt Jennie would tell you to hold it tight, stop the blood if you can."

Dyna hopped down out of a tree and approached them. She said, "Your swords. Did you feel it, Alasdair?"

"Aye," he said with a whisper. He needn't ask how she'd intuited such a thing. He could tell this was one of the things his cousin simply knew.

"I did, too," Alick said, shooting a look at him. "It seemed to make me stronger."

Els shook his head as if in disgust. "What are you fools talking about?"

"Your sword," Alasdair said. "You didn't feel it warm in your hand during the battle?"

"Nay," he said in a tone that made it clear he considered the conversation over. Alasdair wanted to question him more, but this was not the place.

"Emmalin, did you hide the jewels here?" he asked. "Where are they?"

"I have the most valuable ones with me. I hid one in a gown abovestairs, so I'll retrieve them now." She set down the sword as if eager to be rid of it, then disappeared into the manor, Dyna following her to ensure she was safe. A few moments later, they returned with a bag.

Emmalin approached him, her expression resolute. He already knew what she would say. "I have them, but we must return on the morrow or he'll kill my aunt. I must protect her."

"Would he be holding anyone else?" Dyna asked.

"From what he said, he also has Tamsin. She's the serving lass I sent with Aunt Penne. They were to hide in the village."

"Then we'll have to return, will we not?" Alasdair said. He suspected Emmalin wouldn't have it any other way, not that he blamed her. He would have returned for his family, too.

Dyna's expression turned fiercer. "Unless we find them first. Before we do anything, we must take care of our wounded."

"Who's hurt?" Emmalin asked, searching the group. "Besides Alasdair, I mean. You all came here because of me. I'll see each of you to a healer, if necessary." Her gaze paused on a guard who had blood all over his arm. "Yours or someone else's?"

The warrior looked at her sheepishly. "Mine."

"Do not be ashamed," Dyna said. "We took care of over twenty men."

"And we are the only ones still here," Els said, nodding. "You all did a fine job."

Emmalin's gaze searched the area. "Unfortunately, the sheriff and the baron got away. I'd appreciate all you can do to help me ensure that man never sets foot on MacLintock land again."

"Langley was wounded," Dyna said with a fierce grin. "I know this because I shot him in the arse with an arrow. The sheriff had trouble getting him up on the horse, but I couldn't get them again."

"I hear hooves," Alick said, tilting his head. "We need to get the hell out before more come after us. Our horses are just over that hill. Alasdair, you can ride?"

"I'm fine. Emmalin can ride with me," he said after scanning the area. "I don't understand how the fool thinks to keep his secret with so many guards."

Dyna said, "Because if you hire them from the port, they'll do anything for extra coin for one night. They have no idea who he is, though if they'd survived, they would know now." She grinned at Emmalin. "We told them all."

Alick said, "We need to move out of here. Els and I will take most of the guards with us and search the area. Anyone who needs stitching can go with you so Dyna can take care of it. We were told you have the large chamber at The Buck's Inn. We'll meet you there in a bit. Get inside in case someone comes looking for you."

"Whatever you do, keep Emmalin out of view, Alasdair," Els said.

"I know," Alasdair said. "I expect they'll be searching all of Berwick for her. Now that others know about the jewels, anyone could be looking for her. We may have killed some of those guards he hired, but some could have survived. We have to decide what our next step is."

And they couldn't wait long.

CHAPTER EIGHTEEN

E MMALIN WAS STILL IN SHOCK over all that transpired. Her mind kept returning to the violence. She hated that Alasdair and another guard had been injured. What if one of the Grants had died? She hastened to rid her mind of that thought because she just couldn't handle it.

Her mind dipped back to Langley's words. The ones she had not yet shared with the others.

When they arrived at the inn, they hurried up to their chamber, where they could discuss without fear of prying ears.

Bessie came with them and she was frantic. She fussed over everyone, getting fresh water in the basin, finding linen squares, getting drinks for all. Alasdair went straight inside the bed chamber to strip out of his trews so he could check the damage to his leg.

The other two Grant cousins showed up a short time later with no news about the baron or the sheriff. Els headed straight into Alasdair's chamber and came back out, saying, "He needs stitching. Dyna, 'tis up to you. I cut the leg off one side so he'd still be covered. Too many around."

"Fine. Alasdair, come back out here and elevate your leg, putting pressure on the spot that's bleeding. I can't sew if I'm looking at all that blood.

"Aunt Jennie and my mother do it all the time," Els said.

"But I don't. So he needs to slow the bleeding first." She fussed with her saddlebag looking for the tools she would need.

Alasdair limped out, the leg of his trews cut short on one side, a linen square pressed against the wound. "Have you any salve of Aunt Jennie's? I don't wish for it to fester."

"Aye," Dyna said. "I have a small jar."

He settled at the table and said, "Emmalin, please sit. I wish to hear everything Hawkinge said to you when he pulled you aside and whispered to you."

Emmalin attempted to reply, but she couldn't take her eye off the blood pouring down his leg.

"Emmalin. Do not faint on us." Dyna came over to her side and ushered her into a seat. "You turned pale on me. Don't look at it if it bothers you."

She'd seen blood many, many times, but for some odd reason, blood coming from Alasdair's leg unsettled her. Gripping the table, she sat down before her dizziness brought her to the floor.

Els pulled up a chair beside her. "Aye, 'tis most important for us to understand what we're up against."

"I suspect 'twas a set up," Alasdair said, "Someone told him we were coming. Did he give you any inkling about why those men were hidden around the property?"

Emmalin stared at her lap and then quickly glanced at Bessie, hating what she was about to say—and how it would likely be interpreted. "He said there was a traitor who he's had in place all along to tell him of my plans."

"A traitor? He used those exact words?" Alasdair asked.

He and Els stared at each other, exchanging a significant look, while Dyna verbalized their thoughts. "Joya? Do you think 'twas her?"

"I trust her," Alasdair said. "I believe she's a true Scot. If she's been working with him all along, why would she have helped us get into the manor? And she's the one who suspected the counterfeiting arrest. Did he give you any other insight into this traitor? Anything at all?"

The three cousins exchanged significant glances again. They likely considered this confirmation that Joya was the culprit.

She had to tell them the rest of what he'd said. No matter who it implicated. She needed them to know the truth. Swallowing hard, she whispered, "He said he's known all of my steps since he left home."

The Grant cousins seemed to come to the same conclusion at the exact same time, because all three faces turned to stare at Bessie.

Bessie's eyes widened in shock. "Me? You think I am the traitor? I'm not a male." She fell to her knees in front of Emmalin and said, "Nay, my lady. Nay, I would never betray you. I have cared for you since you were a sweet babe in my arms. I loved your mother. Nay, nay, please do not think it was me."

She gripped hold of Emmalin's skirts, twisting them in her hands. "Please."

"Who else could it be?" Els asked. "He could have tried to fool you. It could be a man or a woman, but who knows you are here?"

Emmalin knew one thing for certain: it was *not* her dear maid. "'Tis not Bessie. She has been at my side forever and is the most loyal maid and friend I've ever known. Langley is a lying fool. There could be a traitor, but 'tis not Bessie. Get it out of your minds."

Bessie had broken down into tears. She'd cradled her head in Emmalin's lap, sobbing.

"Allow me to tell you what bothers me most," she said, patting dear Bessie's head.

All faces turned to her. Even Bessie lifted her head to hear her speak.

"Langley Hawkinge married me just to get my land, and he hated me so much he concocted this plan to steal what's mine. He's guilty of treason by creating counterfeit coins and has staged his own death. I will not accept him at his word. The man is a liar and a cheat."

She glanced around the room at everyone. "Look at us. Because of Langley Hawkinge, Alasdair is hurt and so is another Grant guard. Because of him, we're all arguing. Because of him, we fear what will happen if we leave this inn. This is all wrong, and I blame that vile man for everything. No matter what he said, Bessie did *not* betray me. She never would." And she would not allow anyone to say or imply otherwise.

A knock landed on the door, and Alick hastened to answer it. Moments later, he came in with Joya. "I'm told this is the lovely lass who assisted you at the manor?"

Alasdair nodded in confirmation. "She did indeed assist us. We'd have never found him otherwise. We had no idea where his manor home would be."

Which was slightly suspicious. The others seemed to think so, too. They all started arguing again, the cousins putting questions to Joya, who defended herself deftly once she learned about the accusation.

"Aye, I can understand why you might think it was me, except for one problem. I hate the English bastards, so why would I turn your whereabouts over to your enemy? I didn't do it, but I have no way of proving it, except to say that I didn't know any of you a few days ago, so I clearly am not the person who was taking him secrets before then."

There was no denying it made sense. It sounded true. Feeling overwhelmed, Emmalin turned away. "Please, I must get some fresh air," she said.

Dyna said, "I'm going to sew Alasdair up. I think 'twould be best for you to step outside for a spell, Emmalin."

"I'll talk to the guards," Alick said, "have them stand together outside to keep watch. I'll return after I give them some meat pies."

"Go with Emmalin, Els," Alasdair said. "Probably better not to have anyone watch me get sewn up. You know how Dyna is with a needle." He smirked with that last comment.

"You dare to say that before I stitch up your leg? Hmm, I can make you regret that really quickly."

"You know I'd never allow anyone to do it but you, Dyna. You're the best."

Emmalin suddenly had difficulty swallowing past the emotion clogging her throat. The cousins were so comfortable with one another. So close. What would her life have been like if she'd had someone to share her battles? Siblings and cousins to stand by her side and fight for the heritage that was rightly hers. But she was alone. Not wanting to become too melancholy, she decided it was a good time for her to take her leave. She hugged Bessie and said, "Do not fear, Bessie. I believe you. But consider the matter. See if you can think of who it might be. I'll step out if you'll please stay to assist Dyna with her needs."

Els followed her, and she was glad of it. She didn't wish to be alone.

She left then, opening the door and taking in a deep breath. It was dark outside and few people were milling about, but she wasn't afraid. Her husband had been injured, too, and was unlikely to bother them this eve.

Of one thing she was certain. Although everything that had transpired was her husband's fault, she had played a part in it nonetheless. She hated that Alasdair and another man had been hurt trying to save her from her despicable husband.

Els moved over to speak with a few of the guards outside. Leaning against a tree beside the inn, she reflected on everything she'd heard. No matter how much she considered the circumstances, she didn't think Bessie was guilty, but she couldn't come up with any other name.

And that was when she saw him—Gaufried.

"Mistress?" he said, his gaze falling on hers as his face lit up. "Mistress? My lady? 'Tis truly you?"

She moved down the path a ways to greet him, throwing her arms around his neck. "Gaufried. What are you doing here?"

He set her away from him and said, "Oh, my lady. Everything has changed. Your castle has been taken over by ingrates. They ransacked your chamber looking for your mother's jewels. I left because I could not tolerate seeing it that way any longer. I was hoping to find you. I promised your sire I would watch over you and I will."

"But who is there?"

"When I left, Sheriff de Savage and his men were still searching the area for anything of value. He has a party of men searching for you. We mustn't allow them to catch you. I knew you would come here eventually because the king had summoned you."

Els glanced over, his expression full of suspicion, but she indicated all was well.

"Where have you been staying?" she asked.

"There were no rooms available at the Buck's Inn, so I've been in the local stables. I requested to see the king last eve, hoping he'd give me word of you, but he's not in residence. 'Tis all verra strange." Looking about nervously, as if suddenly afraid of being overheard, he said. "Please, my lady, please don't stand in the main path."

She stayed close to the inn but moved out of the way so anyone on horseback could get past. "What is wrong? You look distraught."

He leaned toward her and whispered, "Aye, I am. I'm worried for you. Where will you go, my lady? I will go with you if you wish to reclaim your land, but is it safe to return there yet? How many others are looking for you?"

Els came over and interrupted their conversation. "We will protect the lady. You need not worry. Who are you?"

"Els, this is Gaufried and he was my sire's second. When Langley took over, he made him my steward and installed his own man to be second-in-command."

Gaufried said, "But now that your husband is dead, all the barons are looking for you. I don't know whose men were at the castle, but they were thieves, I tell you." He had a sick look on his face over the situation.

Her eyes widened and her mouth fell open to answer, but words would just not come out. She set her hand on Gaufried's arm. "Langley isn't dead. Those men lied to us. I saw him tonight, and he was quite alive. He intends to kill me if I don't give him my mother's jewels—'twas his intention all along."

Gaufried gasped in shock. "'Struth?"

When she nodded, he shook his head slightly. "I wish to advise you as I would your father, but I fear I am lost. I cannot imagine how you are faring through all of this."

The answer was on her lips—"not well"—but it wouldn't help to admit it. She had no idea what she should do next, and the Grants had surely already done enough for her. She was the one who should come up with a plan.

She was lost in thought when a rider approached them on horseback. The man stopped directly in front of them. "Mistress MacLintock? Know you of her?" he asked, looking from face to face awaiting their answer. "I heard she would be here."

Gaufried searched her gaze, not willing to answer for her, so she took over. "I am the Mistress of MacLintock land." She couldn't help but wonder who would bring a message to her at this location.

The messenger dismounted, holding the reins of his horse, and took a step toward her. "The king's man sent a missive saying you are to meet him at Berwick Castle," he said in an undertone.

"Tell him I am too distraught to come this eve," she responded, making no effort to be discreet.

She glanced at Gaufried, who did his best to hide his smirk.

"He suspected you would say as much," the messenger said. "A banquet will be held at the castle on the morrow. You are invited to partake in the festivities. The king's man will see you there. Do you wish to come now or the morrow?"

She nodded and said, "I will come on the morrow, but my steward will be with me."

"So be it," the man said. He nodded and mounted his horse, riding off toward the royal castle.

"Forgive me, Gaufried," she said, turning to her

steward, "but I don't wish to go alone. Will you come?" If she didn't see what the king wanted, she wouldn't know when she could return to her home. Her wish was to be done with all of this, to leave Berwick, return to her castle, and forget about her husband. Alasdair was not interested in marriage, so she had to start thinking of herself and let her hopes die.

"Of course, but are you sure you wish to go directly to the king's man? Do you know what he wishes?" Gaufried asked his face etched with concern. "Although I am grateful to see you've regained some of your boldness, we must think this through. We need a plan."

She understood his concern for her—indeed, she shared it—but she still intended to go to the castle. One way or another, this had to end.

———◆———

As soon as Emmalin returned to the chamber, he could tell something had transpired outside the inn—and not just because of her new, elderly companion. He bolted out of his chair and asked, "What is it?"

The others waited for her answer, their expressions conveying the same urgency he felt.

She said, "First I must introduce you to my sire's second-in-command, Gaufried. He became my steward when I married because Langley refused to give power to any of my sire's men. Before any of you accuse him of anything, know you that he has been loyal and faithful to my clan for decades.

He came to Berwick searching for me.

"Secondly, the king sent a messenger to the inn, though I know not how he knew where to find me. He advised me to come to Berwick Castle or he would come for me on the morrow. There's a banquet to be held at the castle on the morrow, and he expects my presence there. I agreed to go and Gaufried said he would gladly accompany me, though I know not what the purpose of this is. I need to find out and we don't need to return to Langley's home until sundown."

"This could be his plan to marry you to another baron. I'll accompany you," Alasdair said at once. "Gaufried may attend and help us search the premises, but you'll not go without me." The thought of her being anywhere near another conniving bastard who wanted her land made him wish to punch a wall—or a treacherous Englishman.

Alick winked at her and said, "I think we'll all be going. I do hate to miss a banquet."

"Why?" she whispered.

"The king's man has a reason for this," Dyna said. "We couldn't allow you to go alone. Now, your husband wants your jewels by the morrow, so my suggestion is that going to the castle will keep Langley from kidnapping you."

"I do have the jewels that belonged to my mother," she said. "But they're well hidden." Although she trusted everyone in the room, to an extent, she didn't think it wise to tell them everything.

"Do you think 'tis what the king's man wants?" Els asked.

"It could be, but it could be to form another alliance and a marriage. Either way, I suspect the baron will not attempt to kill you in the middle of Berwick Castle," Alasdair said. "It should be a safe place to meet."

"Be aware of all you do on the morrow. Whatever you do, do not go off to a different location by yourself. If you take such a risk, he could easily kill you," Dyna said. "We must all be verra careful."

Emmalin sighed and said, "I will be. I promise."

She didn't add that she would not risk anyone's life but her own.

Alasdair said, "I suggest we all try to get a good night's sleep. We have much to do yet."

Promises aside, when it came down to it, she'd do what she must.

All she wanted was to be left alone to return to MacLintock Castle.

CHAPTER NINETEEN

EMMALIN, BESSETA, AND GAUFRIED HAD made their way to the entrance of Berwick Castle, uncertain what to expect, but they'd been ushered inside as soon as she gave the guards her name. A servant brought them to a sitting room, where she was greeted by a handsome man several years older than her. "Mistress, I am glad to see you. Word is you have lost your husband. Baron Hawkinge's death has been confirmed by the king's men."

She very nearly corrected the man, but he clearly didn't expect any sort of response. "My name is Baron Eversby," he said, "and I will make sure you have a pleasant visit. I was pleased to hear you would be joining us for the banquet early evening. Would you like a private chamber so you can rest before then? This is your maid?"

"Aye, and my steward. Our guards are off the property."

"Very well. I suspect the king will be eager for you to marry again. You may even meet someone to your liking at our banquet this eve. Someone must be in place to manage your property. We certainly cannot expect you to take charge during such turbulent times."

Emmalin smiled, though she wished to correct most of his statements. She was more than capable of managing MacLintock Castle and all its lands. Her father had taught her well, but he'd also advised her that most men did not view a woman as capable.

She'd do best not to stir up any trouble. Her husband would do enough of that on his own if they found out he was indeed alive. Lying to the king would indeed get him hanged.

"My thanks to you, my lord. I would surely appreciate the chance to rest before the festivities this eve."

"Of course. I'll have someone lead you to your chamber." He snapped his fingers at an older woman dusting a bookcase in the corner, the gesture as obnoxious as it was officious. "I'm sure you must be exhausted from your travels."

She thanked the man and followed one of the housekeepers up to her chamber. Besseta came with her, and Gaufried promised to keep them abreast of all events taking place in the castle.

Emmalin paced the inside of the chamber she'd been given, surprised at the size of it. She'd been ushered inside with the promise of a lovely gown for the evening, though she and Besseta would have to work quickly to instill the necessary pockets inside the garment. As if she cared what she looked like at such a time. Her mind was fixed on the others. Were they inside the castle yet? Dyna had assured her they'd be watching her at all times.

A short time later, someone knocked on the

door. For a moment, Emmalin feared it might be Langley, which was utterly ridiculous that he would dare to show himself here, but a small voice called out to her from behind the thick wood. "I've a platter of food for you, my lady, and some other comforts."

She opened the door to admit the small maid, who was followed by a couple of others. They brought in food, drinks, and a tub.

"I'll take your maid with me so she can locate water and linens for you to freshen up," the first maid said. "The baron has also arranged for a gown to be sent to you and your maid can make the necessary adjustments. May I assist you with anything else?"

"Nay, that will be all. My thanks to you." She didn't know how to feel about being without Bessie, even for a short while, but she couldn't think of a tactful way to say no.

She knew why she was here. The king's greedy barons were eager for her land and would shower her with attention to get it. They were surely oblivious to the fact that her husband still lived.

No one but Bessie, Gaufried, and the Grants knew that.

She couldn't help but wonder if the gown the servants sent up would be a proper mourning gown. Somehow, she doubted it. The men wouldn't wish to be reminded that she'd just lost her husband.

Too anxious to eat, she started pacing the room again, and didn't stop until the lads arrived with steaming water for the tub. Gaufried and Bessie flew in behind them. She hugged her dear maid but said little.

"Did you learn anything about Langley?" she asked them after the lads departed.

"Most of the people I've spoken with believe he's dead," Gaufried said. "But I did hear about the reception this evening in the great hall. The maids say you're to be on display for a new husband."

Emmalin heaved a long sigh. "I've been invited to attend a small gathering before everyone else joins the celebration. The barons likely arranged it so they could speak to me privately."

"And you accepted?" Gaufried asked.

She took a deep breath and said, "Aye. I accept my fate. King Edward wishes to maintain his foothold in the Vale of Leven. He wants access to Loch Lomond, also. He'll not let me escape another marriage. If I meet with the barons, at least I might be able to choose which one I wish to marry once he makes the proclamation."

Although she still hoped to marry Alasdair, she needed to be practical. If he wasn't ready to make a decision now, he might never be. Better to prepare for anything than to find herself in another horrible situation.

"How can I help you?" he asked.

"I would like for you to find out all you can about these barons, starting with their names. Find out who is the kindest, who would suit me best—anything you can. I'll not be tethered to another Langley."

"I will do that, my lady." He grinned. "I'm off to

do your bidding."

Emmalin spent most of the time primping. It seemed there was little time for her and Bessie to talk privately, because someone else kept visiting her chamber. She saw the dressmaker, the man who had prepared the menu seeking her input on the food, and someone who came in to wash the clothes she had worn. The latter servant had arrived without warning, but she'd been allowed to change in privacy, behind a partition, and had managed to remove the ring and necklace from the hidden pocket. She had to be sharp about the jewels. Anyone could steal them to sell, so it was important that she always be aware of her surroundings. She transferred the jewels into a small pouch Besseta had given her and set her dagger on a side table to be placed in whatever clothing she donned later.

After all of the visitors left, she managed to take a small nap. Otherwise, she'd have gone to the banquet with dark circles under her eyes. Sheer exhaustion took over the moment she laid her head down.

"Mistress, you must get ready," Bessie said, shaking her shoulder gently. I must do your hair and get you dressed."

Emmalin sat up, memories of all that had transpired returning to her. It felt as if a shroud had descended on her.

"How long did I sleep?"

"Nearly two hours, my lady. Never fear, your gown is here and 'tis most beautiful, and I already…" She paused to look around before she whispered, "I already added a hidden pocket inside for your mother's jewels. You cannot let them see."

"Thank you, Bessie," she said, removing the small pouch from her grasp and tucking the valuable item into its new hiding place. "This is perfect. I have them all together now."

Emmalin refreshed herself with the water in the basin and Bessie arranged her hair before she stepped into the gown. It was a rich dark blue with gold trimming along the neckline and a trim waist that showed off her soft curves in the best way.

"Oh, my lady. 'Tis a beautiful gown. You look absolutely lovely in it. I shall put gold ribbons in your hair, too. And the beaded slippers match the blue perfectly."

Bessie fussed while Emmalin's mind raced. She bounded back and forth between three thoughts: Alasdair's leg, whether Gaufried would manage to learn anything about the new barons, and the identity of the traitor.

Who was she? Or he?

When the time came, the maid entered and said, "Baron Eversby awaits you at the top of the staircase. He will escort you to the west hall."

Emmalin left the chamber, squeezing Bessie's hands before she stepped out into the wide corridor. Multiple guards were stationed along the passageway leading to the staircase, where Baron Eversby awaited her.

He smiled and gave a slight bow, "Greetings, my lady. You look stunning this eve. I will escort you down to our lavish banquet."

"My thanks, Baron Eversby." She curtsied and took his proffered arm, descending the steps next to him.

Once they were belowstairs, the baron brought her around to meet a couple of other men, all of whom she guessed were interested in marrying her. *Stealing my land*, she thought to herself privately. In addition to being English, they shared another sad failing.

None of them were Alasdair Grant.

Although she didn't understand the barons' games, these men, at least, seemed to genuinely believe Langley was dead. She kept an eye out for her husband, for the man everyone seemed to think was dead, but she saw Alasdair first. Dressed like an Englishman, he outshone every other man in the hall. How she wished to see him in his clan's dress plaid, but she understood why he did not want to draw attention to his heritage. The Scots were not always welcome on English soil.

She sucked in a breath as he drew close to her.

"Have you seen him yet?" Alasdair asked.

"Nay," she said, swallowing a lump in her throat. "All of the barons I've met this eve seem to believe the story about his death. 'Tis another game, I fear. I am here to have my hand and my land auctioned off to the highest bidder is my guess. I've met several barons already. There's been no mention of Langley Hawkinge except for Baron Eversby, the first one I met."

The lump in her throat grew as Alasdair's eyes

locked onto hers. "Then I guess I must spend more time at your side." His eyes glittered with promise, although she didn't dare believe he'd change his mind.

Another baron approached them, gave a slight bow, and said, "My lady, may I invite you for a stroll around the gardens?"

Alasdair bristled and took a step toward her, doing his best to calm his brogue. "Nay, she walks with me."

The man gave them an odd look and left, and Alasdair tucked her a bit closer, his arm going around to the small of her back. Not quite appropriate, but he didn't seem to care. Then again, neither did she.

She quite liked being this close to him. Fresh from a bath, he smelled of sandalwood and mint leaves. She leaned in to inhale more of him as he led her down a passageway and slipped into an alcove, tugging her with him. He pulled a curtain across the alcove, hiding them completely, and wrapped his arms around her.

Emmalin fell against him, and he whispered, "I just had to. You are too enticing for me." He cupped her face and kissed her, his tongue stroking hers until she gave a small moan. Her body melded against his and her nipples peaked against the tight fabric of the gown. If she could have her way, she'd slip the blasted garment off her shoulders and grant him free access to her breasts.

To her surprise, he ended the kiss and dipped his head to her open cleavage, kissing a trail across both breasts while he cupped her through the fabric. One of her hands slid through his thick dark locks, pulling him closer simply because she wanted more of him.

She doubted she could ever get enough.

A male cough from the other side of the curtain interrupted their small tryst. Alasdair pulled away from her with a small smile and leaned in to kiss her cheek before they left the alcove together.

Sheriff de Savage awaited them on the other side of the curtain. He raised his brows, as if they'd offended his sensibilities, and said, "I heard I'd find you here. Your husband wants your jewels. Perhaps he'll leave you be if you give them to me."

She said nothing, her mind scrambling to make sense of the situation. Who'd told him where to find them? One of the barons? Was it all some sick play, staged only for her?

"Do not give them to him, my lady," Gaufried said from behind the sheriff. He must have followed him.

The sheriff glared at her faithful steward, then turned back to her and said, "I'm confident a mutually beneficial arrangement can be reached."

One that involved her death, no doubt.

"But I don't have any jewels," she insisted.

"He says you do."

"The lady said she doesn't have them," Alasdair growled. "Must I beat her answer into you?"

The sheriff cast him a bored look and said, "You can't hide that you're a Scot."

"What the hell does that mean?"

"I have orders to detain all Scots who do not accept King Edward as their king. I could say it was true of you whether it is or not. Keep out of matters that do not concern you."

"Excuse me if I'm mistaken, Sheriff de Savage," Emmalin said sweetly, "but are you not Scottish?"

"True," he said, "but I accept King Edward as my king. I work for him. If you're a loyal subject, you'll heed the husband the king arranged for you to marry."

"Where is the baron?" Gaufried asked. "We were under the impression he wished to meet with my lady this evening."

"You have two hours," the sheriff said, ignoring the question. "Bring the jewels to Hawkinge's manor or your aunt will suffer the consequences." He tipped his head toward Alasdair. "He stays here. She may bring Gaufried only." He spun on his heel and left.

Gaufried fussed with the buttons on his coat, his eyes full of concern. "What are we to do, mistress?"

Just then, Dyna stepped out of the shadows of another alcove. "He's lying. They don't have your aunt with them. She's being kept in a different place."

"Where?" Alasdair asked.

"I don't know that yet. But they'll not kill her there. 'Tis quite impossible."

"We'll meet the bastard. Come to my chamber after the banquet ends. In the meantime, see if you can uncover any other information, especially about where he is keeping Aunt Penne. Or if Tamsin is with her. We still do not know that either." She squared her shoulders knowing she could handle anything with Alasdair by her side. Her rotten husband would not make her cringe in fear."

Her steward nodded and hurried off to do her bidding. As soon as he left, Alasdair immediately said, "I'm going with you."

"I hope you will come with me. Gaufried will attempt to protect me, and I'll have my dagger, but your sword and your cousin's arrows are far more powerful than my small weapon. I fear I have not practiced much with my sword, though I left it at the inn where 'tis of no use to me."

Alasdair narrowed his gaze and said, "My cousins and I will follow you, but I'll stay back until I'm needed."

He leaned down, kissed her cheek and she cupped his face, wanting to keep him by her side forever. "If I could just uncover where my aunt is, I'd be able to handle this better."

"Dyna thinks she's not with him. If that is true, you need not worry."

"I hope you're right. I believe we need to mix amongst the guests, see if we can discover anything else that develops," she said.

He kept his hand at her back as they made their way back into the fray of guests at the banquet, now filled with many from the village. She stayed close to him, but they didn't learn anything new.

She breathed a sigh of relief when the banquet finally ended. Alasdair leaned over and kissed her cheek. "We have one hour. I'll search the periphery of the castle and prepare your mount. Bring Gaufried and meet me on the street in half an hour. 'Tis time to finish this."

Emmalin squeezed his hands, hoping he was right. She wished to be done with this. Now she wanted nothing more than to have her husband gone and preferably dead. She hoped he'd *stay* dead this time. She made her way back out of the hall and down the passageway until she came to the staircase. The wide corridors in the castle allowed for side tables and artwork on the wall. She stopped in front of one beautifully woven tapestry, pleased to see it so well lit up by candles on either side of it, shining on the carefully worked threads in the piece. Her mother would be proud to see her work displayed so well.

She was about to leave when her gaze fell on something odd.

The candlestick holder looked familiar.

She blew the candle out and took it out of the holder so she could look at the silver piece. Gazing at it closely, she searched for something she knew was there, not surprised at all when she found it.

There at the base of the candleholder was the scratch mark she had put in it when she was young. Her mother had been furious with her.

She knew who had betrayed her.

CHAPTER TWENTY

E MMALIN HURRIED UP THE STAIRCASE, placing the holder in her hidden pocket with the jewels, grateful for the voluminous folds in the extravagant gown. Bessie was inside awaiting her. She found her dagger and also put that inside her pocket.

"Bessie, listen carefully. I'm to meet Alasdair and Gaufried soon."

"Has something happened, my lady?"

Her maid's concern went right to her heart. She'd known all along that Bessie was not a traitor, yet she wasn't ready to reveal what she'd uncovered to anyone. "Help me into my breeches, and you must come with me. I don't wish for you to stay here alone. You can go with Dyna."

Bessie, bless her heart, did not question her. "Aye, mistress. I'll ready your things once I've helped you out of that gown."

"Aye, I am meeting with Langley to put an end to this suffering."

"But how will you do that? He will kill you, I fear, once he gets what he wants," Bessie said, her hands trembling as she helped Emmalin out of the gown.

"He wants my mother's jewelry. He may have it.

If it will rid me of him, then I'll gladly relinquish it. He may try to kill me, 'tis true, but Alasdair and his cousins will be there. Langley does not have a large faction of guards. He's doing what he can to keep his identity a secret or he'll be quartered and hanged, I'm sure."

"Please be careful, my lady."

"I need you to go back to the inn, Bessie. I don't want you to be here when the baron returns...*if* he returns."

A knock sounded at the door, but she ignored it for the time being, hurrying to finish her task. Finally, she tucked all her necessities into the hidden pocket in her dress. "Leave through the front entrance right after I depart, Bessie. No one will stop you."

"I will do it, mistress. Please be careful."

She opened the door to a slightly red-faced Gaufried.

"I feared something had happened to you, mistress."

"I'm here. Let's move on, Gaufried," she said after giving Bessie a hug and making her way out the door. Her mind churned as she turned over her various options. Foremost in her mind was the question of whether she should confront her old, and up until now loyal, servant about the candlestick she saw. After all, the last place she'd seen that candle holder was in his hands. He'd told her he would bury it, so how had it ended up at Berwick Castle?

She waited until they were outside before she

tugged on his arm. "Gaufried," she said, reaching for the candleholder in her pocket. "I found this in the castle. You know what that means?"

Gaufried stared at the candleholder in her hand for a long time, then lifted his gaze to hers with tears in his eyes. Something she hadn't expected to see.

"Mistress, 'twas not me. I promised your sire…I know how it must look…I would never…I could not betray you…God would strike me dead."

Some part of her wished to believe the man who'd served her sire for so long. "Did you bury it or did you give it to someone, Gaufried?"

He shifted his feet, then said, "I didn't bury it. I heard the sounds of battle and dropped it on the floor. I ran like the coward I am. But I swear to you in the name of our dear Lord that I did not bring it to Berwick. I did not. I would never give anything to King Edward. Never!"

If she chose to believe him, as she was wont to do, that meant there was still another traitor out there.

"Gaufried, I want to believe you, but…"

He reached for her hand and said, "Never. I promised your sire I would protect you when he lay dying. I could never betray that trust. Or you." His hand fell away from her, and he said, "But I understand if you would prefer to send me away."

She thought about it a moment, but his explanation was feasible, and she did trust him. His every word spoke of sincerity. She gave him a quick hug. "I believe you," she said, "now you must keep Hawkinge from killing me."

"I will protect you with my life, mistress. The baron, he is daft now, I think."

"We must go."

Gaufried moved ahead of her, leaving her with the disturbing thought that someone else wished her dead. Moments later, they reached Alasdair, who had both of their horses saddled and ready. He said, "I found naught of interest. We'll head straight to his home."

They followed a winding route, weaving between paths, until they came to the road near the river. When they neared Langley's manor, Alasdair held back and motioned for her and Gaufried to move forward. They followed the path behind the building, where about ten horses were secured in the stables. Gaufried helped her down and led her in through a side door and into the front room.

There sat her husband, Langley Hawkinge, the man who would not die. He sat on a cushioned chair in an odd position, she guessed because of his injury, and had a small sword in his hand. His gaze locked on hers as soon as she stepped into the room. The only other man she recognized was one of the sheriffs. Sheriff de Savage.

"Surprise!" Langley said with a smirk. "Are you not pleased to see me? I watched you at the banquet from afar. Who are you choosing to replace me? Eversby? I must admit you were a beauty in that gown. Why did you change it? Those breeches under the gown are unbecoming."

"Why are you so evil? Why the constant lies and

deceptions?" She refused to cower to the fool.

Her husband snorted. "You never would have suited me. Even when you pretended to accept your position as a woman, a wife, you rebelled. I saw it in your every move."

Her gaze scanned the room, judging how many men Langley had at his disposal. She counted six guards, but she suspected someone else was hidden within the manor. An accomplice. Langley wouldn't have acted completely alone. He was the kind of man who liked making orders rather than getting his hands dirty. "Are you not worried all these guards will turn you in? Gain coin for turning a traitor in to King Edward?"

"I have far more coin than they would ever gain from the king. Your coffers were mighty rich, I must say. Oh, and your true love couldn't make it. My men found him outside and slit his throat. You have me instead. Now, be a dear and tell me quickly, where are your mother's jewels? The sapphire necklace, of course, but I do believe you have other pieces, too."

How she wished to laugh and tell him her true love was right outside the door, along with his cousin, but she kept her secret.

"You don't have any right to my mother's jewels." She crossed her arms and glared at him, tapping her foot with as much annoyance as she could muster.

"My dear, you're growing stronger. No tears this time? Are you not upset to see me instead of your savage Scot?"

She decided to play a wee game with the bastard.

In the distance, she heard the sound of hoofbeats and she knew without a doubt that it would be more of Alasdair's cousins and men.

She stared directly at Langley. "I *expected* to see you. Why do you think you deserve my jewels? I'm surprised by your sudden interest in them."

Langley gave her an odd look. "Why shouldn't I be interested in jewels? They should be mine by rights as your husband."

"Please," Emmalin said, her voice hard. "I am not finished. Do you recall the time you ambushed us? It happened just outside of your manor…"

Baron Hawkinge stared at her, clearly not understanding where she was going with her reasoning.

"We turned the tables on you." The horses sounded much closer, and there were plenty of them. "After I met with Gaufried, I spoke with the Grants. Guess who's coming? And coming just for you?"

"You foolish bitch," Langley said, bolting out of his chair, only to fall back. The injury he'd taken last eve had clearly incapacitated him somewhat. "Guards! Four of you outside, two of you here to protect me. Ready your weapons."

The din of battle began outside, and two men came for Gaufried, who pulled his weapon out immediately to fight them off. She backed away from Langley, as fast as she could, but Sheriff de Savage lunged forward and grabbed her. He forced her out of the back door.

"Do not let him leave," she yelled back at

Gaufried. "Keep him here until Alasdair arrives."

De Savage yanked on her arm and said, "Shut your mouth. Give me the jewels, and I'll leave you alive," he said through his teeth. Of course, she knew it to be a lie. She'd heard his conversation with Langley. "Where are they? You must have them hidden it on you. Sewn inside your gown? In a pocket in your breeches? I'll rip the garment off of you if I must."

He yanked her along behind him, pulling her into the dark shadows beneath a tree. His mistake was underestimating her. He turned for just a moment, checking on the activity out front, and she acted without hesitation the moment he took his gaze off of her. She reached into her pocket and pulled out the heavy silver candlestick holder, swinging it with all her might and hitting him in his head. "You want your just reward? Here 'tis."

"Ow, you bitch." He stumbled backward but managed to stay on his feet, and moments later, he was coming at her again. She caught sight of another sheriff, de Fry, running toward them from the side of the manor.

De Savage growled, "Give. Me. The. Jewelry."

She shoved away from him. "Fine, here," she said, reaching into her pocket. He was a distance away, but she thought she was close enough. De Savage's eyes glazed over with greed as he watched her retrieve something shiny from her pocket, but the greed quickly changed to shock. She fired her dagger across the short distance between them and it embedded deep in his belly, blood spurting everywhere.

She turned to de Fry, who had stopped his forward progress. "Nicely done, my lady," he said, his words coming as a shock. She'd expected him to retaliate, but he seemed almost...pleased.

De Savage crumpled to the ground, his hand clutching at the dagger, trying to remove it. Pink froth came out of his mouth and he gagged, staring at her. She reached down and pulled it out, wiping the blood on the man's clothing.

Fearful of de Fry, she brandished the dagger at him.

"I'm not here to hurt you," the second sheriff said, raising his hands. "I'm a Scot to my core, but don't tell anyone. Some of us work in secret."

One of the baron's men hurtled around the corner, screaming at de Fry to grab her, kill her, but de Fry spun around and stabbed him instead, confirming that his words were true.

Perhaps de Savage had been the traitor her husband had referred to all along. He was certainly a traitor to the Scots, if nothing else.

Could this be over?

Not yet. Langley still lived.

———◆———

It nearly killed Alasdair to see Emmalin ahead of him riding with Gaufried, but they needed to send her in alone to find out exactly what her husband was about. Dyna had insisted it was the best way. She had ridden ahead of all of them, upon her own insistence, and was already hidden in the trees.

Acting under their younger cousin's directives, Els was riding with Alasdair, and Alick had gathered their men but was hanging back at a distance to avoid being noticed.

They rode down the path as silently as possible because they had no idea how many men they would find in the manor, or if Langley would even be there. He just prayed they got there in time. When they arrived, he made his way over to Dyna's tree and made a bird call. Dyna replied with all the information they needed to know.

"Ten horses outside, but I only count six men besides Langley and de Savage."

He gave Els instructions, which his cousin would pass on to Alick before taking his own position in the manor. Then, without delay, he slipped inside the back entrance of the building.

He didn't see Emmalin anywhere. He moved from chamber to chamber, not surprised to find Langley sitting in the front chamber alone. He'd just seen Gaufried leave and two dead bodies lay not far away from him. He hoped the man was following Emmalin.

Alasdair strode up to the baron and moved in front of him. He wanted with all his heart to plunge his own weapon into the man's rotten heart, but he needed him to stand first. Although the baron held a paltry weapon of his own, he still would not feel comfortable slaying a man who would not defend himself.

"Where's Emmalin?"

"Outside with one of my men. Don't worry,

he'll not hurt her unless I tell him to. He answers to me." The smug expression on his face made Alasdair wish to put his fist in it.

"Hawkinge, get up," he growled.

The man didn't move.

"Go ahead, kill me. Kill a wounded man." He tossed his sword onto the floor and said, "Kill a defenseless, injured man. You sliced me the other day, and it is already festering. The wound will probably cost me my leg. But you're one of those honorable Highlanders, aren't you? You cannot strike me dead unless I'm armed, can you? I'll just sit here and wait for you to kill the rest of my men." He crossed his arms and stared up with a smug grin.

Alasdair bristled—the bastard was right. As much as he wished to kill him, there was a code of honor he could not break. "Pick up your weapon."

"Not touching it. I'll sit here until you all leave."

"Pick it up, you spineless bastard."

Emmalin appeared in the back doorway, stopping short when she saw him.

"Who was with you?" Alasdair asked once he noticed her.

"Sheriff de Savage. He's dead. I had to kill him."

"Well, well, well," Hawkinge sneered, his voice carrying over the din of battle taking place around them. "If it isn't my little whore of a wife. Your lover is here. How many times have you been with him, my dear? Do you have more fire in you with him than you did with me?"

Alasdair stared at Emmalin to see how she would

react. He'd take care of the bastard eventually, but he wanted to give her the chance to confront him first. Something told him it was important.

This entire situation had clearly taken a toll on her, but he could also tell it had made her stronger. He could see it in the lift of her chin, the fire in her eyes, and the square of her shoulders.

She strode over to stand in front of Langley. Judging that he was close enough to get to the man should he try something, Alasdair waited to see what would happen next.

To his surprise, Emmalin spit in her husband's face.

Alasdair knew what she was doing: she was *baiting* him.

The bastard rose to the occasion, letting out a roar and reaching for his sword. Alasdair pulled his dagger from his boot and shot it straight into the man's neck, killing him instantly.

A voice from behind him said, "Nice aim, cousin."

Dyna strode in with the others, holding her arms over her head. "And we are victorious again." Gaufried followed her in, cheering almost as loudly.

Sheriff de Fry came in next, causing Alasdair to reach for his weapon again, but Els stayed his hand. "Nay, don't kill him, Alasdair. He's on our side. He's a Scot."

"Something I'll never forget," the man said seriously. "Unlike de Savage. I must return to the castle." He turned to Emmalin. "The king knew nothing of Langley's lies, but he plans to marry you to another as soon as possible." He stopped to glance at the others in the room. "If I were you, I'd marry yourself to a man of your choice soon. I say that as a Scot."

She nodded to him, staring at her feet, wishing she could disappear into the forest outside.

"I'll advise the king of what happened here," the sheriff added. "Anyone need anything?"

Emmalin said, "Please ask him to grant me a fortnight before I'm forced to marry again."

She could only hope it gave Alasdair enough time to decide.

Sheriff de Fry gave her a slight bow. "I would be pleased to advise him of all you've been through. Since your husband just died a second death, I hope he will honor your request." He nodded to them one more time, then left the manor.

Emmalin whirled around and threw her arms around Alasdair, needing him even if he couldn't give her any promises, and he kissed her hard on the mouth to the cheers of his cousins and their guards. When he pulled back, he asked, "You are not hurt?"

She shook her head. "Nay. The blood is de Savage's. He attempted to steal my mother's jewelry, and I fear he would have killed me afterward. I had a dagger in my pocket. Many thanks to all of you for coming to my aid again. You saw Bessie? She is safe?"

"Aye, she's at the inn," Els said.

"Did you find Aunt Penne?"

"Nay, but I'd be glad to seek out our friend Joya to see what she's learned."

Everyone stared at him. There was something about the way Els said her name that was odd. Almost as if he savored it.

Alasdair said, "Allow Els to see what he can learn, but I think it would be best to get you back to MacLintock land, as far away from the conniving barons as possible. Perhaps your aunt was in the village, after all. He could have used her as an idle threat."

CHAPTER TWENTY-ONE

———

THE TRIP BACK TO MACLINTOCK land was a most quiet one. Alasdair and Els led the group with Emmalin and Bessie between them, while Alick, Dyna, and Gaufried held up the rear. They'd reunited with her guards and brought them along, but no one had any information about Aunt Penne and Tamsin. Not even Joya, who knew everything.

Emmalin clung to the hope they might be back at her castle. It was as far forward as she could bear to look. The king's deadline hung over her head.

Baron Eversby had asked to speak with her before she left Berwick. Knowing exactly what he wanted, she'd preempted him, advising him that she was going home, that she was exhausted, and that she still had a fortnight to make her decision.

She knew where her heart belonged, but Alasdair hadn't mentioned anything about marriage, and he'd heard Sheriff de Fry as well as she had. They were running out of time.

When they neared her castle, she was surprised to see two patrols of warriors in Grant plaids. One of them rode up to Alasdair. "All is well, Alasdair. We've rid the place of marauders, though they took much of the foodstuffs. We've hunted to replace what we could."

Alasdair nodded to him and said, "My thanks. You'll be needed here for at least another sennight, I believe."

Once he left, she turned to him and asked, "Why are they here, Alasdair? Not that I'm ungrateful."

"I'm certain my grandsire must have sent them to rid your castle of any remaining infidels. As you know, he was quite fond of your sire, and he wishes for you to keep your land. It belongs to the Scots, not the English."

She felt ashamed for having ever doubted the man—Alexander Grant was as great as her father had thought him—but most of all she was incredibly happy to be home. For the most part, MacLintock Castle was in good shape.

Clan members waved to her as they passed, many of them shouting greetings.

She waved back at each kind greeting, her eyes tearing up at the beauty of her people and her home. The cottages had been patched, the paths set back to rights, and someone had even planted flowers in front of some of the homes.

Her sire would have been pleased. She also took note of all the attention her clan mates were giving Alasdair. Were they as hopeful as she was for something that would probably never happen?

They were nearly at the stables when a voice she recognized called out to her. "Oh, my dear. I was so worried!"

Aunt Penne stood in the courtyard, looking aggrieved by the weather. Oh, Emmalin had never known she could be this happy to see that sour look.

"Auntie? You are hale? Where have you been?"

Had they not left the village after all? Was everything Langley had said a dirty lie?

Her aunt approached her horse. "Never you mind. Your lying husband kept Tamsin and me prisoner, but we are free of him now. 'Twas such a distressing situation that I wish not to speak of it. What an ingrate! But please, my dear, do not concern yourself. We've heard the news that he is truly dead, and I must say I'm glad of it. 'Tis time for us to put our lives back together. You are well, Emmalin?"

Aye," she said. "Tamsin? Is she here?"

"Aye," Aunt Penne said. "She is fine. Do not worry your pretty head about her. I'll see you inside. 'Tis too cool out here for my old bones."

She wasn't ready for her aunt to leave her sight, but she waved her away, not wanting her to catch a chill. Someday she'd ask about their ordeal with Langley, but not yet. At this point, she wished to never think on him again.

Alasdair drew his horse up behind her, then dismounted near the stables and helped her down. "Em, can we talk privately somewhere?"

The pained look in his eyes told her everything she needed to know. He wasn't ready to marry her, and they both knew she was short on time. She was in no hurry to hear him say the words.

"Aye," she said, "but I'd like to step inside and speak with my people first. We'll feed you and your men before you go on your way."

He arched a brow at her in question.

She let herself touch his arm briefly before pulling away. "I know you're leaving, Alasdair. But I owe you and your guards for all you've done for me and my clan. Please allow me the opportunity to repay some of your kindness."

"Agreed. We'll stay the night and leave on the morrow, first thing, if that suits you."

"It does." She made her way inside, pleased to see much of the mess inside had also been cleaned up. It hurt to see the damage that had been done. To hear about the lives that had been taken. But she was determined to leave Langley in the past and to never, ever subject her people to such a man again. She was taking charge of her life again, putting things back together like Aunt Penne had said.

Still, a deep exhaustion had taken root in her. She was tired of violence, of chaos. Of *fighting*. She wanted peace for her people, and they clearly wished for the same. Many of her clan members had approached her to tell her they were glad Langley would not be returning. They'd hated the way he'd disrespected her and the land they loved.

That eve, the tables were weighed down with crusty warm bread, boar and mutton meat pies, and festive berry tarts. There was plenty of mead and ale for all, the goblets being filled frequently as toast after toast was made to the Grants and to their mistress.

Emmalin had enjoyed watching the Grant cousins bicker and laugh and tell stories, but her heart yearned for a private moment with Alasdair.

She knew she wasn't to get one. He would be leaving with his cousins in the morn, and it was likely the last she'd see of him.

Her heart was broken, but she'd not let him see how much.

At one point in the evening, Dyna cornered her just outside the kitchens. "Do not give up on him," she said.

"What? Who?" Emmalin asked, caught off-guard.

"Alasdair. He's a good man, but he's confused right now."

"How can I help? I would do anything he asked."

"You love him." Dyna didn't ask, just stated the obvious.

"I do, but I honestly don't think he cares."

"He does, but he's had a verra bad year. Have patience. I believe he'll be back."

"I hope you're right," Emmalin said, her heart in her throat. She wished more than anything it were true, but she couldn't forget the way he'd looked at her earlier. He didn't have any hope for them, so how could she?

"Believe in yourself. You both need to be told the same thing. You know you are good for each other, but neither of you will admit it." Dyna said. "Don't give up on him. Not yet."

Dyna spun around and left her standing there, her heart still open and raw from all that had transpired. She made her way back to her table and ate, listening to more of the cousins' banter. How she wished she could join in with the same enthusiasm as before.

After the evening meal, Alasdair held his hand out to her and said, "Would you show me your fine gardens, my lady?"

She smiled and took his hand, leading him out into the cool night after grabbing a shawl by the door. Weaving through the rows of herbs and plants, including some that had been trampled and needed replanting, they found their way over to a bench.

"How is your injury, Alasdair? Not festering, is it?"

"Nay, 'tis fine. Please do not think on it again." He stopped and cleared his throat, something that she didn't like, because she knew where he was going.

He covered her hand with his. "Emmalin, my apologies that I cannot be the man you want me to be."

She put a finger to his lips and fought the tears that begged to fall. "Alasdair Grant, you have naught to apologize for. You have taught me what a true man is, one of honor and loyalty. I owe a debt of gratitude to you and your clan that can never be repaid. Many thanks to you and your cousins. I overstepped my boundaries by proposing to you. Please say no more on it."

"I *do* wish to say more," he said, staring into her eyes. The pain she saw there was heart-wrenching. "I lost my dear grandmother some time ago, and my mother passed suddenly last year. I watched my sire and my grandsire grieve their wives. I did my best to console them, but it was verra difficult watching their pain. I know this is a selfish statement, but I don't know if I could survive that kind of pain. My sire. It ripped him apart."

He paused and she watched him battle with his thoughts, his memories of those he loved. Those he had lost. She understood his grief, so how could she fault him for feeling the way he did? For loving in a way that hurt?

Because she wanted him for herself.

She didn't want another dandy English baron on her land—she wanted a strong, loyal Highlander like Alasdair. But it wasn't to be.

"I would like you to understand, though, I've never felt like this about any other lass. If there is ever anything I can do for you, please send a messenger to Grant land."

Needing to leave lest she fall apart, again, she got to her feet. He did the same. Standing on tiptoes, she kissed his cheek. "If you ever change your mind, know that I have no plans to marry immediately. Whatever happens, I wish you well, and I will always be grateful for your assistance."

She walked away from him and did not look back.

She couldn't. It would be too painful.

CHAPTER TWENTY-TWO

———◆———

THE GROUP DEPARTED IN THE morn, the four cousins taking ten guards with them and leaving the rest behind to protect Emmalin.

"You're a fool, Alasdair," Alick said. "She's the one for you. We all know it. Why the hell don't you?"

The words felt like a sword blow to the head. He shook them off as best he could. "I doubt I'll ever marry," he said.

"I have to agree with Alick," Els said. "Rare though that is. Emmalin is a beautiful Scottish lass with her own land. She could be laird, you could be chieftain. You could use both titles. What more could you want? Strathblane is beautiful land. And if she married a Scottish man, it'll stay with the Scots."

He couldn't argue. Strathblane was beautiful, but the land was not as lovely as its mistress. Nor would he ever find a woman so brave or spirited. He knew all that, but his painful memories held him back. They suffocated him as surely as his fear of small places.

He deliberately changed the subject. "At least this time, I'll carry no bad memories from the battle."

"Aye," Alick said. "Nothing like the battle at Brechin."

"What I went through was nowhere near so bad as what happened to you," Els said, "and I've had a few nightmares, too. What I'd like to know is how Grandsire and our fathers lived through so many battles without any ill effects."

"Who ever said 'twas easy?" Dyna asked. "My sire talks about battles he lived through decades ago, and my mother still has occasional nightmares from her time in Berwick. 'Tis the way of battle. But such pain is only lessened by talking about it. You, Alasdair, need to talk about your last year. Now would be a great time. We're all here to help you."

"Bloody hell, Dyna," he groaned. "Could you not stop pestering me about it?"

He broke into a gallop, needing them to stop pestering him for a time. To leave him to the twists and turns of his own thoughts. Thoughts that seemed to go nowhere.

They set up camp in the forest that night, and the cousins sat around the fire to eat their meager dinner. The guards had gone off on patrol, so they were alone. As if sensing her opportunity, Dyna looked at the three of them, one by one, and said, "'Tis time for us to talk about what happened with your swords in our first battle against Hawkinge."

Alasdair threw a rabbit bone into the fire. Of course she knew. He would have been more surprised if she hadn't known.

"What are you talking about?" Els asked.

"The hilt of my sword grew hot under my fingers. Did it not happen for you?" Alasdair looked back and forth between Els and Alick. Dyna had sensed it. He'd felt it. Why hadn't anything happened for the other two?

"I didn't feel anything. Let it go," Els said, his annoyance at the topic evident.

No one else said anything for a long moment, but Dyna and Alasdair peered at Alick, waiting for his response. "Well?" Alasdair finally said.

Alick looked at all three and let out a huge sigh. "Aye, I felt it. The hilt of my blade warmed up the closer I was to you three. Just like when we were younger."

Alasdair looked back at Els, who said nothing, just played with the rabbit bone he'd been gnawing at. "'Tis nonsense," Els said, his tone sulky. "You must know that."

"Are you sure about that, Els?" Dyna asked, tipping her head back at him. "I saw it. How could you not feel it?"

Els, clearly exasperated, stood up and snapped, "Fine. I felt the heat in the hilt. Now, can we please stop talking about it. I know it happened once when we were young, when Grandsire was with us, but I don't want it to happen again. Can we not just leave it be?"

"I think it likely means something. If it's some form of power we're able to channel, we should try to develop it. Build it to something powerful. Scotland may need our help," Alasdair said.

"Aye, I agree," Dyna said, "But you'll not like what it will take. We'd each need to be in peak condition, inside and out, and we're not."

"Who's not in peak condition?" Els asked. "Not that it matters. I'll still not pursue it."

Dyna tipped her head toward Alasdair.

"Leave me out of your discussion." He knew what Dyna wanted to discuss, and she was right, he wanted no part of it. He gave her a pointed look and narrowed his gaze at her to show her he was in earnest. "Nay."

"We don't need to discuss it now, but you cannot hide from the truth forever," Dyna said to Alasdair.

Thank the heavens above for that. Aye, he had issues. Aye, he'd had a difficult year. Nay, he didn't wish to talk about it. He felt sure that would only make it worse.

They'd nearly made it back to Grant land when Dyna started in on him again. This time, she did not bother with preliminaries. "'Tis time for us to have a discussion."

He cast her a stony glare, hoping it would end the conversation. "By the bloody saints above, could you not let me be?"

"Nay, and in case you're wondering, I sent Alick and Els on ahead. They'll let you off, but I won't. You need to face this."

They rode on in silence for a short time, but he knew she wasn't finished.

A few minutes later, she said, "You must stop hiding from it."

Hellfire, why couldn't she just leave him be? Though her badgering was well-intentioned, sometimes he just wished to throttle her. She knew more than she should, her knowledge had teeth.

"Nay, I don't. I'm not hiding from anything."

"The hell you aren't."

Now she'd started to aggravate him. He decided he'd had enough of her meddling. "Must you continue to nag at me? You're like the midges, always around, always biting. Leave me be, Dyna. I've got naught to say."

"And it's eating at you something fierce," she said, her tone harsh. "I can see it so clearly. Why can't you?"

"What the hell is eating at me? What has you so convinced I'm in need of advice?"

"The fact that you left Emmalin alone to fend for herself. Any fool could see you love her and she loves you. I can see it, she can feel it, but you deny it. *Why?*"

"I didn't leave her there to fend for herself. I left a fine group of Grant warriors there to protect her."

"You may have saved her from one pain," Dyna said, raising her brow, "but you gave her another. Don't you both deserve some happiness? You come so close to the truth, Alasdair, yet you still deny it."

They were nearly at the castle gates. He could see Grant Castle up ahead on the hill, its banners waving strong in the Scottish wind. He was anxious to see his grandsire again, to update him on all that had happened.

To get away from Dyna's questions.

"Tell me the truth," she said. "Tell me how angry you are. Rail at me if you must. You have to get the anger out or it will eat up your insides. I won't let that happen to you."

He ignored her. An odd silence had fallen among the guards around them, as if everyone was waiting to see if he would lose this temper.

"It's been nearly a year. 'Tis time to face the truth." She smirked at him, then whispered, "Or don't you have the courage?"

That was it. He'd had enough. If she wanted to make him mad, she'd succeeded. He yelled to the guards and Els and Alick, who stayed just far enough away to give them privacy, "Go on ahead. Take your horses to the stables and leave us be."

As soon as the others were far enough away, he jumped down from his horse and moved over to grab his cousin's leg out of the stirrup. "Come on. You want to talk? Fine. Get your arse down off that horse and we will talk. But I'm not angry."

She jumped down and stood in front of him, pushing a finger at his chest. "You have a right to be angry."

"Fine. I am angry. It's not fair. I lost my mother and I shouldn't have. She got sick and never got better."

"And?"

He couldn't say it—nay, he just couldn't say the words. He paced around the horses, but he could see how anxious it made Midnight, so he stalked away again. And his cousin followed him, as relentless as a deerhound on a scent.

"What?" He spun around to yell at her. "What the hell do you want me to say?"

"I want you to say it. You know what. *Say it.* If you don't, you'll never be able to move on. Never."

"I don't want to say it. I don't *ever* want to say it."

"You *are* afraid. Fine, then I'll say it. We've all danced around the truth for much too long. 'Tis not helpful to you."

"Don't do it." He pointed his finger at her, backing away despite himself. "I swear to God, do not say those words. Do not, Dyna!"

She moved closer to him and leaned toward him.

"Dyna, I'm warning you. Do. Not. Say. Those. Words."

Her gaze caught his and she whispered the truth. Words he hated to hear. Every time he heard them, they pierced his already broken heart.

"Alasdair, your father's dead, too."

"Nay!" he bellowed. He fell to his knees and yelled a guttural cry that needed to come out. He roared and roared until his throat was raw, hoping he yelled loudly enough that his sire could hear him in heaven.

He knew it needed to be said. She knew it. But he didn't want to believe the truth.

He wanted to be a man like his sire. The laird. The warrior. The wonderful husband. The wise father. But to do that, he would have to face the pain in his heart and he just did not know how. He did not know how to move on.

Unsheathing his sword, he moved over to a group of trees and began to swing it at the branches, the leaves, everything. He wanted to scare Dyna, to convince her to stay away.

He wanted her to stop.

He wasn't sure he could handle any more.

Dyna followed him as he slashed.

"Good, Alasdair. Now tell me why you can't marry Emmalin."

He slashed two more branches, then stabbed his sword into the ground. "Marry her? I'll tell you why not. Because I love her. That's right, I do love her. And I'm not going to go through what the others went through. I won't. I just won't." He paced again.

There, he'd said it. She'd understand now and leave him alone.

"What did they go through? Having a family who loved them? Having bairns? What are you afraid of?"

"Who? My father. I'm an only child. I was the one who held my father when he found out my mother had died. I was the one who had to peel him away from her body because he couldn't let her go. And I did the same with Grandsire. You weren't there when he lost Grandmama. Well, I was. And I'm never going to go through the pain they went through."

Dyna's eyes widened. He'd finally surprised her.

"Aye, I was the one who pulled Grandfather away from Grandmama. No one else would do it. Everyone else was busy crying, but I couldn't stand to see that man sob any more so I pulled him away. And I sat with him every day for the next moon to make sure he would go on."

Dyna had tears running down her cheeks. "You did. I hadn't looked at it that way, but you did. You were older than me, and I suppose I thought you were stronger, too. 'Twasn't fair."

"Aye, I did it for Grandsire, and then I had to go through it again with my sire. Think you I wish to go through the same? I don't."

"But everything you've been through has made you stronger, don't you see? You deserve happiness."

"Nay, I am not strong. My sire was so much stronger than I will ever be, and if he could not survive losing Mama, I know I could not survive such a loss either. Emmalin is better off without me."

"Alasdair, I'm sorry. I hadn't intended to dredge all of that up. I…"

Alasdair sheathed his sword and raced over to his horse, leaping onto Midnight's back and riding hard to the keep. There was one more thing he had to do. He'd wanted to do this for a long time and he hadn't. It was one other thing he had avoided.

When he got to the stables, he jumped off his horse and tossed his sword on the ground, not speaking to anyone. He ran down the path through the inner bailey, gathering stones and putting them in a bag. When he felt he had enough, he hurried into the keep with his collection.

He simply nodded in response to those who greeted him, moving too quickly for anyone to ask him any questions. Up the stairs. Down the passageway. Up the stairs to the parapets. ignored all those who greeted him in the great hall. Grandpapa was not there.

He set his stones down and yelled up to the heavens, "Papa, I need you here right now. Half of my family believes in spirits and ghosts, so I'm telling you to come to me."

He *needed* him. He'd heard plenty of talk about ghosts or ethereal beings, and it was said Aunt Jennie's lasses could hear the dead. Well, if anyone had the right to talk to a dead spirit, he did. He'd waited, praying that his father would send him some sort of message, but nothing had ever happened.

Just like nothing was happening now.

He bellowed two more times. "John Alexander Grant. Jake Grant, married to my dearest mother Aline. I want to talk to you. You owe me this at least. *Please*."

He waited, wishing for his sire's spirit to appear in front of him. If not that, could he at least have a sign? Something?

Why had his father died six moons after his mother? It was too much.

It had been too painful.

The air changed, a light wind appearing out of nowhere, and he was filled with a sense of wonder. "Papa?"

A familiar scent filled the air, the mint leaves his sire had always chewed. The aroma passed by him, no, through him. His father was there. Somehow. Some way.

He picked up his stones and started throwing them as hard as he could into the air. He fired one after the other at an invisible target. "These are for you, Papa. Why did you leave me? I'd just lost Mama, and then you left me. How could you do that to me? They say you died of a broken heart, because you couldn't go on without Mama. What about me?" His throws became more sporadic as pain wrenched at him. "What about me, Papa? I'm all alone. Els has brothers and sisters, and so do Alick and Dyna. But me? I'm alone. I'm *alone*."

He set his face in his hands and forced the tears back, bellowing his frustration.

"Nay, you're not alone, son," said a familiar voice. He whirled around to see his grandpapa standing next to the doorway. "You've never been alone."

The two lairds came out behind Grandpapa. Uncle Jamie and Uncle Connor.

"Alasdair, you're not alone," his grandsire said. "We're all here for you. Aye, you've had a difficult year, losing your mother and your father."

"And I still miss my grandmama." He looked at Grandpapa sheepishly, hating to bring up a painful memory, but he'd loved Grandmama Maddie, too. "Aye, it was five years ago, Grandpapa, but she was my only grandmother." He'd never known his mother's parents.

"Any time you have questions or would like to talk—about anything—you can come to me," Uncle Jamie said. "Jake was my twin brother. I knew him better than anyone, and I'm pretty sure if you ask me something, I'll know how he would answer."

Uncle Connor said, "And he was my dear brother. I always looked up to him. I'm here for you whenever you want."

Alasdair hung his shoulders. He hated to complain, hated to let anyone know how much it hurt. After all, they'd suffered their own losses. But he realized now how much he'd needed to hear this from them. "My thanks to both of you." He noticed his grandfather give a nod to his uncles.

They came over and clasped his shoulder, one at a time, then left him alone with his grandfather.

"He left me alone, Grandpapa. He died of a broken heart, they say. Why couldn't he have waited another year or two for me? I don't have anyone else."

"Son, and I call you that because you remind me so much of my dear son. Aunt Jennie said his heart gave out. In fact, she thinks his heart was too big. She always felt there was something wrong there. His heartbeat didn't sound the way it should. In the end, working in the lists all the time and going to battle was too much for his heart. He didn't leave you on purpose, and if he'd been given the choice, he would have stayed, just for you."

This time, he couldn't stop the tears from flooding his cheeks. He sobbed, moaning at the pain of losing both his mother and father. He had loved them both so much, and the hurt of losing them was nearly unbearable.

He grabbed himself around the waist and shouted, "Grandsire, if Papa were here, what would he tell me to do? I just don't know. I don't know how to move forward."

His grandfather thought for a long time. Finally, he said, "Jake would tell you not to be afraid to live your life. Not once did he ever regret marrying your mother or having you. You brought them both so much joy. He would want you to marry, love someone, and find someone who could love you back…though that may not always be easy."

Alasdair laughed at the jest, finally smiling. "Grandpapa, I wish I could make you stay with us for many more years."

Alexander Grant leaned over the parapets and said, "As long as I'm still needed here, I'm not going to rush off. Aye, I'm an old man, but I have much to do. And Maddie keeps telling me I must stay for a few more years and a few more reasons."

"What? Grandmama talks to you?"

He shrugged his shoulders. "I've told you about the dreams before, when she warns me of things to come. But she also comes just to visit, on occasion. When I wake from those dreams, I can still feel her in my arms…" He paused to gather his composure, clearing his throat. "'Tis wonderful to feel as one with a woman, but 'tis how I always felt with her. She was a special woman, and I like to think she's become a special angel. It may sound foolish to others, but 'tis how I continue on. I know not if it's true, or if it's just my way of keeping her near. Either way, I listen to her. And if you marry someday, you'll listen to your wife, too."

"Why would Grandmama want you to stay?"

"I'll tell you one reason. It's to meet our great-grandbairns and read them her storybooks."

"My bairns?"

"And Els and Alick and Dyna's. All of them. You must remember the picture books your grandmama drew for the young ones. She loved spending time with the young lads and lasses in our clan, just as she did with her bairns and her grandbairns. She always considered herself the protector of bairns."

He couldn't help but smile. He had many loving memories of sitting on his grandmother's lap and listening to her stories. The grandbairns had often fought for the right to be the lucky one allowed to sit on her lap. "I miss her."

"I do, too. But she came to me again a sennight ago and said that one of our grandbairns needed help and I needed to assist."

He turned his head to stare at his beloved grandsire, unable to believe what he had just told him, and then the scent of mint leaves floated to him again, as if his father were attempting to tell him something.

Listen.

Don't be afraid to love.

"She told me I needed to be here for you. I didn't understand why, but now I do." He grasped Alasdair's shoulder and said, "Follow your heart, son."

The two leaned over the parapets, staring out over Grant land in silence, except for a few sniffles left over from Alasdair's bout of tears. "I think I'd like to ask Emmalin to marry me," he said at last.

"Then you need to do it soon, and I'm here to help you do it right. I doubt Edward will bother her again—from what I've heard, he has other issues to settle—but that could certainly change. She's a beautiful, talented Scottish lass. She belongs with a strong Highlander, in my opinion."

He stood up, helped his grandsire do the same, and then hugged the old man, wrapping his arms around him as tightly as he dared. "I love you, Grandpapa. I'm glad you're still here with me. Don't ever leave me."

Alex Grant looked at him and said, "I will someday, but not until you're ready."

CHAPTER TWENTY-THREE

EMMALIN WAS OUT RIDING HER horse, her favorite pastime of late, when she caught sight of Gaufried coming toward her. "What is it?" she yelled to him.

"One of the barons is nearly here. Shall I send him away?"

Emmalin turned her horse in the direction Gaufried had come from, and she recognized Baron Eversby from his posture. He had about ten men with him. "I'll speak with him, Gaufried. My thanks to you."

"I'll follow along, mistress. I don't like that he came here uninvited."

Emmalin rode toward the baron. She'd left the curtain wall far behind for her ride, but she was pleased to see the Grant contingent had followed her closely, along with several of her own guards. Although she doubted the baron meant to force her into marriage—he would have brought more men if that were his intention—she appreciated having them close by. "Greetings to you, Baron Eversby."

When she reached the baron, he grabbed for the reins of her horse. "My lady, you should not be riding this far away from your castle, and who are those savages behind you?"

Emmalin moved her horse away from him intentionally, not surprised to see him bristle when she did so. "I'm fine, my lord, and these men are from Clan Grant. They are visiting for a short time."

"I don't like them here. They don't belong." Although she'd thought the man pleasant enough in Berwick, he'd been on his best behavior there. Now, his gaze was hard and his posture commandeering. She took his measure, not liking what she saw, and cursed herself for thinking that she might possibly accept his suit.

A certain fair-haired archer came to mind, telling her to believe in herself and be patient with the man she loved. "Baron Eversby, I do believe I've made up my mind. I am not interested in accepting your suit."

"What?" he asked, his tone sharp. "But you were agreeable in Berwick. What has changed your mind? Is it the Grant warrior?"

"Nay, *I* changed my mind."

He dropped his voice, taking on a tone she didn't like. "I brought a priest with me because I told him his services would be needed. You'll make a liar out of me if you turn me down. Open your gates."

Gaufried said, "My mistress says be on your way." He'd followed her, not that she was surprised.

"Shut up, you fool. Emmalin, tell your men to open your gates. I'm ordering you."

A small smile tipped up her lips. "Nay, I don't want to open my gates. Had you been more agreeable, I might have invited you in for a brief repast before you take your leave, but I'd like you to leave at once." She'd never been able to speak so bluntly to Langley before he'd left, and it felt wonderful to do so now. Never again would she ignore her own desires. If the king intended to force her to marry, he'd have to come to MacLintock land to do it.

A half circle of warriors in red plaid formed around her, and they unsheathed their swords in unison. Baron Eversby's already pale face lost color as his gaze traveled from one warrior to the next.

"As you wish. We will leave, but King Edward will not be pleased. I'm certain you'll hear from him on this matter." He turned his horse around and left.

Emmalin laughed and spurred her horse to her gates, loosening the plait in her hair to let it fly freely in the wind.

"My thanks, Dyna," she whispered.

Although Emmalin was greatly relieved by her decision, she still felt unsettled after the baron left. In fact, she was so uneasy she spent the next several nights pacing in her chamber. She stood there now, in the middle of the night, having finally identified what was bothering her.

Someone was watching her. It felt like there were constantly eyes on the back of her head, weighing her down.

Her husband had told her someone in her life had betrayed her. And while he'd been a known liar, the facts hadn't lined up. He'd had the candleholders.

He'd known about the jewels. He'd known she would be at the manor with Alasdair.

It wasn't Gaufried—she'd only accused him because he was the one who'd last had the candleholders in his possession. And it wasn't Besseta either. She'd bet her life on that. So who had turned on her?

The answer came to her in a flash, so obvious she wondered why she hadn't figured it out sooner. Uneasy but determined, she prepared to confront her betrayer. She hid her dagger in her pocket and put on her mother's necklace.

The very necklace Langley Hawkinge had so desperately wanted.

When she left her chamber, her first move was to seek out Bessie. Her maid was sitting in front of the hearth in the great hall. Bessie had struggled to sleep lately as well, kept awake by memories of the fighting they'd seen.

"Why are you awake, my lady?" she whispered. "What do you need?"

Wrapping her mantle around her shoulders, she said, "'Tis almost over, Bessie. I need to have a little talk with someone, but there are a few things I'd like you to do." She cleared her throat and gave Bessie her instructions. Her maid hurried off to do as she asked, and Emmalin prepared to leave the great hall. The sight of her father's weapon, which she'd had hung over the hearth again, caught her eye. She smiled, clasping her hands in front of her. "I know what I must do, Papa, and I think you'll approve."

She headed across the courtyard and out into the forest where no one would interrupt them. She found a log and sat down, waiting for her company to join her. Doing her best to get her point across, she leaned back, tipping her head to the moon, hoping the moonlight would reflect against the large sapphire stone in her necklace.

Somehow, she knew the person would follow her. It wasn't long before she heard the soft rustling of the leaves coming from the keep.

As soon as the woman approached her, Emmalin stood up to greet her. "Greetings, Tamsin. Did you think I'd never figure out who the true traitor was?"

The woman, a bit shorter than Emmalin, stood just across from her, her hands on her hips, her hair hanging to her waist, unbound as if she'd just climbed out of bed. "When did you figure out it was me?"

Emmalin unfastened the necklace, moving deliberately slow. "The final indication was Langley knowing the color of my dear necklace. I've always made sure to keep it hidden. Only you, Besseta, and Aunt Penne had seen it before. I knew Besseta and Aunt Penne would never betray me, so that left you."

Tamsin glared at her. "Give it to me. I've had enough of your aunt's incessant nagging, her need to be waited on, giving me orders all the time. And you, too. Just because you were the laird's daughter, you think you have the right to order everyone to do your bidding. Enough is enough. Langley promised to take me away from this horrid place."

"Truly? And what else did he promise you? Were you to marry and stay in Berwick or move to his estate in London?"

"We were going to France. He promised me that he would take me to France and give me coin to live on for a year. But you had to be difficult and keep the necklace with you at all times. If you'd left it here, we would have been in Europe long ago."

Tamsin took several steps toward her.

"Nuh–uh–uh," Emmalin said, waggling her finger at her. "Stay where you are. I may give it to you eventually, but first you'll answer a few questions."

The woman's only response was to stop.

"Did you purposefully implicate dear Gaufried?"

Tamsin shrugged her shoulders and said, "That was my idea. I thought it brilliant."

The callow disregard she had for others was difficult to believe.

"Except it didn't work," Emmalin said, arching an eyebrow. Had greed been the only motivating factor? Had Tamsin truly sold out her own people so cheaply? "Were you in love with my husband? Did he promise to marry you in France?"

"Nay, I don't need a husband. Besides, he had his own plans. They didn't do him much good, did they? But I can still get the necklace for myself. 'Tis the only reason I returned. Give it to me or I will kill your aunt."

"Nay, I don't think I will," she said, stuffing it into her pocket. "'Tis not yours."

A sound echoed through the area, like a single

cracking branch. Tamsin paused and turned her head. "Who's there?"

Emmalin had told Bessie to send Gaufried and another guard out to watch the confrontation from the periphery. She turned her head for just a moment to see who was there.

That was her mistake.

Tamsin grabbed her from behind and held a dagger to her neck. "Gaufried, come out. I see you there. All I want is the necklace. Once Emmalin hands it over, I'll leave you all. 'Tis all I want."

Tamsin had changed. Now that they stood so close together, Emmalin could tell how thin she'd become. The dagger shook in her hand, even piercing Emmalin's skin in two places. Her treachery had cost her—it had poisoned her mind and her body.

Reaching into her pocket, Emmalin collected the necklace. As soon as she knew she had Tamsin's attention, she threw it into the bushes across the glade. "There is your necklace. Fetch it yourself."

Tamsin dove for it, squealing as she searched the ground. "You bitch!"

Emmalin had taken the opportunity to get closer with Gaufried, but Tamsin must have caught her movement out of the corner of her eye. She spun around and charged toward her. "I might not get away, but if I'm to suffer for this, so will you! You'll not get out of this alive!"

Dagger extended, Tamsin charged toward her.

But Emmalin had her own dagger, retrieved from her pocket, and she ducked the slashing weapon and plunged hers deep into Tamsin's belly, stopping her dead in her tracks. The dagger clutched in the betrayer's hand fell to the ground. Her eyes widened as she clutched at the dagger in her torso, gasping for air as she crumpled to the ground, her gaze never leaving Emmalin.

Gaufried clasped her shoulder. "Well done, lass. She deserved it for all the evil she's spread."

And yet, she still felt guilty for having harmed another person, for having ended a life. If only Alasdair were here to comfort her as he'd done the last time. But he wasn't, and he never would be again. She glanced at Gaufried and nodded. "'Tis finally over."

CHAPTER TWENTY-FOUR

EMMALIN FELL INTO A CHAIR in front of the hearth in her great hall. She and the servants had spent the last sennight cleaning the keep and restoring it to its original state, plaids and tapestries and all, and it was starting to feel like her home again. The day after the incident with Tamsin, she'd explained all to her clan members, given them the chance to ask questions, and then pronounced the lass's name was never to be mentioned on MacLintock land again.

The candlestick holder she'd saved sat proudly on a table next to the hearth where it belonged. Tamsin's foolish attempt to implicate Gaufried had forced Emmalin to examine all that had happened.

The keep looked lovely again, and she hoped her mother and sire could see it from the heavens above. All of her sire's sacrifices meant even more to her than before. By restoring the keep, she had restored her sire's heritage.

They'd worked furiously and tirelessly, and the hard work showed, but it hadn't healed the ache in her heart.

She loved Alasdair.

No one could compare with the tall, dark-haired fierce Highlander with the softest touch she'd ever experienced, the man she knew her parents would have been proud to see her marry.

But she hadn't heard from him.

Part of her thought she should be bold. That she should visit him at his keep and risk rejection again. But he knew how she felt—if he wanted her, he would come for her.

Perhaps she'd remain a spinster.

Laughter and cheers rose up from outside, but she didn't have the energy to go to the door. At least they were happy sounds. Her people deserved happiness.

Besseta came inside, her face bright with excitement. "Mistress, you must come outside. Your presence is requested at the curtain wall."

"What? Why?"

"Someone wishes to speak with you at the curtain wall. Hurry so you don't miss it," she said, chuckling.

Another baron must have come with a grand entourage. The polite thing to do would be to offer some sort of response, although she would reject this one just as she had the other. She trudged out the door, across the courtyard, and up the stairs next to the tower on one side of the gates to her castle. All the people she passed giggled as if they knew something she didn't.

She supposed they did.

Would they react as such if some English baron had come to seek her hand? She glanced over her shoulder at the joy on their faces, guessing whatever it was, it wasn't an Englishman.

She climbed the stairs, then leaned on the parapets. A gasp caught in her throat. These were no English knights—below her was a sea of Highland warriors on horseback, all arranged in still rows. Only three of the horsemen were moving, each carrying a flag whipping in the wind as they wove through their assembled comrades.

The gates had been opened, and her clan members had spilled out to watch the show, with fiddlers and flutists gaily playing their instruments. It was a gorgeous early autumn day, the sky a rare blue and the clouds thick and puffy.

Bessie ran up behind her. "Read the banners, my lady," she whispered.

"What?"

"Read the banners. I don't know what they say, but I suspect they're important."

It suddenly dawned on her that the horsemen in front of her wore a sea of Grant plaids, their red and green proudly displayed for all to see. Tears blurred her vision when she recognized the first horseman, or horsewoman, as it was Dyna, carrying a banner with one word on it: "Will." Behind her came Alick and Elshander who carried banners that said, "you" and "marry."

She didn't see the fourth banner until the sea of horses split into two lines and a daft horseman rode straight down the middle toward her, waving a flag that said, "me."

Alasdair charged forward, grinning from ear to ear. He rode his horse right up to the gates, then dismounted, and strode over to the wall directly beneath her.

Bending down on one knee, he bellowed loudly enough for all to hear, "Emmalin MacLintock, will you do me the honor of becoming my wife?"

Emotion clogged her throat, but she nodded her head furiously, which sent four bards into a splendid song about a Highlander who'd brought the force of the Highlands down to propose to his beloved.

She spun around, ran down the stairs, and flew out through the gates, launching herself at Alasdair. He barely managed to catch her as she cried out for all to hear, "Aye! Aye!"

"I love you, Emmalin, and I'm sorry for being such a stubborn fool."

She cupped his face with both hands and whispered, "I love you so much that you are forgiven."

———◆———

Alasdair had never enjoyed himself more than he did that eve. Emmalin's clan had thrown together a splendid celebration for their mistress. The tables were weighed down with vats of venison and lamb stew, loaves of warm bread, and goblets full of mead and ale. The closest family were inside the great hall, while the guards celebrated in the courtyard with plenty of food and ale for all. Alasdair and his cousins had brought plenty of food along with them, knowing the English had likely stolen or destroyed much of their food stores.

They'd decided to send King Edward a missive

after their wedding, but to their surprise, Sheriff de Fry came to visit before they got the chance. He indicated that he would be honored to take their message, but it wasn't necessary.

According to de Fry, the king had already heard of their intention to marry, and he wouldn't interfere so long as the ceremony was done by a priest. Clan Grant was so large that no one wished to anger Alexander Grant or any of his sons or grandsons. The timing was uncanny—how had the king learned of their engagement so quickly?— and Emmalin privately suspected de Fry himself had whispered into Edward's ear. He had helped them in his own way, making a case for leaving the couple alone.

Alasdair had then privately pressed him about his role as sheriff, but de Fry refused to comment beyond confirming that he secretly worked for the Bruce.

It was a proud celebration of two Scottish clans, the MacLintocks and the Grants. Once the food was mostly gone and the minstrels came in for the entertainment and dancing, Emmalin leaned against her betrothed and said, "I hope you don't mind, but it has been a verra long day and we have much to plan on the morrow if we're to marry in a few days. I want everything to be perfect."

He kissed her to the hoots and hollers of the men in the hall, and he couldn't help but grin. Although he never would have expected it, he was excited for the wedding. Excited to call this incomparable woman his wife. He leaned in close to her and whispered, "I love you. Only a few more days, and I'll go up to your chamber with you."

She blushed a very sweet shade of pink and said, "I love you, too." She made a motion to one of the minstrels, who started up a lively tune.

He watched as she left, creeping out of the back doorway to go up the back stairs.

"She left already?"

He turned to look at Dyna. "Aye, she's tired. Has much to prepare. I don't fault her. You know things will keep going down here for a while."

"I expect so. Els and Alick are well into their cups already. But you're not. You've never been into the ale like they have."

He shook his head. "By the way, I wish to thank you for what you did for me."

Dyna scowled and shrugged her shoulders. "I didn't do anything."

She never had been able to accept a compliment.

"Aye, you did, and I think you know it. You forced me to accept my sire's death. It was a difficult day, but I feel much better. Talking to Grandsire, your father, Uncle Jamie, it all helped me come to grips with it."

"Is it true about the mint leaves?" she asked. "Are you sure you didn't create it for Grandpapa's sake?"

"Nay, 'struth. He noticed it, too. I suspect it will happen again someday. Mayhap not for a long while, but I'm hopeful. I never knew the part about his heart, what Aunt Jennie said about it being weaker than many. It was a small thing, but it made me accept what happened a bit better. It helped me move past it."

"I'm glad you worked through it. I think you and Emmalin will be quite happy together."

Besseta came up to stand beside Dyna. "May I have a word with you, my lord?"

"Aye. Do you need help with something?"

She motioned to him. "In the kitchens. I could use your help."

"May I assist with anything?" Dyna asked. "I would be happy to help."

"Nay, nay, just Alasdair." She gave her a sheepish look, but Dyna simply shrugged and moved off.

"Do you need help lifting something?" Alasdair asked as he followed Besseta out of the hall.

She shook her head and held her finger to her lips. "My lady has a secret she wishes to trade with you. She's in her chamber. I'll lead you there."

Alasdair couldn't have been more surprised by this admission, but his interest was piqued so he followed Besseta up the back staircase and down the passageway. When they arrived outside Emmalin's chamber door, the maid motioned for him to go inside.

He opened the door and stepped inside the large chamber. It was totally dark, but he could see the fading embers in the large hearth. A bed sat on one wall, a tub against the other and a partition in the far corner, if he guessed right.

"Emmalin? Is everything all right?"

Her voice came from behind the partition. "I wish to trade a secret. You recall when you promised we would do it again?"

"Aye," he said, watching to see if she would step out from behind the partition or what her game was. Either way, he couldn't help but smile because he was definitely intrigued.

"Then I have two secrets I wish to share, and then you must share one."

"All right. You first."

She stepped out from behind the petition with nothing on but a silver necklace with a large stone, though he couldn't tell the color. "Do you like my sapphire necklace? 'Twas my mother's favorite."

He swallowed hard. "Aye, but I like you more. You take my breath away. You're beautiful, my sweet. I…I…" The light from the hearth cast a golden glow across her curves, her breasts, her hips, causing his mouth to go dry.

"Nay." She shook her finger at him. "My secret first."

Speechless, all he could do was nod.

"I don't want to wait to lie in your arms. It will torture me if I must wait three more days."

"And your second secret?"

She chuckled, tipping her head back, but then said something that completely surprised him. "I don't like the dark, though I did my best to hide it in the tunnels. I didn't want you to think less of me." She lit the candle, set it in a candleholder, and stood next to the light, her hand on her hip. "Your turn. What's your secret?"

He said, "I like you bold." He took three steps until he stood in front of her, loving the way she gulped in a wee bit of air as he came closer. So close. But he didn't touch her yet. He wanted—needed—this to be good for her, and he knew very little about her experience with her first husband. He had planned to ask her about it, but the time had passed.

She lifted her chin a notch and said, "If you'd like to touch me, you must remove one piece of your clothing for each touch."

"And I may touch you wherever I like?"

She tipped her head to the side, lifting a single finger to her lips, then said, "Aye, your choice. Your hands only to start."

"Some rules, please. I wish for you to give your word that if I ever do anything you don't like, you'll tell me."

She smiled and he saw her posture relax just a touch, enough for him to know she had been a bit worried. "Agreed."

He removed one boot and hose and tossed it behind him, where it hit the wall with a loud clunk, making her giggle.

"Excited, my lord?"

He grabbed his other boot, yanked it off, nearly falling over, but threw it behind him. Then he glanced down at his growing arousal under his plaid and said, "Oh, you'll see in a moment."

"That was two pieces," she said as she played with the silver chain.

"That's because I have two hands," he said, reaching for her breasts, but then he stopped. "Agreed?"

"Agreed."

She stood tall, and he reached for her chest with a growl. "My sweet, you are lovely."

He ran his hands along the outside of her breasts, then cupped and lifted the full mounds before bringing his thumbs up to tease her dark nipples until they peaked. She closed her eyes, her head falling back as a small whimper released from the back of her throat while she leaned into him.

He took it as a good sign when she pulled back abruptly, lifting her head with a start, and cleared her throat. Her cheeks were flushed, and the haze of desire in her eyes was not lost on him.

"Another piece," she said.

He waggled his brow at her and quickly unlatched the pin holding his plaid at his shoulder, dropping the fabric to the floor with a whoosh.

Her eyes widened with delight and she reached for him, wrapping her hand around his hard member, her mouth forming a perfect small circle. "Oh, Alasdair."

He reached for her wrist and shook his finger at her. "You touching me was not part of the deal. My turn again." But first he tugged his tunic off over his head, leaving his body totally bare.

Her eyes locked on the dark hairs of his chest, traveling to his nipples and then continuing downward. She held her hands out to him, begging him. "Please?"

"Nay, not part of our bargain."

"But you have nothing left," she whined.

"Two pieces of clothing means two places I get to touch."

She stepped closer to him, and although he was still a head taller than her, he loved that she was tall enough that he could look her nearly in the eye. He noticed she stepped close enough so their sexes touched, and he grinned, waggling a finger at her. "You play with fire, lass."

She gently moved her soft mound against him.

He had to close his eyes, but he would do as he intended. He reached behind her, placing his hands on the cheeks of her bottom and caressing each one lightly, moving her slowly closer, and she moaned with pleasure, her head falling against him as she gave in to her desire.

CHAPTER TWENTY-FIVE

SHE WAS IN HEAVEN, IN a world she hadn't known existed, in the playful, skilled hands of the man she loved. Falling against him, she gave in to the fire he'd stoked inside her, enjoying each caress as if she'd never been touched so.

For she had not.

He scooped her up in his arms, lifting her as easily as if she weighed nothing at all, and lowered her down on the bed.

"You want this, love?" he asked as he settled himself over her.

"Aye, please. I need you, Alasdair." Her arm snaked around his neck, her fingers running through his long locks. "Now."

"Not yet..." He kissed her deeply, stroking her tongue with his, then moved his lips to her neck, planting kisses down the long, elegant length of it, and then ran his tongue down to her nipple. He teased the tip with the edge of his teeth, and she pushed against him in wild abandon, her need so great she cared not what he thought. She bucked against him to enter her, to give her what she needed.

She wanted his heat, needed his hardness inside her. She reached for him, grabbing him fully in her hand and positioning him at her slick entrance.

"You're mine forever now, Emmalin," he whispered in her ear.

"Aye, forever," she whispered, her fingers digging into his shoulder as he teased her, his hands everywhere as he drove her closer and closer to the edge of something.

He entered her swiftly and she cried out with pleasure, welcoming his invasion, giving him the chance to fill her completely. "Alasdair, we were meant for each other. More, please…"

She arched against him, wanting more, wanting everything he had, and he increased his pace, hitting her harder until everything changed, euphoric waves of pleasure sending her spiraling into a climax she clung to, gasping his name.

He finished with a roar and they clung to each other, enjoying the shared pleasure, gasping for air until she heard what she'd always wished to hear.

"Aye, lass, we were meant for each other. Forever."

———◆———

The marriage took place three days later at MacLintock Castle, after the Grant's new carriage arrived bearing Alasdair's grandfather, his aunt Jennie, and several young bairns. The rest arrived on horseback.

Alasdair stood at the front of the chapel near the altar. Although his sire could not be by his side, three people took his place. His grandsire stood strong between his uncles Jamie and Connor, all three dressed in their finest Grant plaids.

Emmalin walked down the aisle alone, looking beautiful in a pale lavender gown with a long train, carrying a bouquet of lavender and white flowers, her hair decorated with green and lavender ribbons, done especially by Besseta.

When she made it to his side, he looked at her and said, "I can't believe you're mine. You are absolutely gorgeous." He wished so badly to kiss her cheek, but the priest cleared his throat, bringing both of their eyes back to the front.

The doors stood open at the back of the church, and as soon as the priest started, a warm breeze carried through the crowd.

Emmalin lifted her face to the wind and whispered, "I smell mint leaves."

Alasdair broke into a wide smile. "'Tis just my Da."

EPILOGUE

———————

A month later...

ALEXANDER GRANT LED THE GROUP out to the lists, though he used his wooden stick to assist him across the uneven terrain, a son on either side of him for extra support. The rest followed them. He led the way to the exact spot he'd seen in his dream. He stopped, looked around him, and pointed with his stick. "Here. This is the place."

"Grandsire, what is this about?" Alasdair asked. He'd come home for a brief visit at his grandfather's insistence, although Alex had not yet explained why he was to come. The lad's lovely wife stood beside him. Everyone was here, just as they should be. Els with Jamie and Gracie, Alick with Finlay and Kyla, while Dyna was there with Connor and Sela.

"Humor an old man. I had a dream. You will do as I instruct," he said to his three grandsons and one granddaughter, their parents surrounding them.

"Papa, you're scaring me," Kyla said.

"Be patient, daughter." He took his time because he was quite sure his dear wife watched their bairns and grandbairns over his shoulder. How proud she would be if she were there with him.

Silence settled as he gathered his thoughts. "Alasdair, you are to spar with Connor, Alick with your sire, and Els with your sire."

"What about me, Grandpapa?" Dyna asked.

"Stand to the side for a moment. Let them spar a bit, get their swords warmed up."

"Papa, it's nearly dark out. This is not safe," Jamie said. "I don't wish to strike my son by accident just because you had a dream."

"Then make it a light sparring. You'll see, Jamie. Trust me."

They spread apart and began to do as instructed. Less than five minutes had gone by when Connor said, "Is it really that warm out here or are you that good, Alasdair?"

Alex grinned and crossed his arms with satisfaction. His dream had been another prediction, although this one was not from Maddie. It had been revealed to him that he had one last purpose. One position to fulfill before the end. The sparring continued for another few moments before Finlay stepped back abruptly and dropped his sword.

"What the hell? The hilt is hot. 'Tis burning my flesh."

Alex chuckled but said nothing, motioning for Finlay and Alick to stand back and wait. Jamie followed suit a few minutes later.

"Papa, explain yourself. The hilt of my sword is also hot."

"Mine isn't," Els said.

Alick tipped his blade back and forth in his hand.

"Mine was warm, but not hot."

Alasdair looked at Connor, who nodded and said, "'Tis getting warm."

"Good enough," Alex said. "Everyone stand back except my three grandsons, please."

Giving him some rather odd looks, they did as he asked, but he could tell none of them had guessed at what he was about to reveal.

The dream had come to him a sennight ago, but he remembered it as if he'd lived it yester eve. Maddie had come to him first and said, "You remember how I told you there are things you must do before you may leave? Here is the primary reason you must stay. This man will explain everything to you."

A strange man in long robes had stepped out from behind his dear wife and said, "You were the finest swordsman of the Highlands. Your country is in a state of turmoil. We sent you your grandsons on the same night, at the same time. You will guide them on how to help the Scots, and we grant them spectral swords. Help them learn how to use them."

"But I cannot travel with them, so how can I guide them?" Alex had asked.

"Through your granddaughter. You will have the ability to communicate with her directly, no matter where she goes. Do not doubt her power. There will be others to assist your quest, one who can use daggers, one expert with horses, an expert at spying, another archer. Your granddaughter's skills you shall learn eventually, if she can develop them properly. And her mate is completely secret. You'll know them by their strengths. Each strength will be necessary and obvious. The group, together, will be indestructible, if they choose to handle their strengths properly together."

He'd thought about the strange man's claims many times, along with what he'd seen his grandbairns do in the past, and while his mind doubted, the only way to be certain was to test it.

"Alick, Elshander, Alasdair, arrange yourselves in a triangle facing each other, your swords in front of you, pointed toward the ground."

They did as he asked and stood in the formation he'd suggested. "Step back three steps each."

Again the three followed his instructions. "Now hold your swords over your heads, pointed toward the sky," he directed. "Make sure you have a solid grip on your weapons."

The lads exchanged looks, but they did as he suggested. As soon as their swords were lifted over their heads, a bright streak of lightning shot across the sky, followed by the rumble of thunder. The longer they held them up, the more the lightning fired across the night sky, beginning to fire with a fury so powerful the three had trouble hanging on to their swords.

"Grandsire, I cannot hold it any longer," Els said, gasping. He dropped the sword tip to the ground, his two cousins following him.

"What does this mean?" Alasdair asked with awe, glancing over his shoulder at Emmalin.

He held his hand up to all and said, "Patience." He gave them a few moment's rest and then said, "Do it again please, one more step back."

They did as he asked and the same lightning show dominated the dark sky, illuminating the entire area.

"Dyna, step in the middle, and bring your bow with you, please."

She stared up at her grandfather, wide-eyed, moving closer but clearly hesitant to do as he asked. Sela clutched Connor's arm, waiting to see what would happen.

When Dyna stepped inside, the lightning moved a bit closer, focused more above the four of them instead of into the distance, but still not harnessed. For some reason, he knew this wasn't right.

"Emmalin. Do you have your dagger?"

"Aye," she said, pulling it out of her pocket to show him.

"Stand next to Alasdair with your weapon in your hand, please."

She did as he asked, and the lightning emanating from the lads' swords changed to a golden glow, an aura that shrunk until it settled around the five young people. But it wasn't quite what he'd seen before in a dream.

The energy bursting from the five young people in front of him held the promise of even more power.

"We have much to learn, but I'm certain you can see why this is worth pursuing." Alex paced in a circle around the group, watching and feeling the raw power emitted by the group.

Dyna smiled. Elshander seemed less pleased, but he gave a short nod.

His three children stared at him, and he shrugged. "I dreamed of the forthcoming turmoil in Scotland. We were blessed with the three lads for a reason. But they need more guidance than mine alone. Dyna will be their center of reason, and a few others will be brought into the group to assist them. 'Tis what I was told, and what we will do."

Alex said, "I give you the Highland Swords. We have a duty to save the Scots from the English wherever we can."

THE END

Dear reader,
   Stay tuned for at least three more stories in this series: Els, Alick, and, Dyna. I hope you enjoyed your journey with Alasdair and Emmalin, although painful at times. Life goes on in Grant Castle, and I may even come up with a couple of more stories to add to this series. It will stay primarily historical, but with a wee bit of paranormal added.

And yes, Alexander Grant is immortal.

Thank you for reading! As always, reviews would be greatly appreciated. Sign up for my newsletter on my website at *www.keiramontclair.com*. I send newsletters out with each new release.

Another way to receive notices about my new releases is to follow me on BookBub. Click on the tab in the upper right-hand side of my profile page. You can also write a review on BookBub.

Keira Montclair

www.keiramontclair.com
www.facebook.com/KeiraMontclair
www.pinterest.com/KeiraMontclair

NOVELS BY KEIRA MONTCLAIR

THE CLAN GRANT SERIES
#1- RESCUED BY A HIGHLANDER-
Alex and Maddie
#2- HEALING A HIGHLANDER'S HEART-
Brenna and Quade
#3- LOVE LETTERS FROM LARGS-
Brodie and Celestina
#4-JOURNEY TO THE HIGHLANDS-
Robbie and Caralyn
#5-HIGHLAND SPARKS-
Logan and Gwyneth
#6-MY DESPERATE HIGHLANDER-
Micheil and Diana
#7-THE BRIGHTEST STAR IN THE
HIGHLANDS-
Jennie and Aedan
#8- HIGHLAND HARMONY-
Avelina and Drew

THE HIGHLAND CLAN
LOKI-Book One
TORRIAN-Book Two
LILY-Book Three
JAKE-Book Four
ASHLYN-Book Five
MOLLY-Book Six

About the Author

KEIRA MONTCLAIR IS THE PEN name of an author who lives in Florida with her husband. She writes fast-paced historical romance, often with children as secondary characters.

If she's not writing, she prefers to spend time with her grandchildren. She's worked as a high school math teacher, a registered nurse, and an office manager. She loves ballet, mathematics, puzzles, learning anything new, and creating new characters for her readers to fall in love with.

She considers her work done well when her readers shed tears over her stories, but there's always a happy ending!

Her bestselling series is a family saga that follows two medieval Scottish clans through three generations and now numbers over thirty books.

Contact her through her website,
www.keiramontclair.com